HYPOTHERMIA

ALSO BY

Arnaldur Indriðason in English translation

Fiction

Tainted Blood
(first published with the title Jar City)

Silence of the Grave

Voices

The Draining Lake

Arctic Chill

Arnaldur Indridason

Hypothermia

TRANSLATED BY

Victoria Cribb

RANDOM HOUSE CANADA

www.randomhouse.ca

Random House Canada and colophon are registered trademarks.

Library and Archives Canada Cataloguing in Publication

Arnaldur Indriðason, 1961–
Hypothermia / Arnaldur Indriðason ; translated by Victoria Cribb.

Translation of: Harðskafi.
ISBN 978-0-307-35781-6

I. Cribb, Victoria II. Title.

PT7511.A67H3713 2009   839'.6934   C2009-901834-9

Text design: SX Composing DTP, Rayleigh, Essex

Printed in the United States of America

10 9 8 7 6 5 4 3 2 1

'The elder brother recovered from his frostbite but
was said to be left gloomy and withdrawn by his ordeal.'

Tragedy on Eskifjördur Moor

María hardly registered what was happening during the funeral. She sat numbly in the front pew, holding Baldvin's hand, barely conscious of her surroundings or the service. The vicar's address, the presence of the mourners and the singing of the little church choir all blurred into a single refrain of grief. The vicar had come round to see them beforehand to make notes, so María already knew the contents of her address. It focused for the most part on María's mother Leonóra's academic career, the courage she had shown in fighting the dreaded illness, the wide circle of friends she had collected during her life, and María herself, her only daughter, who had to some extent followed in her mother's footsteps. The vicar touched on Leonóra's eminence in her field and the care she took to cultivate her friendships, as witnessed by the attendance on that miserable autumn day. Most of the mourners were fellow academics. Leonóra had sometimes mentioned to María how rewarding it was to belong to the intelligentsia. There was an arrogance implicit in her words that María had chosen to ignore.

She remembered the autumn colours in the cemetery and the frozen puddles on the gravel path leading to the grave, the crackling sound as the thin film of ice broke under the feet of the pall-bearers. She remembered the chilly breeze and making the sign of the cross over her mother's coffin. María had pictured herself in this situation countless times before, ever since it became clear that the disease would kill her mother, and now here she was. She stared at the coffin in the grave and recited a brief mental prayer before making the sign of the cross with her outstretched hand. Then she lingered motionless at the graveside until Baldvin led her away.

She remembered people coming up to her at the reception afterwards to pay their respects. Some offered their assistance, asking if there was anything they could do for her.

María's mind did not return to the lake until all was quiet again and she was left alone with her thoughts, late that night. It did not occur to her until then, when it was all over and she was thinking back over that gruelling day, that no one from her father's family had turned up to the funeral.

1

The emergency line received a call from a mobile phone shortly after midnight. An agitated female voice cried:

'She's . . . María's killed herself . . . I . . . it's horrible . . . horrible!'

'What's your name, please?'

'Ka – Karen.'

'Where are you calling from?' the emergency operator asked.

'I'm at . . . it's . . . her holiday cottage . . .'

'Where? Where is it?'

'. . . At Lake Thingvallavatn. At . . . at her holiday cottage. Please hurry . . . I . . . I'll be here . . .'

Karen thought she would never find the cottage. It had been a long time, nearly four years, since her last visit. María had given her detailed directions just to be on the safe side, but they had more or less gone in one ear and out the other because Karen had assumed she would remember the way.

It was past eight in the evening and pitch dark by the time she left Reykjavík. She drove over Mosfellsheidi moor where there was little traffic, just the odd pair of headlights passing by on their way to town. Only one other car was travelling east and she hung on its red rear lights, grateful for the company. She didn't like driving alone in the dark and would have set off earlier if she hadn't been held up. She worked in the public-relations department of a large bank and it had seemed as if the meetings and phone calls would never let up.

Karen was aware of the mountain Grímannsfell to her right, although she couldn't see it, and Skálafell to her left. Next she drove past the turning to Vindáshlíd where she had once spent a two-week summer holiday as a child. She followed the red tail lights at a comfortable speed until they drove down through the Kerlingarhraun lava field, and there their ways parted. The red lights accelerated and disappeared into the darkness. She wondered if they were heading for the pass at Uxahryggir and north over the Kaldidalur mountain road. She had often taken that route herself. It was a beautiful drive down the Lundarreykjadalur valley to Borgarfjördur fjord. The memory of a lovely summer's day once spent at Lake Sandkluftavatn came back to her.

Karen herself turned right and drove on into the blackness of the Thingvellir national park. She had difficulty identifying the landmarks in the gloom. Should she have turned off sooner? Was this the right turning down to the lake? Or was it the next? Had she come too far?

Twice she went wrong and had to turn round. It was a Thursday evening and most of the cottages were empty. She had brought along a supply of food and reading material, and María had told her that they had recently installed a television in the cottage. But Karen's main intention was to try to sleep, to get some rest. The bank was like a madhouse after the recent abortive takeover. She had reached the point where she could no longer make any sense of the infighting between the different factions among the major shareholders. Press releases were

4

issued at two-hourly intervals and, to make matters worse, it transpired that a severance payment of a hundred million krónur had been promised to one of the bank's partners, someone whom a particular faction wanted to fire. The board had succeeded in stirring up public outrage, and it was Karen's job to smooth things over. It had been like this for weeks now and she was at the end of her tether by the time it occurred to her to escape from town. María had often offered to lend her the cottage for a few days, so Karen decided to give her a call. 'Of course,' María had said at once.

Karen made her way slowly along a primitive track through low-growing scrub until her headlights lit up the cottage down by the water. María had given her a key and told her where they kept a spare. It was sometimes useful to have an extra key hidden at the cottage.

She was looking forward to waking up tomorrow morning amidst the autumn colours of Thingvellir. For as long as she could remember people had flocked to the national park in the autumn, since few places in the country could boast such a brilliant display of colour as here by the lake where the rust-red and orange shades of the dying leaves extended as far as the eye could see.

She started to ferry her luggage from the car to the sun deck beside the door. Then, putting the key in the lock, she opened the door and groped for the light switch. The light came on in the hallway leading to the kitchen and she took her little suitcase inside and placed it in the master bedroom. To her surprise, the bed was unmade. That was not like María. A towel was lying on the floor of the lavatory. When she turned on the light in the kitchen she became aware of a strange presence. Although she was not afraid of the dark, she felt a sudden sensation of physical unease. The living room was in darkness. By daylight there was a superb view of the lake from its windows.

Karen turned on the living-room light.

Four solid beams extended across the ceiling, and from one of them a body was hanging, its back turned to her.

Shock sent her crashing back against the wall and her head slammed into the wood panelling. Everything went black. The body hung from the beam by a thin blue cord, mirrored in the dark living-room window. She didn't know how long it was before she dared to inch closer. The tranquil surroundings of the lake had in an instant been converted into the setting for a horror story that she would never forget. Every detail was etched on her memory. The kitchen stool, out of place in the minimalist living room, lying on its side under the body; the blue of the rope; the reflection in the window; the darkness of Thingvellir; the motionless human body suspended from the beam.

Karen approached cautiously and caught sight of the swollen blue face. Her ghastly suspicion proved correct. It was her friend María.

2

An extraordinarily short space of time seemed to pass between Karen's phone call and the arrival on the scene of the paramedics, accompanied by a doctor and some police officers from the neighbouring town of Selfoss. The Selfoss CID, who had been assigned the case, knew only that the woman who had committed suicide was from Reykjavík, lived in the suburb of Grafarvogur and was married but childless.

The cottage was full of people conversing in low voices. They stood around like awkward strangers.

'Was it you who called?' a young detective asked.

The woman who had found the body had been pointed out to him where she sat in the kitchen, staring dejectedly at the floor.

'Yes. My name's Karen.'

'We can get you a trauma counsellor if you—'

'No, I think . . . it's all right.'

'Did you know her well?'

'I've known María ever since we were children. She lent me the cottage. I was going to spend the weekend here.'

'You didn't see her car behind the cottage?' the detective asked.

'No. I didn't think there was anyone here. Then I noticed that

the bed hadn't been made and when I went into the living room
. . . I've never seen anything like it before. Oh God, poor María!
Poor thing!'

'When did you last speak to her?'

'Only a few days ago. When she lent me the cottage.'

'Did she say that she intended to be here herself?'

'No. She didn't mention it. She said of course she'd lend me
the place for a few days. No problem.'

'And was she . . . on good form?'

'Yes, I thought so. She seemed her usual self when I went
round to pick up the key.'

'She'd have known you were coming here?'

'Yes. What do you mean?'

'She knew that you'd find her,' the detective said.

He had pulled up a stool when he'd started talking to Karen.
She grabbed his arm, staring at him.

'Do you mean . . .?'

'Maybe you were meant to find her,' the detective said. 'Not
that I know anything about it.'

'Why would she have wanted that?'

'It's only a guess.'

'But it's true; she knew I'd be here over the weekend. She
knew I was coming here. When . . . when did she do it?'

'We haven't been given an exact time of death yet but the
doctor thinks it can't have been much later than yesterday
evening. So probably about twenty-four hours ago.'

Karen hid her face in her hands.

'God, it's so . . . it's so unreal. I should never have asked to
borrow the cottage. Have you spoken to her husband?'

'The police are on their way to see him now. They live in
Grafarvogur, don't they?'

'Yes. How could she do this? How could anyone do a thing like this?'

'From sheer despair,' the detective said, beckoning the doctor over. 'Mental torment. You weren't aware of anything like that in her case?'

'Maria lost her mother two years ago – to cancer,' Karen said. 'It was a terrible blow to her.'

'I see,' the detective said.

Karen's lips trembled. The detective asked if the doctor could do anything to help her. She shook her head, saying she was all right but would like to go home if that was allowed. It was not a problem. They would talk to her later if necessary.

The detective escorted her out to the drive in front of the cottage and opened the car door for her.

'Will you be all right?' he asked.

'Yes, I think so,' Karen answered. 'Thank you.'

The detective watched her turn the car and drive away. By the time he went back into the cottage they had cut down the body and laid it on the floor. He knelt down beside it. The dead woman was dressed in a white T-shirt and blue jeans but was wearing no socks. She was slim and had a thin face and short dark hair. He could see no signs of a struggle, either on her body or in the house; only the overturned kitchen stool on which the woman must have stood to tie the noose round the beam. The blue rope could have been bought from any DIY shop. It had cut deep into her slender neck.

'Lack of oxygen,' announced the district medical officer, who had been talking to the paramedics. 'Unfortunately for her, her neck's not broken. That would have been quicker. She suffocated when the noose tightened round her neck. It would have taken some time. They're asking when they can take her away.'

'How long would it have taken?' the detective asked.

'Two minutes – maybe less – before she lost consciousness.'

The detective stood up and looked around the cottage. From what he could see it was a very ordinary Icelandic holiday home with its leather three-piece suite, handsome dining table and newly fitted kitchen. The walls of the living room were lined with books. He walked over to the shelving unit and noticed the brown leather spines of five volumes of Jón Árnason's *Collected Folk Tales*. Ghost stories, he thought to himself. Other shelves contained French literature titles and Icelandic novels, interspersed with china or ceramic ornaments and framed photos, including three of the same woman at different ages as far as he could tell. The walls were hung with graphic prints, a small oil painting and watercolours.

The detective went through to what he assumed was the master bedroom. There was a body-shaped indentation in the bedclothes, on one side. There was a pile of books on the bedside table, with a volume of poetry by Davíd Stefánsson from Fagriskógur on top. Beside them was a small bottle of perfume.

His tour of the cottage was not motivated by mere curiosity. He was searching for signs of a struggle, any clue that the woman had not gone voluntarily into the kitchen, fetched the stool, positioned it under the beam, climbed on to it and put the rope round her own neck. All he found were the signs of a terribly quiet – almost polite – death.

He was interrupted by a colleague from the Selfoss CID.

'Found anything?' the man asked.

'Nothing. It's suicide. Pure and simple. There's no indication of anything else. She must have killed herself.'

'It certainly looks that way.'

'Hadn't I better cut down the rope before we leave? She's got a husband, hasn't she?'

'Yes, please take it down. He'll have to come here at some point.'

The detective picked up the noose from the floor and turned it over in his fingers. It was not a very professional effort: the knot had been tied inexpertly and the rope did not slide smoothly through the loop. It occurred to him that he could have done a better job himself, but perhaps it was unreasonable to expect a superior noose from an ordinary housewife from Grafarvogur. It was not as if she would have made a special study of the method and prepared for her suicide in detail. It had probably been the result of a moment of madness rather than a carefully premeditated act.

He opened the door on to the decking. It was only two steps down and a couple more yards to the edge of the lake. There had been a freeze over the past few days and a thin film of ice covered the water nearest the shore. In some places it had frozen to the rocks, like a paper-thin sheet of glass beneath which the water swirled.

3

Erlendur drove up to an unassuming detached house in the suburb of Grafarvogur. It stood on its own at the end of a cul-de-sac in a street of handsome villas. Most of them were identical, painted white, blue or red, with a garage and two cars per house. The street was well lit and clean, the gardens were neatly tended, the lawns mown, and the trees and bushes tidily pruned. There were box-trimmed hedges wherever you looked. The house in question appeared older than the other buildings in the street; it was built in a different style, with no bay windows or conservatory and with no pretentious columns flanking the front door. It was a white building with a flat roof and a large picture window in the sitting room that faced on to Kollafjördur fjord and Mount Esja. Around the house there was an extensive, beautifully lit garden that was clearly well tended. The shrubby potentilla and alpine cinquefoil, as well as the Hansa roses and pansies had all died back with the autumn.

It had been unusually cold recently, with a northerly wind and bitter temperatures. A dry gust blew the leaves along the road to the end of the cul-de-sac. Erlendur parked his car and looked up at the house. He took a deep breath before going inside. This was the second suicide in a week. Perhaps it was due to the onset of autumn and the thought of the long dark winter ahead.

It had fallen to him to contact the man on behalf of the Reykjavík police, as was the custom. The Selfoss force had already decided to transfer the case to Reykjavík for 'appropriate handling', as they called it. A priest had been sent to see the man. They were sitting in the kitchen when Erlendur arrived. The priest opened the door to him and showed him into the kitchen, explaining that he was the vicar of Grafarvogur. María had attended a different church but they had been unable to contact her vicar.

The husband, a lean, strongly built man wearing a white shirt and jeans, was sitting very still at the kitchen table. Erlendur introduced himself and they shook hands. The man's name was Baldvin. The vicar stood by the kitchen door.

'I must go to the cottage,' Baldvin said.

'Yes, the body has been—' Erlendur started, but got no further.

'I was told that . . .' Baldvin began.

'We'll go with you if you like. Though the body has in fact been transferred to Reykjavík. To the morgue on Barónsstígur. We thought you would prefer that to the hospital in Selfoss.'

'Thank you.'

'We'll need you to identify her.'

'Naturally. Of course.'

'Was she alone at Thingvellir?'

'Yes, she went there two days ago to do some work and was due back in town this evening. She said she'd be late. She'd lent the cottage to a friend for the weekend. Or that's what she told me. Said she might hang around and wait for her.'

'It was her friend Karen who found her. Do you know her?'

'Yes.'

'Were you here at home?'

13

'Yes.'

'When did you last speak to your wife?'

'Yesterday evening. Before she went to bed. She had her mobile phone at the cottage.'

'So you hadn't heard from her at all today?'

'No, not at all.'

'She wasn't expecting you at Thingvellir?'

'No. We were going to spend the weekend in town.'

'But she was expecting her friend this evening?'

'Yes, so I gathered. The vicar told me that María probably . . . did it . . . yesterday evening?'

'The pathologist hasn't given us a more accurate time of death yet.'

Baldvin was silent.

'Had she tried to do this before?' Erlendur asked.

'This? Suicide? No, never.'

'Did you know she was in a bad way?'

'She's been a bit depressed and down,' Baldvin said. 'But not so . . . this is . . .'

He broke down in tears.

The vicar met Erlendur's eye and signalled that that was enough for the moment.

'I'm sorry,' Erlendur said and rose from the kitchen table. 'We'll talk more another time. Do you want to call someone to come and be with you? Or a grief counsellor? We can . . .'

'No, it's . . . Thank you.'

On his way out Erlendur walked through the sitting room, which was lined with large bookcases. He had noticed a smart SUV in front of the garage when he parked in the drive.

Why die and leave a home like this? he wondered. Is there really nothing here to live for?

He knew that such thoughts were futile. Experience showed that motives for suicide could be unpredictable and unrelated to a person's financial situation. The act itself frequently came as a total shock and could be committed by people of all ages: adolescents, the middle-aged and elderly, people who decided one day to end it all. Sometimes there was a long history of depression and failed attempts. In other cases the act took friends and family completely by surprise. 'We hadn't a clue he was feeling like that.' 'She never said anything.' 'How were we to know?' The family were left devastated, their eyes full of questions, their voices full of disbelief and horror: 'Why? Should I have seen it coming? Is there something I could have done better?'

The husband accompanied Erlendur to the hall.

'I gather she lost her mother not long ago.'

'Yes, that's right.'

'Was María badly affected by her death?'

'It hit her very hard,' the man said. 'But this is incomprehensible. Even though she's been depressed lately it's still utterly incomprehensible.'

'Of course,' Erlendur said.

'I expect the police deal with a lot of cases?' Baldvin said. 'Of suicide, I mean?'

'Sadly, it's always happening,' Erlendur said.

'Was she . . . Did she suffer?'

'No,' Erlendur said firmly. 'She didn't.'

'I'm a doctor,' Baldvin said. 'You don't have to lie to me.'

'I'm not,' Erlendur said.

'She'd been depressed for quite some time,' Baldvin said, 'but she didn't try to get any help. Maybe she should have done. Maybe I should have been more aware of what she was going

through. She and her mother were very close. María had difficulty reconciling herself to her loss. Leonóra was only sixty-five;
she died far too young. Of cancer. María nursed her and I'm not
sure she had got over her death. She was Leonóra's only child.'

'I imagine that would be hard to bear.'

'It's probably difficult to put oneself in her shoes,' Baldvin
said.

'Yes, of course,' Erlendur replied. 'And her father?'

'He's dead.'

'Was María religious?' Erlendur asked, seeing a statue of Jesus
on the chest of drawers in the hall. There was a Bible beside it.

'Yes, she was,' the other man said. 'She went to church. Much
more religious than me. More so with age.'

'You're not religious?'

'I can't say I am.'

Baldvin sighed heavily.

'It's . . . it's so unreal, you must excuse me, I . . .'

'Yes, I'm sorry,' Erlendur said. 'I'm done.'

'I'll go down to Barónsstígur then.'

'Good,' Erlendur said. 'The police pathologist will need to
examine her. It has to be done in circumstances like these.'

'I understand,' Baldvin said.

Soon the house was empty. Erlendur followed a little way
behind the vicar and Baldvin. As he was turning out of the drive
he glanced in the rear-view mirror and thought he saw the
sitting-room curtains move. He braked and stared in the mirror.
He could see no movement at the window and by the time he
took his foot off the brake and continued on his way he was sure
that he must have been mistaken.

María was prostrate with grief for the first weeks and months after Leonóra's death. She refused all visits and stopped answering the phone. Baldvin took a fortnight's leave from work but the more he wanted to do for her, the more she insisted on being left alone. He procured her drugs to combat the lethargy and depression, but she wouldn't take them. He knew a psychiatrist who was willing to see her but she refused. She said she needed to work through her grief on her own. It would take time and he would have to be patient. She'd done it before and would do it again now.

María was familiar with the anxiety and depression, the lack of appetite and weight loss, and the feeling of mental paralysis that drained her of energy and made her indifferent to anything but the private world of her grief. She allowed no one in. She had been in a similar state after her father died. But then her mother had been there as a pillar of strength. María had dreamed of her father incessantly during the first years after his death and many of her dreams had turned into nightmares that she could not shake off. She suffered from delusions. He appeared to her so vividly that she sometimes thought he was still alive, that he hadn't died after all. She sensed his presence when she was awake, even smelled his cigars. Sometimes she felt as if he were standing beside her, watching her every move. Because she was only a child, she believed he was visiting her from heaven.

Her mother Leonóra, who was a rationalist, said that the visions, the sounds and the smells were a natural reaction to grief, part of her mental response to her father's death. They had been very close and his death had been so traumatic that her senses were conjuring up his presence; sometimes his image, sometimes a smell associated with him. Leonóra called it the inner eye that was capable of bringing her mental pictures to life; she was susceptible after the shock and her senses were hypersensitive and fragile and conjured up abnormal sensations that would disappear with time.

'What if it wasn't the inner eye, as you always said? What if what I saw when Dad died was on the boundary between two worlds? What if he wanted to visit me? Wanted to tell me something?'

María was sitting on the edge of her mother's bed. They had discussed death openly after it became obvious that Leonóra would not be able to escape her fate.

'I've read all those books you brought me about the light and the tunnel,' Leonóra said. 'Maybe there is something in what people say. About the tunnel to eternity. Eternal life. I'll soon find out.'

'There are so many vivid accounts,' María said. 'Of people who have died and come back to life. Of near-death experiences. Of life after death.'

'We've discussed this so often . . .'

'Why shouldn't they be true? At least some of them?'

Leonóra looked through half-closed eyes at her daughter who was sitting beside her, utterly shattered. The effect of her illness on María had been almost worse than it had been on herself. The thought of her mother's approaching death was unbearable to María. When Leonóra had gone she would be alone in the world.

'I don't believe them because I'm a rationalist.'

They sat for a long time in silence. María hung her head and Leonóra kept drifting into a doze, worn out by her three-year battle with the cancer that had now finally defeated her.

'I'll give you a sign,' she whispered, half-opening her eyes.

'A sign?'

Leonóra smiled faintly through the haze of drugs.

'Let's keep it . . . simple.'

'What?' María asked.

'It'll have to be . . . it'll have to be something tangible. It can't be a dream and it can't just be some vague feeling.'

'Are you talking about giving me a sign from beyond the grave?'

Leonóra nodded.

'Why not? If it's anything other than a figment of the imagination. The afterlife.'

'How?'

Leonóra seemed to be sleeping.

'You know . . . my favourite . . . author.'

'Proust.'

'It . . . it'll be . . . keep an eye out . . .'

Leonóra took her daughter's hand.

'Proust,' she said, exhausted, and fell asleep at last. By evening Leonóra was in a coma. She died two days later without ever regaining consciousness.

Three months after Leonóra's funeral, María woke with a jolt in mid-morning and got out of bed. Baldvin left early for work in the mornings and she was alone in the house, feeling weak and worn out from bad dreams and serious long-term stress and debility. She was about to go into the kitchen when she felt instinctively that she was not alone in the house.

At first she looked around her in a panic, believing that a burglar had broken in. She called out to ask if anyone was there.

She was standing there, frozen into immobility, when suddenly she smelled a faint hint of her mother's perfume.

María stared straight ahead and saw Leonóra standing by the bookshelves in the semi-darkness of the sitting room, speaking to her. But she could not make out the words.

She stared at her mother for a long time, not daring to move, until Leonóra vanished as suddenly as she had appeared.

4

Erlendur turned on the light in the kitchen when he got home to his apartment-block flat. A heavy bass beat was pounding from the floor above. A young couple had recently moved in and they blasted out loud music every evening, sometimes deafeningly loud, and threw parties every weekend. Their visitors tramped up and down the stairs well into the early hours, often making an appalling noise. The couple had received complaints from the residents on their staircase and had promised to mend their ways but so far had not kept their word. To Erlendur's mind, what the couple played was not really music so much as the relentless repetition of the same heavy bass beat, interspersed with raucous wailing.

He heard a knock on the door.

'I saw your light on,' his son Sindri Snaer said, when Erlendur opened the door.

'Come in,' Erlendur said. 'I've just got back from Grafarvogur.'

'Anything interesting?' Sindri asked, closing the door behind him.

'It's always interesting,' Erlendur said. 'Coffee? Something else?'

'Just water,' Sindri said, taking out a packet of cigarettes. 'I'm on holiday. I'm taking two weeks off.' He looked up at the ceiling, listening to the thudding rock music upstairs that Erlendur had already ceased to notice. 'What's that racket?'

'New neighbours,' Erlendur called from the kitchen. 'Have you heard from Eva Lind at all?'

'Not recently. She had a fight with Mum the other day.'

'A fight with your mother?' Erlendur said, coming to the kitchen door. 'What about?'

'You, from what I could hear.'

'What can they be fighting about me for?'

'Talk to her.'

'Is she working?'

'Yes.'

'On drugs?'

'No, I don't think so. But she still won't come to any meetings with me.'

Erlendur knew that Sindri attended AA meetings and found them helpful. Despite his tender years, Sindri had suffered from major drink and drug problems, but had single-handedly turned over a new leaf and taken the steps necessary to master his addiction. His sister Eva had not been using recently but refused to consider rehab and meetings in the belief that she could stand on her own two feet.

'What was going on in Grafarvogur?' Sindri asked. 'Some incident?'

'A suicide,' Erlendur said.

'Is that a crime, or . . .?

'No, suicide's not a crime,' Erlendur said. 'Except perhaps to the living.'

'I knew a bloke who killed himself,' Sindri commented.

'Really?'

'Yeah, Simmi.'

'Who was he?'

'He was all right. We worked together for the council. Very easygoing bloke, never said a word. Then he just went and hanged himself. Did it at work. We had a shed and he hanged himself in it. The foreman found him and cut him down.'

'Do you know why he did it?'

'No. He lived with his mother. I went out on the piss with him once. He'd never touched alcohol before, just puked up.'

Sindri shook his head.

'Simmi,' he said. 'Weird bloke.'

It seemed as if the pounding bass line upstairs would never let up.

'Aren't you going to do anything about that?' Sindri asked, glancing up at the ceiling.

'That lot won't listen to anyone,' Erlendur said.

'Do you want me to talk to them?'

'You?'

'I could ask them to turn off that crap. If you like.'

Erlendur considered.

'You can certainly try,' he said. 'I haven't bothered to go up. What did you say they were fighting about, Eva and your mother?'

'I didn't get involved,' Sindri said. 'Was there something strange about this suicide? The one in Grafarvogur?'

'No, just a tragedy. The worst kind. The husband was at home in town when his wife killed herself at their holiday cottage.'

'And he didn't have a clue?'

'No.'

Shortly after Sindri left, the rock music upstairs ceased its pounding. Erlendur looked up at the ceiling. Then he went and

23

opened the front door. He called out to Sindri Snaer but Sindri had gone.

A few days later Erlendur received the pathologist's report on the body from Thingvellir. It showed nothing unnatural apart from death by hanging: no physical injuries or foreign bodies in the blood. María had been healthy and free from disease. There were no biological explanations for why she had chosen to put an end to her own life.

Erlendur went back to see the husband, Baldvin, to inform him of the findings. He drove up to Grafarvogur after lunch and knocked at the door. Elínborg had come along for moral support. She almost couldn't be bothered, claiming that she had enough on her plate. Sigurdur Óli was on sick leave, at home in bed with flu. Erlendur glanced at his watch.

Baldvin invited them into the sitting room. He had taken leave from work for an unspecified period. His mother had stayed with him for a couple of days but had now left. Colleagues and friends had come round or sent messages of condolence. He had arranged the funeral and was aware that some people were planning to write obituaries. He told Erlendur and Elínborg all this as he was making coffee. He was subdued and went about everything slowly but seemed to have himself well under control. Erlendur explained the results of the post-mortem. His wife's death had been registered as suicide. He reiterated his condolences. Elínborg hardly spoke.

'It can be a good idea to have somebody with you,' Erlendur said. 'In circumstances like these.'

'My sister and mother are taking good care of me,' Baldvin said. 'But it's good to be alone sometimes, too.'

'God, yes,' Erlendur said. 'For some people that's the best therapy.'

Elínborg darted a glance at him. Erlendur prized solitude above anything else in life. She wondered what she was doing with him at this house. All he had said was that he had to deliver the pathologist's report. It would take no time. Yet now he was chatting to the man as if they were old friends.

'You blame yourself,' Baldvin said. 'I feel as if I should have done something. As if I could have done something better.'

'That's a natural reaction,' Erlendur said. 'We come across it a lot in our line of work. The family have usually already done everything or nearly everything in their power by the time something like this happens.'

'I didn't see it coming,' the man said, 'I can assure you. I've never been so shocked in my life as when I heard what she'd done. You can't imagine how I felt. I'm used to all sorts of things as a doctor, but when . . . when something like this happens . . . I don't believe anyone could be prepared for it.'

Baldvin seemed to feel the need to talk and informed them that he and his wife had met at the university. María had read history and French. He had dabbled in acting in the sixth form and had attended the drama school for a while before deciding to change tack and take up medicine.

'Was María a professional academic?' Elínborg asked. She herself had a degree in geology but had never worked in the field.

'Yes, she was,' Baldvin said. 'She worked from home. We have a study in the basement. She taught a bit and undertook history projects for institutions and businesses. She did her own research and wrote articles.'

'When did you move to Grafarvogur?' Erlendur asked.

'We've always lived in this house,' Baldvin said, looking round the sitting room. 'I moved in with her and Leonóra while I was still a student. María was an only child and inherited the house when her mother died. It was built before plans were drawn up for the area and they started building here on a large scale. You'll have noticed that the house is set back a little from the others.'

'It looks older than the rest,' Elínborg remarked.

'Leonóra died here,' Baldvin continued. 'In one of the bedrooms. It took three years from when she was diagnosed with cancer until she died. She really didn't want to go into hospital. She wanted to die at home. María nursed her throughout.'

'That must have been tough on your wife,' Erlendur said. 'You told me that she was religious.'

He caught Elínborg sneaking a glance at the clock.

'Yes, she was. She held on to her childhood beliefs. She and her mother used to talk a lot about religion after Leonóra fell ill. Leonóra was like that. Open. She wasn't shy about discussing her illness and death. I think it must have helped a lot with the grief. I think she was resigned to dying in the end. Or as resigned as anyone can be in the circumstances. I'm familiar with it from my job. Of course, no one's truly reconciled to having to die like that, but it is possible to die feeling reconciled to yourself and your family.'

'Are you saying that her daughter was reconciled to dying as well?' Erlendur asked.

Baldvin thought.

'I don't know,' he said eventually. 'I doubt whether anyone who does what she did can be truly reconciled.'

'But she thought about death a lot.'

'All the time, I think,' Baldvin said.

'What about her father?'

'He died a long time ago.'

'Yes, you told me.'

'I never met him. She was only a little girl when it happened.'

'How did he die?'

'He drowned at their summer cottage. At Thingvellir. He fell out of a small boat. Apparently it was very cold and he was a heavy smoker and led a sedentary lifestyle and . . . he drowned.'

'Tragic to lose a parent that young,' Elínborg said.

'María was there,' Baldvin said.

'Your wife was?' Erlendur asked.

'She was only ten. It had an enormous impact on her. I don't think she ever really got over it. So when her mother developed cancer and died, it hit her doubly hard.'

'She had a lot to bear, then,' Elínborg said.

'Yes, she had a lot to bear,' Baldvin agreed, bowing his head.

5

Several days later Erlendur was sitting in his office with a cup of coffee, going over an old missing-person file, when he was informed that someone was asking for him at the front desk: a woman called Karen. Recalling that this was the name of the friend who had found María's body at Thingvellir, Erlendur went down to reception where a woman wearing a brown leather jacket and jeans was waiting. Under her jacket she wore a thick white roll-neck jumper.

'I wanted to talk to you about María,' she said after they had exchanged greetings. 'You are the one handling the case, aren't you?'

'Yes, but it's hardly a case as such, it's been—'

'Could I have a quick word with you?'

'How did you know each other, again?'

'We were childhood friends,' Karen said.

'Oh yes, of course.'

Erlendur showed her into his office where she took a seat opposite him. She did not remove her leather jacket despite the heat in the room.

'We didn't find anything out of the ordinary,' he said, 'if you're after information of that sort.'

'I can't get her out of my head,' Karen said. 'I keep seeing her in front of me the whole time. You can't imagine what a shock it was that she should do this. That I should find her like that. She used to tell me everything but she never talked about anything like this. We confided in each other. If anyone knew María, it was me.'

'And what? You don't think she could have committed suicide?'

'Exactly,' Karen said.

'Then what did happen?'

'I don't know – but she could never have done that.'

'Why do you say that?'

'I'm just sure. I knew her and I'm certain she would never have committed suicide.'

'Suicide generally takes people by surprise. The fact that she didn't tell you anything doesn't make it impossible that she could have killed herself. There's no indication to the contrary.'

'Also, I find it a bit strange that Baldvin should have had her cremated,' Karen added.

'What do you mean?'

'Her funeral's already been held. Didn't you know?'

'No,' Erlendur said, mentally counting the days since he had first visited the house in Grafarvogur.

'I never heard her say that she wanted to be cremated,' the woman said. 'Never.'

'Would she have told you?'

'I think so.'

'Did you and María ever discuss your funerals – what you wanted done with your remains?'

'No,' Karen said stubbornly.

'So you don't really have any proof of whether she wanted to be cremated or not?'

'No, but I just know. I knew María.'

'You knew María. Have you come to this office to put it on record that you believe there's something suspicious about her death?'

Karen considered for a moment.

'I find the whole thing very odd.'

'But you have no actual evidence to back up your suspicion that something strange occurred.'

'No.'

'Then there's very little we can do,' Erlendur said. 'Do you know anything about María's relationship with her husband?'

'Yes.'

'And?'

'It was okay,' Karen said reluctantly.

'So you don't think her husband had anything to do with what happened?'

'No. Perhaps someone came to the door of the cottage at Thingvellir. There are all sorts wandering about there. Foreign tourists, for example. Have you checked up on that angle at all?'

'There's nothing to suggest it,' Erlendur said. 'Did María intend to be at the cottage when you arrived?'

'No,' Karen said. 'Not that we discussed.'

'She told Baldvin she was going to wait for you.'

'Why should she have told him that?'

'Perhaps to be left in peace,' Erlendur said.

'Did Baldvin tell you about Leonóra, her mother?'

'Yes,' Erlendur said. 'He said her death had been a terrible loss to her daughter.'

'Leonóra and María had a special bond,' Karen said. 'I've never known such a close relationship, ever. Do you believe dreams can tell the truth?'

'I don't know if that's any of your business,' Erlendur said. 'With all due respect.'

The woman's vehemence had taken him by surprise. Yet he understood what drove her. A dear friend had committed an act that she found impossible to understand and accept. If María had been in such a bad way, Karen felt that she, Karen, ought to have known and done something about it. Now, even though it was too late, she still wanted to do something – if nothing else, then at least to have an opinion about the tragic event.

'What about life after death?' the woman asked.

Erlendur shook his head.

'I don't know what you—'

'María believed in it. She believed in dreams, that they could tell her something, guide her. And she believed in life after death.'

Erlendur was silent.

'Her mother was going to send her a message,' Karen said. 'You know, if there was an afterlife.'

'No, I'm not quite sure I follow,' Erlendur said.

'María told me that Leonóra was going to let her know if what they talked about so much towards the end turned out to be true. If there was life after death. She was going to send her a sign from the next world.'

Erlendur cleared his throat.

'A sign from the next world?'

'Yes. If there turned out to be an afterlife.'

'Do you know what it was? What sort of sign she was going to give her?'

Karen didn't answer.

'Did she do it?' Erlendur asked.

'What?'

'Did she send her daughter a message from the next world?'

Karen gave Erlendur a long look.

'You think I'm a fool, don't you?'

'I really couldn't say,' Erlendur said. 'I don't know you at all.'

'You think I'm talking a load of gibberish!'

'No, but I don't know how all this concerns the police. Would you care to explain? A message from the afterlife! How are we supposed to investigate something like that?'

'I think the least you could do is to listen to what I have to say.'

'I *am* listening,' Erlendur said.

'No, you're not.' Karen opened her bag, took out a cassette and laid it on his desk. 'Maybe this will help you,' she said.

'What is it?'

'Listen to it and then talk to me. Listen to it and tell me what you think.'

'I can't . . .'

'Don't do it for me,' Karen said. 'Do it for María. Then you'll know how she felt.'

She stood up.

'Do it for María,' Karen said, and left.

Erlendur took the tape home with him that evening. It was an ordinary, unmarked cassette tape. Erlendur had an old radio cassette player. He had never used it to play a tape and didn't know if it worked. He stood for a long time with the tape in his hand, wondering if he should listen to it.

He found the machine, pressed 'open', inserted the cassette, then pressed 'play'. At first he heard nothing. Several more seconds passed and still nothing happened. Erlendur expected to hear the dead woman's favourite music, probably church music, since María was religious. Then there was a tiny click and the tape began to hiss.

'. . . After falling into a trance,' he heard a deep masculine voice say.

He turned up the volume.

'After that I won't be aware of myself,' the man's voice continued. 'It's the dead who choose either to speak through me or to reveal things to me. I am merely their channel for making contact with their loved ones. How long it lasts varies according to the nature of the contact.'

'Yes, I see,' a high female voice replied.

'Did you bring what I asked?'

'I've got a jumper that she was very fond of and a ring Dad gave her that she always wore.'

'Thank you. I'd better take that.'

'Here you are.'

'Remind me to give you the tape afterwards. You forgot to take it the other day. It's easy to forget oneself.'

'Yes.'

'Right, let's see what happens. You're not afraid, are you? You told me at first that you were a little nervous. Some people are anxious about what might come out in these sessions.'

'No, not any more. I wasn't really afraid, just a little uncertain. I've never done anything like this before.'

Long pause.

'There's a gleam of water.'

Silence.

'It's summer and there are bushes and the gleam of water. Like sunlight on a lake.'

'Yes.'

'There's a boat by the lake – does that sound familiar?'

'Yes.'

'It's a small boat.'

'Yes.'

'It's empty.'

'Yes.'

'Does that sound familiar? Do you know this boat?'

'Dad had a small boat. We have a holiday cottage by Lake Thingvallavatn.'

Erlendur turned off the cassette player. He realised that the recording was of a seance and he was certain that the high voice belonged to the woman who had killed herself. Not that he knew anything about it, beyond remembering her husband saying that her father had drowned in Lake Thingvallavatn. Hearing her voice felt peculiar somehow, as if he were prying into someone else's private life. He stood by the cassette player for a long time without moving, until curiosity overcame his doubt and he pressed 'play' again.

'I can smell cigar smoke,' he heard the medium say. 'Did he smoke?'

'Yes. A lot.'

'He wants you to take care.'

'Thank you.'

A long pause followed the woman's words. Erlendur listened to the silence. The hissing of the tape was the only sound audible. Then suddenly the medium began to speak again but now in a completely different voice, deep, harsh and gruff.

'Be careful! . . . You don't know what you're doing!'

Erlendur was startled by the anger in the voice. But in the next breath it had changed.

'Was that all right?' the medium asked.

'I think so,' said the high-voiced woman. 'What was . . .?'

She hesitated.

'Did anyone you recognise make contact?' the medium asked.

'Yes.'

'Good, I . . . Why am I so cold . . .? My teeth are chattering.'

'There was a different voice . . .'

'Different?'

'Yes, not yours.'

'What did it say?'

'It said I should be careful.'

'I don't know what it was,' the medium said. 'I don't remember any—'

'It reminded me . . .'

'Yes?'

'It reminded me of my father.'

'The cold . . . doesn't come from there. The intense cold that I'm feeling. It's directly connected to you. There's something dangerous about it. Something you should beware of.'

Erlendur reached out and turned off the tape. He couldn't face listening to any more. It felt disrespectful. The recording contained material that touched his conscience. He felt as if he were listening at a door. He couldn't bear to dishonour the woman's memory by eavesdropping any further.

6

The old man was waiting for Erlendur at the front desk. He used to come to the police station with his wife but now that she had passed away he came to see Erlendur alone. The couple had dropped by his office regularly for nearly thirty years now, first every week, then every month, then several times a year, then once a year and finally at two- to three-yearly intervals on their son's birthday. Over the years Erlendur had become well acquainted with them and with the sorrow that drove them to seek him out. Their younger son, Davíd, had walked out of their house in 1976 and had never been heard from again.

Erlendur shook the old man's hand and showed him to his office. On the way he asked him how he was doing. The old man said he had moved into a nursing home some time ago but was not happy there. 'It's full of nothing but old people,' he said. He had come down to the station by taxi and asked if Erlendur could call a car to pick him up when their meeting was over.

'I'll get someone to give you a lift home,' Erlendur said, opening the door of his office for him. 'So the nursing home's not very lively, then?'

'Not very, no,' the old man said as he took a seat.

He had come to enquire after news of his son, although he

knew, and had long known, that no news would be forth-coming. Erlendur understood this extraordinary persistence and had always received the couple civilly and shown them the consideration of listening to them. He knew that they had always followed the news – read the papers, listened to the radio and watched the television – in the faint hope that someone had somewhere found a clue relating to their son's disappearance. But in all these years there had not been a single lead.

'He would have been forty-nine today,' the old man said. 'The last birthday he celebrated was his twentieth. He invited all his college friends over, and Gunnthórunn and I had to leave the house for the duration. The party went on till the early hours. He never got to celebrate his twenty-first.'

Erlendur nodded. The police had never found any clues relating to their son's disappearance. It had been reported thirty-six hours after Davíd had left home. He sometimes studied at a friend's house till late at night and went in to school with him in the morning, and had mentioned to his parents that he was going round to see him that evening and might stay over. They were revising for their final exams and were due to finish sixth-form college that spring. He had also mentioned that he needed to go to a bookshop. When he didn't come home from school the following day, his parents began to ring around and ask after him. It transpired that he had not turned up to classes that morning. They called his friend who said that Davíd had not visited him, nor had he mentioned his plans for that evening. The friend had asked Davíd if he felt like going to the cinema, but Davíd had said that he had other fish to fry, without stating what. Other friends and acquaintances proved ignorant of Davíd's whereabouts. He had been lightly dressed when he had left home.

Notices were placed in the papers and appeals were made on television but to no avail and as time wore on his parents' and brother's hopes faded. They refused point-blank to listen to any suggestion of suicide, adamant that the very idea would have been alien to Davíd. But after weeks and months had elapsed with no explanation of Davíd's disappearance, Erlendur said that they should not rule it out. He himself could not see many other possibilities in this case, given that the young man had not been planning to go climbing or to travel into the interior. Another possible explanation was that he had accidentally fallen foul of someone in the criminal fraternity who had disposed of him, for reasons that were obscure, and had hidden the body. His parents and friends had flatly denied that he'd had a quarrel with anyone or could have been involved in any criminal activity that might explain his disappearance. Police checks confirmed that he had not left the country by plane, nor was his name present on the passenger lists of any ships. And no staff at any of the country's bookshops had noticed him in their stores on the day he had vanished.

The old man took a mug from Erlendur and slurped his coffee noisily, though it was not particularly hot. Erlendur had attended his wife's funeral. They did not seem to have many friends or a large family. Their other son was divorced and had no children. A small women's choir had stood at the organ, singing: 'Hark, Heavenly Creator . . .'

'Is there any news of our case?' the old man asked, having half-emptied his cup. 'Has anything new emerged?'

'No, I'm afraid not,' Erlendur said, for the umpteenth time. He did not find the old man's visits a trial. For him, the worst part was that there was little he could do for him except listen to his repeated protestations of what a dreadful thing it was about their dear boy and how could something like that happen and how could there be no news of him?

'Of course, the police have enough on their plates,' the old man said.

'It comes in waves,' Erlendur said.

'Yes, well, no, anyway, best be making tracks,' the old man said, without moving, as if there were something more to be said. Yet they had gone over everything that mattered.

'I'll be in touch if anything comes up,' Erlendur promised, sensing the old man's hesitation.

'Yes . . . erm . . . the thing is, Erlendur, I may not be bothering you again,' the old man said at last. 'It's probably time to let sleeping dogs lie. You see, they've found something . . .' He coughed. 'They've found some muck in my lungs. I've always smoked like an idiot and apparently it's all coming home to roost, so I don't know what . . . And all that cement dust can't have helped, either. So I wanted to say goodbye, Erlendur, and to thank you for everything, everything you've done for us ever since you first came to see us that terrible day. We knew you would help us and you have done, although we're no nearer. He's dead, of course, and has been all these years. I think we've known that for a long time. But one . . . we . . . where there's life there's hope, isn't there?'

The old man stood up. Erlendur rose too and opened the door.

'There's always hope,' he agreed. 'How do you feel with that stuff in your lungs?'

'I'm an old crock these days, anyway,' the old man said. 'Worn out all the time. Utterly worn out. And since I was given the diagnosis, breathing seems to have become more of an effort too.'

Erlendur helped him down to reception and found a squad car to take him back to the nursing home. They said their goodbyes on the steps in front of the police station.

'So long, Erlendur,' the old man said. He was thin and stooped from hard physical labour, with a mop of thick grey hair. He had been a mason and his face was now as grey as cement dust.

'Look after yourself,' Erlendur said.

He watched as the old man climbed into the police car, then followed the vehicle with his eyes until it disappeared round the corner.

The vicar with whom María had had the most dealings was called Eyvör. She served not in Grafarvogur but in a neighbouring parish. She was shocked and saddened by María's fate and by the fact that she should have felt she had no choice but to take her own life.

'It goes without saying that it's heartbreaking,' she told Erlendur who was sitting in her office in the church at the end of the day. 'To think that someone in the prime of life should kill herself as if she had no other option. Experience has shown that it's possible to help people who suffer mental distress and hardship if one intervenes early enough in the process.'

'You didn't have any inkling of what sort of state María was in?' Erlendur asked. 'I gather that she was a believer and attended this church.'

'I knew she was in a bad way after losing her mother,' Eyvör said. 'But there was nothing to suggest that she would resort to a desperate measure like this.'

The vicar was around forty, well dressed in a purple suit and wearing masses of jewellery: three rings, a gold chain round her neck and large earrings. She had been surprised to receive a visit from the police to ask about a parishioner who had committed suicide. She asked immediately if it was a police matter.

'No, of course not,' Erlendur said and invented an excuse on the spot about wrapping up his report on the case. He had heard that María had been in touch with the vicar and wanted to see if he could have a chat with her, take advantage of the opportunity in case it could help with future incidents. Unfortunately, suicide was one aspect of life that landed on a policeman's desk, not the most pleasant, and Erlendur wished to learn more about the causes and effects in case it could help him in his job. Eyvör took a liking to this gloomy policeman, immediately sensing that there was something trustworthy about him.

'Did she talk to you about death?' Erlendur asked.

'Yes, she did,' Eyvör replied. 'About her mother and also about an incident from her childhood that I don't know if you're aware of.'

'You mean when her father drowned?' Erlendur asked.

'That's right. María was in a dreadful state after losing her mother. I officiated at that funeral too, in fact. I got to know mother and daughter quite well, especially after Leonóra fell ill. She was a brave woman, a remarkable woman – nothing ever daunted her.'

'What did she do?'

'Do you mean her job? She was a professor at the university, a professor of French.'

'And her daughter was a historian,' Erlendur said. 'That explains the large number of books in the house. Was María depressed?'

'Let's just say she was very low. I do hope you won't repeat this. I really shouldn't be discussing it with you. She didn't exactly turn to me in her grief, but I got the impression that she was under a great deal of strain. She used to come to church but never opened up to me. I tried to console her but it was actually quite difficult. She was very angry – angry that her mother should have had to die like that. Angry with the powers that be. I think she might have lost a little of her faith, the childlike faith she'd always had, after watching her mother waste away and die.'

'But God moves in mysterious ways, doesn't he?' Erlendur said. 'He alone knows the point of all this suffering?'

'I wouldn't be doing this job if I didn't believe that faith can help us. If we didn't have faith, where would we be?'

'Were you aware at all of her interest in the supernatural?'

'No, I can't say that I was. But, as I say, she was quite reticent and guarded when it came to her private life. Or certain aspects of it.'

'Such as?'

'She believed in dreams, that they could give her an insight into things we can't see in our waking life. Her belief grew stronger over time until I got the impression that she believed dreams were some kind of door into another world.'

'The afterlife?'

'I don't know exactly what she meant.'

'And what did you say to her?'

'What we preach in church. We believe in the resurrection on the Day of Judgement and in eternal life. The reunion of loved ones is the essence of the Easter message.'

'Did she believe in that sort of reunion?'

'I felt that she derived a certain consolation from the idea, yes.'

*

Elínborg was again in tow when Erlendur paid another short visit to María's husband, Baldvin. It was the day after he had spoken to the vicar. He invented some pretext involving a notebook that he had mislaid. Elínborg stood at his side in the sitting room of the house in Grafarvogur, watching him explain his visit. Erlendur had never in his life owned a notebook.

'I haven't seen anything of the kind here,' Baldvin said, after a cursory glance round the room. 'I'll let you know if I find it.'

'Thank you,' Erlendur said, 'I'm sorry to bother you.'

Elínborg smiled awkwardly.

'Tell me: I know it's none of my business, but did María regard death as the end of it all?' Erlendur asked.

'The end of it all?' Baldvin repeated, surprised.

'I mean, did she believe in life after death?' Erlendur asked.

Elínborg stared at him. She had never heard him ask such questions before.

'I think so,' Baldvin said. 'I think she believed in the resurrection, like other Christians.'

'When people are having a hard time or experience the loss of a loved one, they often search for answers, sometimes even from mediums or psychics.'

'I wouldn't know about that,' Baldvin said. 'Why are you asking?'

Erlendur was on the verge of telling him about the recording that Karen had given him but changed his mind. Another time. He suddenly felt it would be unwise to drag Karen into this and mention her concerns. He ought to keep faith with her.

'Just thinking aloud,' he said. 'We've inconvenienced you enough, I'm sorry for the intrusion.'

Smiling, Elínborg took the man's hand and said goodbye with a few words of condolence.

'What was that all about?' she asked angrily once they were seated in the car and Erlendur was driving away slowly. 'The woman committed suicide and you start talking some crap about life after death! Have you no sense of decency?'

'She went to see a medium,' Erlendur said.

'How do you know?'

Erlendur took out Karen's tape and handed it to her. 'It's the recording of a seance that his wife attended.'

'A seance?' Elínborg said in astonishment. 'She went to a seance?'

'I haven't listened to the whole tape. I was going to let him hear what's on it, but . . .'

'But what?'

'I want to track down the medium,' Erlendur said. 'I suddenly wanted to know what game the medium was playing and whether he might have done something to trigger this tragedy.'

'You think he was playing with her?'

'I do. He pretended to see a boat on a lake, to smell cigar smoke. That sort of rubbish.'

'Was he alluding to her father's drowning?'

'Yes.'

'You don't believe in mediums?' Elínborg asked.

'No more than I believe in fairies,' Erlendur said, turning out of the cul-de-sac.

7

When Erlendur got home that evening he buttered himself a flat-cake and topped it with smoked lamb, turned on the coffee-maker, then put Karen's cassette back in the machine.

He thought about María's suicide, about the despair required to precipitate such an act and the sheer mental torment that must have lain behind it. Erlendur had read notes from people who had taken their own lives, some consisting of only a few lines, maybe only a sentence, a single word; others longer, with a detailed enumeration of the reasons for the act, an apology of sorts. Sometimes the letter would be left on the pillow in the bedroom. Sometimes on the floor of the garage. Fathers, mothers, adolescents, pensioners, people who were alone in the world.

He was about to press 'play' when he heard a knock at the door. He went and opened it. Eva Lind slipped past him and came inside.

'Is it a bad moment?' she asked, taking off her knee-length black leather coat. Under it she was wearing jeans and a thick jumper. 'It's bloody cold outside,' she said. 'Isn't this gale ever going to let up?'

'I doubt it,' Erlendur replied. 'It's forecast to last the week.'

'Did Sindri come round?' Eva Lind asked.

'Yes. Do you want some coffee?'

'Yes, please. What did he say?'

Erlendur went into the kitchen and fetched the coffee. He had tried to cut down on his caffeine intake in the evenings because he sometimes had trouble sleeping if he drank more than two cups. Not that he minded wakeful nights; they were the best time for grappling with problems.

'He didn't really say much, though he did mention that you'd had a row with your mother,' Erlendur said when he returned. 'He thought it was something to do with me.'

Eva Lind fished a packet of cigarettes from her leather coat, plucked one out with her nails and lit up. She blew the smoke in a long cloud across the living room.

'The old bag went mental.'

'Why?'

'I told her you two should meet up.'

'Your mother and I?' Erlendur said in surprise. 'Whatever for?'

'That's exactly what Mum said. "Whatever for?" To meet. To talk. To stop this bollocks of never talking. Why can't you two do that?'

'What did she say?'

'She told me to forget it. End of story.'

'Was that what the row was about?'

'Yes. What about you? What do you say?'

'Me? Nothing. If she doesn't want to, that's that.'

'That's that? Can't you even talk to each other?'

Erlendur thought for a moment.

'What are you trying to achieve, Eva?' he asked. 'You know it was all over a long time ago. We've hardly spoken for decades.'

'That's the point – you haven't really talked since Sindri and me were born.'

'I bumped into her when you were in hospital,' Erlendur said. 'It wasn't pleasant. I think you should forget it, Eva. Neither of us wants this.'

Eva Lind had had a miscarriage a few years back and it had taken her a long time to get over the grief. She had been a drug addict for years but Sindri had told Erlendur that she had recently, on her own initiative, started to sort herself out and was doing well.

'You're quite sure?' Eva asked, looking at her father.

'Yes, quite sure,' Erlendur said. 'Tell me, how are you? You look somehow different, more grown up.'

'More grown up? Getting old, am I?'

'No, that's not what I meant. More mature, maybe. I don't know what I'm trying to say. Sindri said you were sorting yourself out.'

'He's talking crap.'

'Is he right?'

Eva Lind didn't answer immediately. She inhaled the smoke of her cigarette and held it in her lungs for a long time before finally expelling it through her nose.

'My friend died,' she said. 'I don't know if you remember her.'

'Who?'

'Her name was Hanna. Your lot found her behind the rubbish bins at Mjódd.'

'Hanna?' Erlendur whispered, thinking back.

'She overdosed,' Eva Lind said.

'I remember. It wasn't long ago, was it? She was on heroin. We don't see much of that here, at least not yet.'

47

'She was a good mate.'

'I didn't know.'

'Do you ever?' Eva Lind said. 'It was either do what she did or . . .'

'Or?'

'Try to do something different, try to drag myself out of the pit. Do it for real for once.'

'What do you mean by doing what she did? Do you think she did it deliberately? Took an overdose?'

'I don't know,' Eva Lind said. 'She didn't care. About anything.'

'Didn't care?'

'Couldn't give a shit about anything.'

'What was her history again?' Erlendur asked. He remembered a wretched-looking girl of about twenty who had been found with a syringe in her arm outside the shopping centre at Mjódd the previous winter. The binmen had found her early in the morning, lying frozen with her back to the wall.

'Why do you always have to talk like a professor?' Eva Lind said. 'What the fuck does it matter? She died. Isn't that enough? What does her "history" matter? What does it matter that there was no one there for her? Anyway, she wouldn't have wanted help because she hated herself. So why should anyone have bothered to help her?'

'She seems to have mattered to you,' Erlendur commented warily.

'She was my mate,' Eva Lind replied. 'Anyway, I didn't mean to talk about her. Will you agree to meet Mum?'

'You feel that I wasn't there for you?' Erlendur asked.

'You've done more than enough,' Eva Lind said.

'I never manage to deal with you – I can never help you in any way.'

'Don't worry. I'll cope.'

'She hated herself?'

'Who?'

'Your friend. You said she hated herself. Was that why she took an overdose? Are you saying she despised herself?'

Eva Lind slowly stubbed out her cigarette.

'I don't know. I think she'd lost all self-respect. It didn't matter to her any more what became of her. She hated a lot of things but most of all I think she hated herself.'

'Have you ever been in that situation?'

'Only about a thousand times,' Eva Lind replied. 'Are you going to meet Mum?'

'I really don't think it would achieve anything,' Erlendur said. 'I've no idea what to say to her and last time we talked she bit my head off.'

'Couldn't you do it for me?'

'What do you expect to get out of it? After all these years?'

'I just want you two to talk,' Eva Lind said. 'To see you together. Is that so bloody hard? You have two children, Sindri and me.'

'Surely you're not hoping we'll get back together?'

Eva Lind contemplated her father for a long moment.

'I'm not an idiot,' she said. 'Don't think I'm some kind of idiot.'

Then she stood up, collected her belongings and said goodbye.

Erlendur sat there remembering how Eva Lind would some-times flare up abruptly like this. He thought he would never get the hang of talking to her without putting her back up. To him, the idea that he should meet up with Halldóra, his ex-wife and the mother of his children, was absurd. That chapter of his life was long finished, in spite of what Eva Lind might say or let herself dream. He and Halldóra had nothing to say to one another. She was a total stranger to him.

Remembering the tape, he went over to the machine and turned it on. He rewound a little to refresh his memory of what he had listened to before. He heard the medium's voice become deep and gruff as he almost growled 'You don't know what you're doing!' Then it changed in the next breath and the medium talked of feeling cold.

'There was a different voice . . .' the woman said.

'Different?'

'Yes, not yours.'

'What did it say?'

'It said I should be careful.'

'I don't know what it was,' the medium said. 'I don't remember any—'

'It reminded me . . .'

'Yes?'

'It reminded me of my father.'

'The cold . . . doesn't come from there. The intense cold I'm feeling. It's directly connected to you. There's something dangerous about it. Something you should beware of.'

Silence.

'Is everything all right?' the medium asked.

'What do you mean, "beware of"?'

'I don't know. But the cold doesn't bode well. I do know that.'

'Can you summon my mother?'

'I don't summon anyone. She'll appear if it's appropriate. I don't summon anyone.'

'It was so brief.'

'I'm afraid there's not much I can do about that.'

'He seemed very angry. He said: "You don't know what you're doing."'

'You'll have to decide for yourself what you want to read into that.'

'Can I come again?'

'Of course. I hope I've been able to help you a little.'

'You have, thank you. I thought perhaps . . .'

'What?'

'My mother died of cancer.'

'I understand,' Erlendur heard the medium say sympathetically. 'You didn't tell me. Is it long since she died?'

'Nearly two years.'

'And did she make contact here?'

'No, but I can sense her. I can sense her presence.'

'Has she given you any sign? Have you been to any other psychics?'

A lengthy silence followed the question.

'I'm sorry,' the medium said. 'Of course, it's none of my business.'

'I've been waiting for her to come to me in a dream but she hasn't.'

'Why have you been waiting for that?'

'We made . . .'

Pause.

'Yes?'

'We made a pact.'

'Oh?'

'She . . . we talked about . . . that she would give me a sign.'

'What sort of sign?'

'If there was life after death she was going to send me a message.'

'What kind of message? A dream?'

'No, not a dream. But I've been waiting to dream about her. I do so long to see her again. Our sign was a bit different.'

'You mean . . . Has she done it, has she given you a sign?'

'Yes, I think so – the other day.'

'What was it?' the medium asked, the eagerness evident in his voice. 'What was the sign? What kind of sign was it supposed to be?'

There was another long pause.

'She was Professor of French at the university. Her favourite author was Marcel Proust and his work *In Search of Lost Time*. She had all seven volumes in French in a beautifully bound edition. She said she would use Proust. The sign would mean yes, there was life after death.'

'And what happened?'

'You think I'm mad.'

'No, I don't. People have been preoccupied with the question of whether there is life after death since time immemorial. We've been trying to find the answer for thousands of years, both scientifically and on a personal level, like you and your mother. It's not the first time I've heard a story like this. And I don't judge people.'

His words were followed by a long hiatus. Erlendur sat in his chair, engrossed. There was something strangely alluring about the dead woman's voice, something unwavering and steadfast that Erlendur believed in. He was extremely sceptical about what she was saying and convinced that seances like the one he was listening to were of no use to anyone, and yet he was certain that the woman genuinely believed what she was saying, that what she had experienced was real to her.

Finally the silence was broken.

'At first, after my mother died, I sat in the living room staring at Proust's works, not daring to take my eyes off them. Nothing happened. Day after day I sat watching the bookcase. I even slept in front of the books. Weeks passed. Months. The first thing I did when I woke up in the morning was to look at the bookcase. The last thing I did at night was to check if anything had happened. Gradually I realised that it was pointless and the more I thought about it and the longer I stared at the book-shelves, the better I understood why nothing was happening.'

'And why was it? What did you realise?'

'It dawned on me over time and I was immensely grateful. My mother was helping me through my grief. She'd given me some-thing to focus on after her death. She knew I'd be devastated, whatever she said. She did her best to prepare me for her death; we used to have long conversations until she became too weak to talk. We discussed death and how she would send me a sign. But of course all that happened was that she made the process of grieving easier for me.'

Silence.

'I don't know if you understand me.'

'I do. Go on.'

'Then the other day, almost two years after my mother died – I'd given up watching the bookshelves and Proust by then – I woke up one morning and went to put on the coffee and fetch the paper, and when I was on my way back to the kitchen I happened to glance into the living room and . . .'

The machine hissed in the silence that followed the woman's words.

'What?' the medium whispered.

'It was lying open on the floor.'

'What was?'

'*Swann's Way* by Marcel Proust. The first volume in the series.'

Another long silence.

'Is that why you came to me?'

'Do you believe in life after death?'

'Yes,' Erlendur heard the medium whisper. 'I do. I believe in life after death.'

8

When Erlendur woke up early next morning, his thoughts returned to the old man who had visited him at the police station to ask for news of his son, almost thirty years after the boy's disappearance. It was one of the first cases that Erlendur had kept open long after everyone else had given up on it. In those days the CID had been based in an industrial estate in Kópavogur. He remembered from around the same time two other missing-person cases that he had not investigated himself but whose details he was familiar with nonetheless. One, which had occurred several weeks earlier, involved a young man who had left a party in Keflavík with the intention of walking to the neighbouring village of Njardvík, but had never arrived there. It was winter and a blizzard had blown up during the night. Search parties were sent out and after three days one of his shoes was found down by the tide-line. He had been on the right track but seemed to have been driven by the storm towards the sea. Nothing had been heard of him since. He had been wearing a shirt, with no coat or sweater, when he left the party and had been drunk, according to his fellow partygoers.

The other case concerned a young girl from the northern town of Akureyri. She was studying at the university and rented a flat in Reykjavík but it was impossible to tell exactly when she had disappeared. When her landlord did not receive his rent in advance for the month, he went round to chase up the money but found no one home. She did not have any compulsory classes at the university because she was writing up her biology dissertation at the time. Moreover, she was an only child and her parents were abroad on a two-month trip around Asia and were only in sporadic contact with her. By the time her parents came home and went to visit their daughter in town, she had vanished. The landlord let them into the flat. Everything was as it should have been, as if she had just popped out for a moment. Her textbooks lay open on the tables where she had been working on the dissertation. There were a couple of glasses in the sink and she had not made the bed. She had been in telephone contact with her friends in Akureyri some time before and two of her fellow students had heard from her and assumed that she had gone north to Akureyri some weeks earlier. To lend support to this theory, the battered old Austin Mini that she drove was also missing.

Erlendur went into the kitchen and turned on the coffee-maker. He put some bread in the toaster, buttered it when it was done, then brought out the cheese and marmalade. He pondered what he had heard on the tape that Karen had lent him and wondered what to do about it. He now had a better appreciation of María's state of mind before she'd killed herself.

His thoughts moved on to Sindri and Eva and his ex-wife Halldóra. He couldn't envisage a meeting between Halldóra and himself, whatever importance Eva Lind might place on bringing them together. Erlendur very rarely thought of Halldóra because when he did so it raked up memories of all the fights and quarrels they had had before he'd walked out on her and their two children. The divorce had been brewing for a long time. He had wanted to do everything in his power to mitigate its effects but every time he had hinted to her that he wished to end the relationship and move out, she'd cut him off, saying it was absurd, that they could work through their problems, and anyway she wasn't aware of any problems and had no idea what he was talking about.

Erlendur flicked through the papers but couldn't shake off the memory of María's voice and her words to the medium. The seance could not have been held long ago; on the tape she had talked of it being just under two years since her mother died, and neither, clearly, had it been her first meeting with the medium. He contemplated the powerful bond between María and her mother. It must have been exceptional. They had probably been brought even closer by the father's death at Lake Thingvallavatn and had supported each other through thick and thin. Could it be anything other than coincidence that María had found the book on the floor, the same book that they had agreed would be a sign of the afterlife? Or had someone else taken a hand in events? Had María told someone, her husband or someone else, about the pact with her mother in the interval between Leonóra's death and the book's falling from the shelf, and subsequently forgotten the fact? Had she herself unwittingly removed the book from the shelf and failed to put it back properly? He couldn't say. The recording ended with María explaining that she had come to the medium because of the sign that she thought she had been sent by her mother; she had wanted to receive confirmation, to make contact with her mother if possible and to learn to be reconciled to her death. The suicide indicated that María had not been reconciled; that, on the contrary, the whole business had finally tipped her over the edge.

Erlendur tried to find a reason for the strangely powerful urge that had gripped him when he'd listened to the tape. An urge to know more, to become better acquainted with the woman who had taken her life, with her friends and family, and to find out why her life had followed the path that was to end in a noose at the holiday cottage. He wanted to get to the bottom of the matter, wanted to track down the medium and interrogate him, dig up the story of the accident on Lake Thingvallavatn, find out who María was. He thought about the voice that had warned María to be careful, that she didn't know what she was doing. Where had that deep, gruff voice come from?

Erlendur sat at the kitchen table, his coffee forgotten, unsure why he was wasting time on this, and his thoughts strayed back to his mother in the basement flat where she had moved after his father's death. She had worked in a fish factory, as tirelessly industrious as ever, and Erlendur used to visit her regularly, sometimes bringing along his dirty laundry. She would feed him and then they used to sit and listen to the radio or else he would read to her; his mother with her eternal knitting – perhaps a scarf that she would later give him. They had little need to talk; the companionable silence was enough for them.

She had still only been middle-aged when his father had died but there was never anyone else in her life. She said she enjoyed being alone. She kept in touch with friends and relatives out east, and former neighbours who had also moved to Reykjavík. Iceland was changing; people were drifting away from the countryside. She assured Erlendur that she never felt lonely in the city but he bought her a television anyway. She was always self-reliant and rarely asked him to do anything for her.

They hardly ever talked of Bergur who had been snatched from them with such shocking suddenness. At times she would make some general remark about the boy or both brothers, but she never talked of the loss of her son. To her, it was a private matter and Erlendur respected her reticence.

'Your father would have liked to know before he died,' she once remarked when he was with her. They had been sitting in silence most of the evening. Erlendur always visited his mother on the anniversary of the day it had happened, the day when he and his younger brother had been caught in the blizzard with his father.

'Yes,' Erlendur replied. He knew what his mother meant.

'Do you think we'll ever know?' she asked, looking up from the book that he had brought her. He had finally summoned up the courage to show it to her late that evening, unsure if he was doing the right thing.

'I don't know,' Erlendur said. 'It was a long time ago.'

'Yes,' she said. 'It was a long time ago.'

She carried on reading.

'What a pack of nonsense this is,' she commented eventually, looking up from the book again.

'I know,' Erlendur said.

'What business is it of other people's, this stuff about me and your father? What has it got to do with anyone else?'

He didn't answer.

'I don't want anyone to read this,' his mother said.

'Well, we can't stop them,' he pointed out.

'And the stuff he says about you.'

'It doesn't bother me.'

'Has this just been published?'

'Yes, it's the third volume in the series. The final volume. It came out just before Christmas. Do you know the man who wrote it? This Dagbjartur?'

'No,' she said. 'He must have been talking to the local farmers.'

'Yes, that's what I thought. It's very detailed and most of what he says is correct.'

'He has no right to say that about your father and me.'

'Of course not.'

'It's not fair on him.'

'No, I know.'

'Where did the man get it from?'

'I don't know.'

His mother closed the book.

'It's a load of nonsense; I don't want anyone to read it,' she repeated.

'No,' he said.

'No one,' she said, handing him the book. He saw that she was fighting back tears. 'As if it was his fault,' she said. 'As if it was anybody's fault. It's nonsense!'

Erlendur took the book. Perhaps he should not have shown it to her. Or should at least have prepared her better for 'Tragedy on Eskifjördur Moor', as the chapter was called. He didn't intend to show anyone else the account. His mother was right; there was no need to draw attention to what was written there.

The winter that the volume containing the story of the brothers' ordeal was published, Erlendur's mother came down with flu. He wasn't aware of it, being wholly taken up with work, and she was unwilling to put him to any inconvenience. She went back to work before she was fully recovered, suffered a relapse and took to her bed again, seriously ill this time. When she finally got in touch with Erlendur she was more dead than alive. The infection had seriously affected her heart. He forced her to go to hospital but there was little they could do. She was only in her early sixties when she died.

Erlendur took a sip of his coffee and found it was cold. He stood up, went into the living room and took down the third volume from the bookcase. It was the same copy that his mother had been reading all those years ago. She had been aggrieved with the author of the account, feeling that he had been too hard on the family. Erlendur agreed; the book contained assertions about matters that were nobody else's business – however true they might have been. His children, Sindri and Eva, knew of the existence of the account but he had been reluctant to show it to them. Perhaps for his father's sake. Perhaps because of his mother's reaction.

He replaced the book on the shelf and the puzzle of the woman from Grafarvogur returned to haunt him. What had led her to that noose? What had happened at Lake Thingvallavatn the day her father died? He wanted to know more. It would have to be his own private investigation and he would have to proceed cautiously, so as not to arouse suspicion; talk to people, make deductions, just as he would in any other case. He would need to lie about the reason for his prying; invent some fictional assignment. But then, it wouldn't be the first time he had done something of which he was not exactly proud.

Erlendur wanted to know why the woman had suffered such a cruel, lonely fate by the lake where her father had also met his chilly end.

The point where the book opened, the sentence about the sky, was also significant.

María's meeting with the medium had lent her a degree of strength. She was convinced that her mother had given her a sign by pulling Swann's Way *out of the bookcase. She couldn't imagine any other explanation, and the medium, the gentlest, most understanding of men, had seemed to agree with her. He told her examples of similar cases of the dead making contact, either directly or else via dreams, sometimes even the dreams of other people rather than of their nearest and dearest.*

What María did not tell the medium was that a few months after Leonóra's death she had begun to see extraordinarily vivid apparitions, and yet she was not frightened by them, despite her fear of the dark. Leonóra would appear to her in the bedroom doorway or on the landing or even sitting on the edge of her bed. If María went into the living room she might see Leonóra standing by the bookshelves or sitting in her chair in the kitchen. She even appeared to her when she left the house, as a faint reflection in a shop window or a face disappearing into the crowd.

To begin with, these visions did not last long, perhaps only for an instant, but they became increasingly prolonged and vivid, and Leonóra's presence grew stronger, just as María had experienced after her father's death. She had read up on this type of grief-related hallucination and knew that the visions could be connected to loss and emotions such as guilt and chronic anxiety. She also knew that studies of the phenomenon suggested that they were projections of her own mind, her inner eye. She was an educated woman; she did not believe in ghosts.

And yet she did not want to close off every avenue. She was no longer confident that science had the answers to all mankind's questions.

The passing of time only reinforced María's belief that her visions were something more than mere psychological delusions produced by a mind oppressed with suffering. At one point they became so realistic that she felt they must originate in another world, despite what science would have her think. Little by little she began to believe that another world might exist. She immersed herself once more in the accounts that Leonóra had read at her urging about near-death experiences and the golden radiance and the love associated with it, about the divine figure in the light, the weightlessness in the dark tunnel that led towards the light. Instead of seeking help for her suffering, she tried to analyse her own condition by using her innate logic and common sense.

Almost two years passed in this way. María's visions grew less frequent over time and her obsession with Proust faded. Her life was returning to an even keel although she knew it would never be the same as it had been when her mother was alive. Then one morning she woke up early and happened to glance in passing at the bookcase.

Nothing had changed.

Or . . .

She looked back at the books.

She felt dizzy when she realised that the first volume was missing. Moving closer she saw that Swann's Way *was lying on the floor.*

Not daring to touch the book, she stooped and peered at the open pages, reading:

'The woods are black now,
yet still the sky is blue . . .'

9

Sigurdur Óli returned to work, coughing and fastidiously blowing his nose into a paper tissue. He said he couldn't face hanging around at home any longer, though he hadn't completely shaken off the bloody flu yet. He was wearing a new, light-coloured summer coat in spite of the autumnal chill and had already been to the gym and barber's at the crack of dawn that morning. When he bumped into Erlendur he looked as fit as ever, despite his lingering virus.

'Everything hunky-dory?' he asked.

'How are you?' Erlendur asked in return, ignoring the irritating phrase that Sigurdur knew always got on his nerves.

'Oh, you know. Anything happening?'

'The usual. Are you going to move back in with her?'

It was the same question that Erlendur had asked Sigurdur Óli before Sigurdur came down with flu. He liked Sigurdur's wife Bergthóra and was saddened by the failure of their marriage. They had once briefly discussed the reasons for the separation and Erlendur had got the impression from his colleague that all hope was not yet lost. But Sigurdur Óli had not answered him then and nor did he do so now. He couldn't stand Erlendur's interfering.

'Still obsessed with missing-person cases, I hear,' he said and disappeared round the corner.

There was less to do than usual, so Erlendur had dug out the files on the three missing-person cases that had occurred in quick succession nearly thirty years ago and had arranged them on the desk in front of him. He clearly remembered the girl's parents. He had gone to visit them two months after their daughter had been reported missing, when the search had yielded no results. They had travelled down from Akureyri and were staying in Reykjavík at the house of some friends who were away. Erlendur could see that they had been going through sheer hell since their daughter's disappearance; the woman looked haggard and the man was unshaven, with black shadows under his eyes. They were holding hands. He knew they had been to see a therapist because they blamed themselves for what had happened; for going on that long trip and only keeping in intermittent contact with their daughter. The trip had been the fulfilment of an old dream of theirs to visit the Far East. They had travelled to China and Japan and even deep into Mongolia. The last contact they'd had with their daughter was via a poor telephone line from a hotel in Beijing. They'd had to book the phone call a long time in advance and the connection was bad. But their daughter had said that things were going very well at her end and that she was looking forward to hearing all about their adventures.

'That was the last time we heard from her,' the woman said in a low voice when Erlendur came to see them. 'We didn't come home until two weeks later and by then she had vanished. We called again when we got to Copenhagen and when we landed at Keflavík, but she didn't answer. When we reached her flat, she had disappeared.'

'We couldn't really make proper telephone contact until we got back to Europe,' her husband added. 'We tried to call her then but she didn't answer.'

Erlendur nodded. A comprehensive search had been organised for their daughter, who was called Gudrún, nicknamed Dúna, but with no success. The police had interviewed her friends, fellow students and relatives but no one could explain her disappearance or begin to imagine what could have become of her. They combed the beaches in Reykjavík and the surrounding area. Crews in inflatable lifeboats scoured the coastline and divers dragged the sea. No one seemed to have noticed the movements of her Austin Mini; an aerial search of the entire Reykjavík area, the route north to Akureyri and all the main roads had failed to produce any results.

'It was just an old banger, really, that she bought herself up north,' her father said. 'You could only get in through the driver's door; the passenger door was stuck, the handles for winding the windows were broken and the boot didn't open, but she was very fond of it all the same and drove it everywhere.'

The parents talked about their daughter's hobbies, one of which was studying lakes. She was reading biology and had a special interest in lakes and aquatic life. The search for her had taken account of this and encompassed the lakes near Reykjavík and Akureyri and on the road north, but to no avail.

Erlendur looked up from the file. He didn't know where the couple were living these days. They were probably still based in Akureyri, both in their seventies by now and hopefully enjoying their retirement. They had got in touch with him every so often for the first few years but he had not heard from them for a long while.

He picked up another file. The disappearance of the young man from Njardvík seemed to have a more obvious explanation. He had been underdressed for the walk between the villages and although the distance was short, a violent blizzard had been raging and seemed likely to have caused his death. In all probability he had stumbled into the sea and been dragged away from shore by the waves. The amount he'd had to drink, which by all accounts had been excessive, must have hampered his ability to save himself, blunting his judgement, energy and willpower. Local rescue teams and the young man's family and friends had combed the entire coastline from the Gardskagi lighthouse to Álftanes in the following days. The young man had left no trail and the search had to be postponed again and again due to extreme weather conditions. All efforts to find him proved in vain.

Erlendur got in touch with María's friend Karen to tell her that he had listened to the tape she'd left in his office. They had quite a long conversation during which Karen gave him the names of several people connected to María. She didn't ask Erlendur why he wanted to examine the case further but seemed pleased with his reaction.

One of the people Karen mentioned was a man named Ingvar. Erlendur decided to pay him a visit. He was friendly and did not query Erlendur's explanation of why he was asking questions about María. They met late one afternoon as freezing showers lashed the city. Erlendur claimed that the police were taking part in a comprehensive study of suicide in collaboration with the other Nordic countries. It was not a complete lie. A study of the kind was being carried out by the Nordic ministries of social affairs and the police had contributed information to it. The aim was to try to uncover the root of the problem, as a Swedish report put it: to examine the causes of suicide, the distribution according to age, gender

68

and social class, and to try to identify any common factors.

Ingvar listened attentively as Erlendur churned out his spiel. Ingvar was in his sixties, an old family friend and companion of María's father Magnús. He came across as rather a passive, sedate sort of man. Naturally he had been shattered by the news and had attended María's funeral, which he described as beautiful. He found it incomprehensible that the girl should have resorted to such a desperate measure.

'Though I knew she was under a lot of strain.'

Erlendur sipped the coffee that the man had offered him.

'I gather she was badly affected by her father's death,' he said, putting down his cup.

'Dreadfully,' Ingvar replied. 'Dreadfully badly. No child should have to go through an ordeal like that. She witnessed the whole thing, you know.'

Erlendur nodded.

'Magnús and Leonóra bought the holiday cottage shortly after they married,' Ingvar continued. 'They often invited me and my dear late wife Jóna to stay with them at weekends and so forth. Magnús spent a lot of time out in his boat. He was mad about fishing, could carry on for days at a time. I used to go along sometimes. He tried to get little María interested but she didn't want to go with him. It was the same with Leonóra. She never went on Magnús's fishing trips.'

'So they weren't with him on the boat?'

'No, certainly not. Magnús was alone; anyway, you'll be able to read that in your reports. In those days people didn't bother so much about wearing or carrying life jackets. Magnús had nothing of the sort with him when he went out on the lake. From what I can remember the boat came equipped with two life jackets, but Magnús always said he didn't need them and kept them in the boat shed. He only went a short way out as a rule; hardly left the shore.'

'But he went a bit further out that last time?'

'He did, yes, from what I've heard. It was unusually cold that day. It was about this time of year, autumn.'

Ingvar fell silent.

'I lost one of my best friends in him,' he added, momentarily distracted.

'That's tough,' Erlendur said.

'His boat had an outboard motor and we gathered from the police afterwards that the propeller fell off and the boat lost its steering and stopped. Magnús had no oars and fell overboard while fiddling with the engine. He was overweight and a heavy smoker and didn't take any exercise, so I don't suppose that helped. Leonóra said the wind had picked up; a cold blast from Mount Skjaldbreid had whipped up the waves, and Magnús drowned in a matter of minutes. Lake Thingvallavatn is freezing cold at this time of year. No one can survive in it for more than a few minutes.'

'No, of course,' Erlendur said.

'Leonóra told me the boat couldn't have been more than a hundred and fifty metres or so from shore. They didn't see what happened. Just caught sight of Magnús in the water and heard his shouts, which were soon cut off.'

Erlendur glanced out of the living-room window. The city lights glittered in the rain. The traffic was building up. He could hear its rumble from inside the house.

'Naturally his death came as a crushing blow to his wife and daughter,' Ingvar continued. 'Leonóra never remarried. She and María lived together for the rest of her life, even after the girl married. Her husband, the doctor, simply moved in with them.'

'Were they religious, the mother and daughter, that you were aware?'

'I know that Leonóra derived a certain comfort from religion after what happened at Thingvellir. It helped her and no doubt the girl too. María was a little angel, I have to say. Leonóra never had the slightest trouble with her. Then she met that doctor – who seems a very decent chap to me. I don't actually know him very well but I had a word with him after María died and of course he was distraught, just as we all are, all of us who knew her.'

'María had a degree in history,' Erlendur remarked.

'Yes, she was interested in the past; she was a great reader. She got that from her mother.'

'Do you know what her particular field was?'

'No, I don't, actually,' Ingvar said.

'Could it have been religious history?'

'Well, I understand that her interest in the afterlife intensified after her mother died. She immersed herself in spiritualism, in ideas about life after death and that sort of thing.'

'Do you know if María ever visited mediums or psychics?'

'No, I know nothing about that. If so, she never told me. Have you asked her husband?'

'No,' Erlendur said. 'It's just something that occurred to me. Did she seem very depressed to you? Could you have imagined that she would do something like that?'

'No, I couldn't. I met her several times and talked to her on the phone but she didn't give the impression that this would . . . in fact, quite the opposite. I thought she was beginning to pick up. The last conversation I had with her was a few days before she . . . before she did it. She seemed more decisive than often before, more optimistic, if anything. I thought I sensed signs of an improvement. But I gather that's sometimes the case.'

'What?'

'That people in her position rally once they've taken the decision.'

'Can you imagine what effect it might have had on her as a young girl to witness the accident at Thingvellir?'

'Well, naturally one can't put oneself in her shoes. In María's case she clung to her mother and drew all her strength and comfort from her after the accident. Leonóra hardly dared take her eyes off the child in those first months and years. Of course, an event like that would have a profound impact and remain with you for the rest of your life.'

'Yes,' Erlendur said. 'So they mourned him together.'

Ingvar was silent.

'Do you know why the motor packed up?' Erlendur asked.

'No. They said the propeller came off. That's all we knew.'

'Had he been fiddling with it, then?'

'Magnús? No. He didn't have a clue about that sort of thing. Never touched an engine in his life as far as I'm aware. If you want to know more about Magnús you could talk to his sister, Kristín. She might be able to help you. Have a chat to her.'

Later that day Erlendur went to see an old schoolfriend of María's. His name was Jónas and he was finance manager of a pharmaceuticals company. He sat in his spacious office, impeccably dressed in a tailor-made suit and wearing a loud yellow tie. He himself was tall and slim with a three-day beard shadow, not unlike Sigurdur Óli. When Erlendur called beforehand, Jónas expressed himself a little surprised by the inquiry into his schoolfriend's suicide and puzzled as to how it concerned him, but he asked no awkward questions.

Erlendur waited for Jónas to finish a phone call that he

explained he had to take; some urgent outside matter, from what Erlendur could gather. He noticed a photo of a woman and three children on a shelf and assumed they were the finance manager's family.

'Yes, about María – is it true what I've heard?' Jónas asked when he finally put down the receiver. 'Did she commit suicide?'

'That's correct,' Erlendur said.

'I could hardly believe it,' Jónas said.

'You met her at college, didn't you?'

'We went out for three years, two at sixth-form college and one at university. She read history, as you probably know. She was into that kind of research.'

'Did you live together or . . .?'

'For the last year. Until I'd had enough.'

Jónas broke off. Erlendur waited.

'No, her mother was . . . to put it bluntly, she was extremely interfering,' Jónas elaborated. 'And the strange thing was that María never seemed to see anything odd about it. I moved into her place in Grafarvogur but quickly gave up on the whole thing. Leonóra was all-important and I never felt I had María to myself. I discussed it with her but María didn't get it; she wanted her mother to live with her and that was that. We quarrelled a bit and in the end I simply couldn't be bothered any more and walked out. I don't know if María ever missed me. I've barely seen her since.'

'She got married later on,' Erlendur said.

'Yes – to some doctor, wasn't it?'

'So you didn't lose touch completely?'

'Well, I just happened to hear and can't say I was surprised.'

'Did you ever see her after you broke up?'

'Maybe two or three times by chance, at parties and that sort of thing. It was all right. María was a great girl. It's absolutely terrible that she should have chosen to end her life like that.'

The mobile phone in Erlendur's pocket began to ring. He apologised and answered it.

'She's prepared to do it,' he heard Eva Lind say at the other end.

'What?'

'Meet you.'

'Who?'

'Mum. She's prepared to do it. She's agreed to meet you.'

'I'm in a meeting,' Erlendur said, glancing at Jónas, who was patiently stroking his yellow tie.

'Aren't you up for it, then?' Eva Lind asked.

'Can I talk to you later?' Erlendur asked. 'I'm in a meeting.'

'Just say yes or no.'

'I'll talk to you later,' Erlendur said.

He ended the call.

'Did death have any particular meaning for María?' Erlendur asked. 'Was it something she gave much thought to, from what you can remember?'

'Not particularly, I don't think. We didn't discuss it – we were only kids, after all. But she was always very scared of the dark. That's the main thing I remember about our relationship, her absolute terror of the dark. She could hardly be alone in the house after nightfall. That was another reason why she wanted to live with Leonóra, I think. And yet . . .'

'What?'

'In spite of her fear of the dark, or perhaps because she of it, she was forever reading ghost stories, all that sort of stuff, Jón Árnason's Icelandic folk tales and so on. Her favourite films were horror movies about ghosts and all that crap. She lapped it up, then would hardly dare go to sleep in the evenings. She was incapable of being alone. Always had to have somebody with her.'

'What was she so afraid of?'

'I never really knew because I couldn't give a toss about that sort of thing. I've never been scared of the dark. I don't suppose I listened to her properly.'

'But she actively indulged her fear?'

'It certainly seemed like that.'

'Was she sensitive to her surroundings – did she see or hear things? Was her fear of the dark rooted in something she had experienced or knew?'

'I don't think so. Though I remember that she used to wake up sometimes and stare fixedly at the bedroom door as if she could see something. Then it would pass. I think it was something left over from her dreams. She couldn't explain it. Sometimes she thought she saw human figures. Always when she was waking up. It was all in her mind.'

'Did they speak to her?'

'No, it was nothing – just dreams, like I say.'

'Might it be relevant to ask about her father in this context?'

'Yes, of course. He was one of them.'

'One of those that she saw?'

'Yes.'

'Did she attend any seances when you were with her?'

'No.'

'You'd have known?'

'Yes. She never did anything like that.'

'Her fear of the dark – what form did it take?'

'Oh, the usual, I expect. She didn't dare go down to the

washing machine in the basement on her own. She would hardly go into the kitchen alone. She always had to have all the lights on. She needed to be able to hear me if she was moving around the house in the evenings, especially if it was very late at night. She didn't like it if I went out, if I couldn't spend the night with her.'

'Did she try to get any help for it?'

'Help? No. Isn't it just something that . . . Can you get help for fear of the dark?'

Erlendur didn't know. 'Maybe. From a psychologist or someone like that,' he said.

'No, nothing like that, at least not while I was with her. Maybe you should ask her husband.'

Erlendur nodded.

'Thanks for your help,' he said, standing up.

'No problem,' Jónas said, again running a small hand down his yellow tie.

10

The old man's visit to the police station to ask for news of his missing son continued to prey on Erlendur's mind. Despite wishing passionately that there was something he could do for him, he knew that there was precious little he could achieve in practice. The case had been shelved long ago. An unsolved missing-person case. The most likely explanation was that the young man had killed himself. Erlendur had tried to discuss this possibility with the old couple but they wouldn't hear of it. Their son had never entertained such an idea in his life and had never attempted anything of the kind. He was a happy, lively soul and would never have dreamed of taking his own life.

Their opinion was seconded by his friends whom Erlendur had interviewed at the time. They utterly rejected the idea that Davíd could have killed himself, dismissing it as ridiculous, but could provide little enlightenment otherwise. He had not mixed with any types who might conceivably do him harm; he was simply a very ordinary youth who was finishing sixth-form college and planning to start a law course at university with his two best friends the following autumn.

At the present moment, Erlendur was sitting in the office of Thorsteinn, one of those two friends. It was decades since they had last spoken about the young man's disappearance.

Thorsteinn had taken a law degree, been appointed Supreme Court advocate and now ran a large legal practice with two partners. He had thickened out considerably since his early twenties, lost most of his hair and now had bags under his eyes from fatigue. Erlendur remembered the youth he had met some thirty years before, a young, slim, muscular figure about to embark on the life that had now set its mark on him, transforming him into a worn-out middle-aged man.

'Why are you back here asking questions about Davíd? Has there been some news?' the lawyer asked. Then he buzzed his secretary and instructed that he was not to be disturbed. Erlendur had encountered the secretary, a smiling middle-aged woman, in the corridor.

It was two days since he had spoken to María's ex-boyfriend. Elínborg complained that he did nothing at work these days except waste his time on old missing-person files. Erlendur told her not to worry her head about him. 'I'm not worried about you,' Elínborg retorted, 'I'm worried about the taxpayers' money.'

'No, no news,' Erlendur said in reply to Thorsteinn. 'I believe his father's dying. It's the last chance to do something before he passes away.'

'I think of him from time to time,' the lawyer said. 'Davíd and I were great mates and it's sad not knowing what happened to him. Very sad.'

'I believe we did everything we could,' Erlendur said.

'I don't doubt it. I remember how dedicated you were. There was another officer with you . . . ?'

'Marion Briem,' Erlendur said. 'We handled the case together. Marion has since died. I've been going through the old files. Were you away in the countryside when he vanished?'

'Yes, my parents are from Kirkjubaejarklaustur. I went there on a visit with them. We were away for a week or so. I only heard about Davíd when I came back to town.'

'You mentioned a telephone conversation that you had with him, your last conversation. While you were in Kirkjubaejarklaustur. He called you there.'

'Yes. He was asking when I was coming back to town.'

'He wanted to tell you something.'

'Yes.'

'But he wouldn't say what it was.'

'No. He was very secretive, but he seemed elated. It was good news that he wanted to tell me, not bad. I asked him specifically. He giggled. Told me not to worry, that it would all become clear.'

'And he was elated about his news?'

'Yes.'

'I know we asked you all this at the time.'

'You did. I couldn't help you. Any more than I can now.'

'And there's nothing else apart from what you said then: that he had some news to tell you, which he was happy about.'

'That's right.'

'His parents didn't know what it could be.'

'No, he doesn't seem to have told them.'

'Do you have any idea what it could have been?'

'Only guesses. Sometime much later it occurred to me that it might have been a girl, that he'd fallen for some girl, but I'm just guessing. I don't suppose the idea crossed my mind until I met Gilbert again.'

'Davíd didn't have a girlfriend at the time he vanished?'

'No, none of us did,' the lawyer said, with a smile. 'Somehow I have the feeling that he would have been the last of us lads to get a girlfriend. He was terribly shy about that sort of thing. Did you ever talk to Gilbert?'

'Gilbert?'

'He moved to Denmark around the time when Davíd disappeared. He's back in Iceland now. I imagine he's probably the only person you never interviewed.'

'Oh yes, I vaguely remember,' Erlendur said. 'I don't think we ever managed to get hold of him.'

'He was going to work at a hotel in Copenhagen for a year but liked it so much that he stayed on. Married a Danish woman. It's about ten years since he came home. I hear from him occasionally. I got the impression once, from what he said, that Davíd had met a girl. At least, that's what Gilbert thought, but it was all very hazy.'

'Hazy?'

'Yes. Very.'

That evening, after Erlendur had eaten and settled down in his chair to read, his girlfriend Valgerdur phoned. She was trying to drag him out to the theatre. The National was staging a popular comedy that she wanted to see and she was keen for Erlendur to come with her. His reaction was unenthusiastic as the theatre bored him. Valgerdur had had no more luck in trying to persuade him to go to the cinema. The only cultural activity he was not entirely averse to was concerts: choral music, solo performances and concerts by the Symphony Orchestra. The last event he had attended with her had been an evening's entertainment by a mixed choir from Svarfadardalur in the countryside. Valgerdur had a cousin in the choir. Erlendur had thoroughly enjoyed the occasion. The programme had featured the poems of Davíd Stefánsson set to music.

'The play's supposed to be hilarious,' Valgerdur told him over the phone. 'A light farce. It would do you good.'

Erlendur grimaced.

'All right,' he said. 'When is it?'

'Tomorrow evening. I'll pick you up.'

He heard a knock at his door and said goodbye to Valgerdur. Eva Lind was standing on the landing with Sindri. They greeted their father, then entered and sat down in the living room. Both took out cigarettes.

'What did you say to that lot upstairs? I haven't heard a peep from them since you had a word with them.'

Sindri grinned. Erlendur had been astonished not to hear the heavy rock blasting out from upstairs any longer and had been wondering what on earth Sindri could have said to make the couple belatedly show their neighbours some consideration.

'Oh, they were pretty harmless: a girl with a ring in her nose and a bloke with a bit of an attitude. I told them you were a debt collector. That you did regular spells inside for GBH and were getting pissed off with the noise.'

'I thought maybe they'd moved,' Erlendur said.

'You dickhead,' Eva Lind said, her gaze fixed on her brother. 'Have you started telling lies for him now?'

'It was a hell of a racket,' Sindri said apologetically.

'Have you thought about it?' Eva Lind asked Erlendur. 'About Mum. You *are* going to meet her, aren't you?'

Erlendur didn't answer immediately. He'd had little time to give any thought to what Eva was trying to arrange. He had no desire to see his ex-wife, the mother of his children. But, then again, he didn't want to appear dismissive of Eva's initiative now that she seemed to have developed a new interest.

'What are you trying to achieve?' he asked.

81

His gaze swung back and forth between brother and sister as they sat on the sofa facing him. Their visits had gradually become more frequent: first Sindri, after he'd moved back to Reykjavík from the east where he had been working in a fish factory, then Eva Lind, after she had cut back on her drug intake. Their visits meant a great deal to Erlendur, especially when they came together. He liked to observe their relationship. As far as he could tell it was good. Eva Lind was the bossy big sister and sometimes adopted the parental role. She would give Sindri an earful if she was displeased. Erlendur suspected that she had been put in charge of her brother at times when they were younger. And although Sindri gave back as good as he got, he displayed no ill feeling or impatience.

'I just think it would be good for you both,' Eva Lind said. 'I don't understand why you can't even talk to each other.'

'Why do you want to interfere?'

'Because I'm your daughter.'

'What did she say?'

'Oh, you know, that she'd do it. She'd meet you.'

'Did you have to apply much pressure?'

'Yes. You're as bad as each other. I don't know why you ever broke up.'

'Why is this so important to you?'

'You ought to be able to talk to each other,' Eva Lind said. 'I don't want things to go on like this any more. I've . . . Sindri too, we've never seen you two together. Not once. Don't you find that weird? Do you think it's normal? That your children have never even seen the pair of you together? Their own parents?'

'Is that anything unusual these days?' Erlendur asked. Then he directed his words to Sindri. 'Are you just as set on this?'

'I really couldn't give a toss,' Sindri said. 'Eva's trying to drag me into it but I really—'

'You don't have a fucking clue,' Eva Lind interrupted.

'No, right. There's no point trying to tell her this is a load of crap. If you and Mum had the slightest interest in talking, you'd have done it by now. Eva's just sticking her nose in, like always. She can't stop. Sticks her nose in everywhere, especially when it has sod-all to do with her.'

Eva Lind looked daggers at her brother.

'You're a twat,' she said.

'I think maybe you should leave it, Eva,' Erlendur said. 'It's . . .'

'She's up for it,' Eva Lind said. 'It's taken me two months to talk her round. You have no idea what shit I've had to go through.'

'Look, I understand what you're trying to do but in all seriousness I don't think I can bring myself to.'

'Why not?'

'It's . . . It was over between your mother and me a long time ago and it won't help anyone to rake the whole thing up now. It's past. Finished. Over. I think maybe it would be better to think of it like that and try to concentrate on the future instead.'

'I told you,' Sindri said, with a look at his sister.

'Concentrate on the future! Bollocks!'

'Have you thought it through, Eva?' Erlendur asked. 'Is she planning to come here? Am I supposed to visit her? Or are we to meet on neutral territory?'

He looked at her, reflecting on the fact that he had started to use Cold War terminology when talking about his ex-wife.

'Neutral territory!' Eva Lind snorted. 'What do you think it's like trying to deal with you two? You're off your trolleys, both of you.'

She stood up.

'We're nothing but a sodding joke to you. Me and Mum and Sindri – we're nothing but a joke!'

'That's not true at all, Eva,' Erlendur said. 'I really didn't—'

'You've never taken the slightest notice of us!' Eva Lind said. 'Never listened to a word we had to say!'

Before Erlendur and Sindri knew it, she had stormed out of the door, slamming it so hard that the entire building echoed.

'What . . .? What happened?' Erlendur asked, looking at his son.

Sindri shrugged.

'She's been like this ever since she quit using; incredibly touchy. You can't say a word without her going mental.'

'When did she start this business about wanting your mother and me to meet?'

'She's always talked that way,' Sindri said. 'Ever since I can remember. She thinks . . . oh, I don't know, Eva's so full of crap.'

'I've never heard her talk crap,' Erlendur said. 'What does she think?'

'She said it might help her.'

'What? What might help her?'

'If you and Mum . . . If things didn't have to be so bad between you and Mum.'

Erlendur stared at his son.

'She said that?'

'Yes.'

'It might help her to get a grip on her life?'

'Something like that.'

'If your mother and I tried to make up?'

84

'She just wants you to talk to each other,' Sindri said, stubbing out the cigarette he had smoked down to the end. 'Why's that so complicated?'

Erlendur lay awake after their visit, thinking about a house in the east of the country that had once been reputed to be haunted. It was a two-storey wooden house, built by a Danish merchant towards the end of the nineteenth century. In the 1930s a family from Reykjavík had moved in and shortly afterwards stories began to circulate about the woman of the house, who kept hearing the sound of a child crying behind the panelling in the sitting room. No one had mentioned anything of the kind before and no one could hear the crying except the housewife when she was alone at home. Her husband talked dismissively of local cats but his wife obstinately insisted it was nothing of the sort. She became fearful of the dark and of ghosts, suffered from nightmares and generally felt ill at ease in the house. In the end she could no longer bear it and persuaded her husband to move away from the district. They returned to Reykjavík after only three years in the east. The house was sold to some locals who never noticed anything unusual.

Shortly after 1950 a man became interested in the story of the housewife from Reykjavík and the crying child, and started researching the history of the house. A number of families had lived there since the Danish merchant sold it, including three families simultaneously in one period, but there was never any mention of a child crying behind the sitting-room panelling. On delving further back into the early history of the house in search of any link to a child, the man discovered that the Danish merchant who built it had had three daughters who all lived to a ripe old age. The merchant's servants had no children. But when finally he turned to the story of the house's construction he found out that there had been two head carpenters, one of whom had taken over the job from the other. The former, who resigned from the job, had had a two-year-old daughter who was killed in an accident on the site where the sitting room was later built. A pile of timber had fallen on her from a height, killing her instantly.

Erlendur had heard the story of the haunted house in his youth. His mother had it first-hand from the man who had dug up the tale of the carpenter's daughter. He completely ruled out the possibility that the housewife from Reykjavík could have known anything about the building of the house. Erlendur didn't know what to make of the story. Nor did his mother.

What did it tell one about life and death?

Was the woman from Reykjavík more receptive to supernatural influences than other people or had she heard the story of the carpenter's daughter and responded as she had because she suffered from an overactive imagination?

And if she was more receptive than other people, what on earth was it that had lurked behind the panelling?

11

The woman remembered clearly the period when María and Baldvin had started dating. Her name was Thorgerdur and she was tall and big-boned, with a mane of dark hair. She had studied history with María at university but had given up after two years and switched to a degree in nursing. She had kept in close touch with María ever since their student days and was chatty and not at all shy about talking to a police officer like Erlendur. She even volunteered the information that she had once witnessed a crime; she had been at the chemist's when a hooded man had burst in with a knife and threatened the sales lady.

'He was pathetic, really,' Thorgerdur explained. 'A druggie. They caught him immediately and we bystanders had to identify him. It was easy. He was still wearing the same shabby clothes. Needn't have bothered with the hood. A stunning-looking boy.'

Erlendur smiled privately. A member of the underclass, Sigurdur Óli would have said. It was one of those terms he had picked up in America. To Sigurdur Óli's mind it applied not only to criminals and drug addicts, whom he described as total losers, but also to anyone else he disliked for whatever reason: uneducated employees, shop assistants, labourers, even trades-men, all of whom drove him up the wall. He had once flown to

Paris for a weekend break with Bergthóra. They had taken a charter flight and he had been disgusted when most of the other passengers, who were on their annual work outing, became rowdy and drunk and, to cap it all, broke into applause when the plane landed safely in Paris. 'Plebs,' he'd sniffed to Bergthóra, full of disdain at the behaviour of the underclass.

Erlendur eased the conversation round to María and her husband and before Thorgerdur knew it she was telling him all about the history course that she had dropped out of and about her friend María who had met the future doctor at a student disco.

'I'm going to miss María,' she said. 'I can still hardly believe that she went like that. The poor thing, she can't have been in a good way.'

'You got to know one another at the university, you say?' Erlendur prompted.

'Yes, María was absolutely fascinated by history,' Thorgerdur said, folding her arms across her chest. 'Fascinated by the past. I was bored out of my skull. She used to sit at home, typing up her notes. I didn't know anyone else who bothered. And she was a good student, which you certainly couldn't say about all of us who did history.'

'Did you know Baldvin?'

'Well, only after he and María got together. Baldvin was a great guy. He was studying drama but had more or less given up by the time they started going out. Didn't really have what it took to be an actor, apparently.'

'Oh?'

'Yes, or so I heard – that he was better off opting for medicine. They were a terrific gang, the drama students, always having a laugh. People like Orri Fjeldsted, who's obviously one of the big

88

names today. Lilja and Saebjörn – they got married. Einar Vífill. They all became stars. Anyway, Baldvin switched to medicine and carried on acting alongside his studies for a while, but eventually gave up.'

'Did he regret it, do you know?'

'No, not that I've heard. Though he's still very interested in the theatre. They went to a lot of plays and knew loads of people in showbiz, had friends at all the theatres.'

'Do you know what sort of relationship Baldvin and Leonóra had?'

'Well, of course he moved in with María, and Leonóra, who was a very strong character, was living there too. María sometimes said her mother tried to boss them around and it got on Baldvin's nerves.'

'What about María, what period of history was she interested in?'

'She only had eyes for the Middle Ages, the stuff I found deadliest of all. She studied incest and bastardy and the laws and punishments associated with them. Her final dissertation was about drownings at Thingvellir. It was very informative. I got to proofread it for her.'

'Drownings?'

'Yes,' Thorgerdur said. 'The execution of adulteresses in the Drowning Pool and so on.'

Erlendur was silent. They had found a seat in the lounge at the hospital where Thorgerdur worked. An old lady inched past them on a Zimmer frame. An assistant nurse in white clogs hurried along the corridor. A group of medical students stood nearby, comparing notes.

'Of course, it fits,' Thorgerdur remarked.

'What fits?' Erlendur asked.

'Well, I heard she'd . . . I heard she'd hanged herself. At her holiday cottage at Thingvellir.'

Erlendur looked at her without answering.

'But of course it has nothing to do with me,' Thorgerdur said awkwardly on receiving no reaction.

'Do you know if she had any particular interest in the supernatural?' Erlendur asked.

'No, but she was terrified of the dark. Always had been, ever since I first knew her. She could never go home from the cinema alone, for instance. You always had to go with her. Yet she went to see all the scariest horror movies.'

'Do you know why she was so frightened of the dark? Did she ever talk about it?'

'I . . .'

Thorgerdur hesitated. She glanced out into the corridor as if to make sure that no one was listening. The old lady with the Zimmer frame had reached the end of the corridor and was standing there as if she didn't know what to do next, as if the purpose of her trip had eluded her somewhere during her painfully slow progress up the corridor. In the distance an old favourite was playing on the radio: *He loved the sea, did old Thórdur . . .*

'What was that?' Erlendur asked, leaning forward.

'I have the feeling she didn't . . . there was something about what happened at Lake Thingvallavatn,' Thorgerdur said. 'When her father died.'

'What?'

'It's a feeling I had, that I've had for a long time about what happened on Lake Thingvallavatn when she was a little girl. María could be very subdued at times and in very high spirits at others. She never mentioned that she was taking any medication but her exaggerated mood swings didn't seem normal to me sometimes. Once, a long time ago when she was very depressed, I was sitting with her at her house in Grafarvogur when she started talking about Lake Thingvallavatn. It was the first I'd heard about it; she'd never raised the subject before in my hearing, and I immediately got the sense that she was crippled with guilt about what had happened.'

'Why should she have felt guilty?'

'I tried to discuss it with her later but she never opened up again like she did that first time. I felt she was always on guard because of what had happened but I'm absolutely convinced that there was something gnawing away at her, something she couldn't tell anyone.'

'Naturally, it was a terrible thing to happen,' Erlendur said. 'She watched her father drown.'

'Of course.'

'What did she say?'

'She said that they should never have gone to the holiday cottage.'

'Was that all?'

'And . . .'

'Yes?'

'That perhaps he was meant to die.'

'Her father?'

'Yes, her father.'

The audience exploded with laughter, Valgerdur among them. Erlendur raised his eyebrows. The husband had appeared unexpectedly at the third door and let out a peculiar bark on spotting his wife in the arms of the butler. His wife thrust the butler away, crying that he had tried to have his wicked way with her. The butler gave the audience a look as if to say, 'In your dreams!' Cue more gales of laughter from the audience. Valgerdur, beaming from ear to ear, glanced at Erlendur, only to sense his boredom. She stroked his arm and he smiled at her.

After the show they went to a café. He ordered a chartreuse with his coffee. She ordered chocolate cake served hot with ice cream, and a sweet liqueur. They discussed the play. She had enjoyed it but he was unimpressed, merely pointing out inconsistencies in the plot.

'Oh, Erlendur, it was only a farce. You're not supposed to take it so seriously,' Valgerdur said. 'You're supposed to laugh and forget yourself. I thought it was hilarious.'

'Yes, people certainly laughed a lot,' Erlendur said. 'I'm not used to going to the theatre. Are you familiar with an actor called Orri Fjeldsted?'

He remembered what Thorgerdur had said about Baldvin's actor friends. He himself knew next to nothing about the celebrity world.

'Of course I do,' Valgerdur said. 'You saw him in *The Wild Duck*.'

'*The Wild Duck*?'

'Yes, he was the husband. A bit old for the role, perhaps, but . . . a very good actor.'

'Yes, he is,' Erlendur said.

A keen theatregoer, Valgerdur had managed to drag Erlendur along with her on a handful of occasions. She chose weighty plays, Ibsen and Strindberg, in the hope that they would appeal to him, but discovered that he was bored. He fell asleep during *The Wild Duck*. She tried comedies. They were beyond the pale, in his opinion. However, he did enjoy a dreary production of

Death of a Salesman, which did not come as a particular surprise to Valgerdur.

The café was fairly empty. Easy-listening music was playing from somewhere above their heads. It sounded like Sinatra to Erlendur: 'Moon River'. He had a record of Sinatra singing it. He had once seen a film in the cinema – he had forgotten the name – in which the song was sung by a beautiful actress. There were few people out in the chilly autumn weather. The odd figure darted past their window, bundled up in a down jacket or winter coat; faceless, nameless people who had business in town at this late hour.

'Eva wants me and Halldóra to meet,' Erlendur announced, sipping his liqueur.

'Oh,' Valgerdur said.

'She wants us to try to improve our relationship.'

'That makes sense, doesn't it?' Valgerdur said. She always took Eva Lind's side when her name came up in conversation. 'You have two children together. It's natural for you to have some sort of contact. Is she prepared to meet you?'

'So Eva says.'

'Why haven't you been in contact for all these years?'

Erlendur paused for thought.

'Neither of us wanted it,' he answered.

'It must have been difficult for them. For Sindri and Eva.'

Erlendur did not reply.

'What's the worst that could happen?' Valgerdur asked.

'I don't know. It's become so remote, somehow. Our relationship. The way we were. A whole lifetime has passed since we lived together. What would we talk about? Why rake it all up?'

'Maybe time has healed the wounds.'

'It didn't seem like that when I bumped into her a few years ago. She hadn't forgotten anything.'

'But now she wants to meet you?'

'Apparently, yes.'

'Maybe it's a sign that she's willing for there to be a reconciliation.'

'Maybe.'

'And it's important to Eva.'

'That's the point. She's pushing pretty hard for it but . . .'

'What?'

'Nothing,' Erlendur said. 'Except . . .'

'Yes?'

'I couldn't bear any sort of score-settling.'

The foreman called down to Gilbert who was standing at the bottom of a vast, cavernous foundation pit. He was dressed in blue overalls and smoking a cigarette. The foreman informed Erlendur that they were building an eight-storey block of flats with a basement car park, which was why the foundations had to be so wide and deep. He didn't ask why Erlendur wanted to speak to Gilbert, who stood for a long time looking up at them on the edge of the pit before flicking away his cigarette and starting to climb a large wooden ladder that rose from the depths. It took him quite some time. The foreman made himself scarce. The site was up by Lake Ellidavatn. Yellow cranes reared into the gloomy grey afternoon sky as far as the eye could see, like giant square brackets thrust into the ground by the gods of industry. There was a roar from an unseen dumper truck. From somewhere else came the electronic beeping of a reversing lorry.

Erlendur introduced himself, shaking Gilbert by the hand.

Gilbert didn't know what to make of it. Erlendur asked if they could sit down somewhere quiet, out of this din. Gilbert studied him, then nodded towards a green hut. It was the contractors' cafeteria.

Inside the suffocating heat of the cafeteria, Gilbert half-unzipped his blue overalls.

'I can't believe you're asking about Davíd after all this time,' he said. 'Has there been some new development?'

'No, nothing,' Erlendur said. 'It's a case I handled back in the day and for some reason . . .'

'It won't go away. Is that it?' Gilbert finished for him.

He was a tall, lanky man of around fifty who looked older; a little hunched as if he had grown used to avoiding door lintels and low ceilings. His arms were long like his body; his eyes sunken in his gaunt face. He hadn't bothered to shave for several days and his stubble rasped when he scratched it.

Erlendur nodded.

'I'd just moved to Denmark when he went missing,' Gilbert said. 'I didn't hear about it till later and was totally shocked. It's sad that he's never been found.'

'It is,' Erlendur said. 'An attempt was made to track you down at the time but with no success.'

'Are his parents still alive?'

'His father is, but he's old and in poor health.'

'Are you doing this for him?'

'No, not for anyone in particular,' Erlendur said. 'It emerged the other day that you're the only one of his friends we never talked to because you'd moved abroad.'

'I meant to spend a year in Denmark,' Gilbert said, fishing a new cigarette from inside his overalls. His movements were slow and methodical. He found a lighter in another pocket and tapped the cigarette on the table. 'But ended up staying for twenty. It was never the intention but . . . that's life.'

'I gather you spoke to Davíd shortly before you left the country.'

'Yes, we were always in contact. Have you been talking to Steini – Thorsteinn, I mean?'

'Yes.'

'I met him at one of those reunions. Apart from that I've lost all contact with the gang I knew in the old days.'

'You told Thorsteinn it was conceivable that Davíd had met a girl. That information never emerged during the original investigation. I wanted to find out if you know who it was and if I can get hold of her.'

'Steini didn't have a clue. I assumed he knew more than I did,' Gilbert said, lighting the cigarette. 'I don't know who the girl was. I don't even know if there was a girl. Did nobody come forward when Davíd went missing?'

'No,' Erlendur said.

His mobile phone began to ring. He asked Gilbert to excuse him and took out his phone.

'Yes, hello.'

'Are you questioning people about María?'

Erlendur was taken aback. The voice was grave and severe, and contained a note of cold accusation.

'Who is this?' Erlendur asked.

'Her husband,' the voice on the phone said. 'What the hell are you up to?'

A number of answers flashed through Erlendur's mind, all of them lies.

'What's going on?' Baldvin asked.

'Perhaps we should meet,' Erlendur said.

'What are you investigating? What are you doing?'

'If you're home later today I could—'

Baldvin hung up. Erlendur smiled awkwardly at Gilbert.

'Sorry,' he said. 'We were talking about the girl. Do you know anything about her, anything you could tell me?'

'Next to nothing,' Gilbert said. 'Davíd called me the day before I flew to Denmark to say goodbye and told me it was probably okay to tell me a secret since I was going abroad. He wasn't going to let the cat out of the bag, though, not until I grilled him and asked him straight out. Then he told me there might be some news about his love life when I came home again.'

'Was that all he said, that there might be some news about his love life later?'

'Yes.'

'And he'd never been in a relationship with a girl before that?'

'No, not really.'

'And you got the impression he'd met a girl?'

'That's what I thought. But, you know, it was only a feeling I got from what he said.'

'You didn't get the sense that he was in a suicidal mood at all?'

'No, quite the opposite; he was very cheerful and in high spirits. Unusually cheerful, because he could sometimes be a bit on the quiet side – thoughtful and serious.'

'And you can't think of anyone who would have wanted to do him harm?'

'No way.'

'But you don't know who the girl was?'

'No idea, I'm afraid.'

12

Erlendur drove up to the house in Grafarvogur. It was getting dark, a reminder that winter would soon be here after the short, wet summer. Erlendur felt no dread at the thought. He had never dreaded the winter as so many did, not like those who counted the hours until the days would start to lengthen again. He had never regarded winter as his enemy. Time seemed to slow down in the cold and darkness, enfolding him in peaceful gloom.

Baldvin met him at the door and Erlendur wondered as he followed him into the sitting room whether he would carry on living in the house now that both Leonóra and María were gone. He did not get a chance to ask him. Baldvin wanted an explanation for why Erlendur was going around town interrogating people about him and María; why he had to learn about it from his friends and what on earth it was all about; were the police launching an investigation?

'No,' Erlendur said, 'it's nothing like that.'

He told Baldvin that the police had received a tip-off, as sometimes happened in connection with suicides, suggesting that something suspicious might have happened. Due to pressure from one of María's friends, whom he would prefer not to name, he had taken it upon himself to speak personally to several individuals, but this in no way changed the fact that María had taken her own life. Baldvin had no need to worry. There was no question of a formal inquiry, nor was there any need for one.

Erlendur talked along these lines for some time, slowly and deliberately, in an apologetic tone that generally worked well with people when it was employed by the police. He noticed that Baldvin was growing somewhat calmer. He had been standing angrily by the bookcase but sat down in a chair once most of his tension had evaporated.

'What's the status of the case, then?'

'It has no status,' Erlendur said. 'There is no case.'

'It's an uncomfortable feeling, knowing that people are talking,' Baldvin said.

'Of course,' Erlendur agreed.

'It's hard enough as it is,' he said.

'Yes,' Erlendur said. 'I heard it was a beautiful funeral.'

'She gave a very good address, the vicar. They knew each other well. A lot of people turned up. María was very popular everywhere she went.'

'You had her cremated?'

Baldvin had been staring down at the floor but now he raised his gaze to Erlendur.

'It was what she wanted,' he said. 'We discussed it. She didn't want to lie in the ground and . . . you know . . . she felt it was a better solution. I agreed; I'm going to be cremated too.'

'Do you know if your wife was interested in the supernatural, attended seances or anything of that sort?'

'No more than anyone else,' Baldvin said. 'She was terribly afraid of the dark. You've probably heard about that.'

'Yes.'

'You've asked me about this before,' Baldvin said. 'About the afterlife and psychics. What are you driving at? What do you know?'

Erlendur gave him a long look.

'What do you know?' Baldvin repeated.

'I know she went to a medium,' Erlendur said.

'She did?'

Erlendur took the tape from his coat pocket and handed it to Baldvin.

'This is the recording of a seance that María attended,' he said. 'I suppose it's one reason why I wanted to find out more about her.'

'The recording of a seance?' Baldvin said. 'How . . . how come you've got it?'

'I was given the tape after María died. She'd lent it to a friend.'

'A friend?'

'Yes.'

'Who?'

'I'll ask her to get in touch with you if she wants to.'

'Have you listened to it? Isn't that a violation of her privacy?'

'What the recording tells *you* is probably more the issue. Are you sure you didn't know about the seance?'

'She never told me about any seance and I'm not prepared to discuss it under the circumstances. I don't know what's on the tape and I find the whole thing highly irregular.'

'Then I apologise,' Erlendur said, standing up. 'Perhaps you'll have a word with me when you've listened to it. If not, it doesn't matter. It may be that the whole thing hinges on Marcel Proust.'

'Marcel Proust?'

'You didn't know?'

'I don't know what you're talking about.'

'I gather María preferred not to be alone,' Erlendur said. 'Because she was afraid of the dark.'

'I . . .'

'Yet she was alone on a dark autumn night at Thingvellir.'

'What is this? What are you implying? I expect she didn't want anyone with her when she killed herself!'

'No, probably not. Perhaps you'll get in touch,' Erlendur said and left Baldvin with the recording of the seance in his hands.

The old man had been moved to a geriatric ward. Erlendur had not called beforehand and had to ask the nursing staff for directions before he eventually found him. The old man was struggling ineffectually to put on a dressing gown. Erlendur hastened to help him.

'Oh, thank you. It's you, is it?' the old man said when he recognised Erlendur.

'How are you?' Erlendur asked.

'Bearing up,' the old man answered. Then he asked, 'What are you doing here?' and Erlendur heard the growing excitement in his voice. 'It's not about Davíd, is it? You haven't found out something?'

'No,' Erlendur said hastily. 'Nothing like that. I was just passing and thought I'd look in.'

'I'm not really supposed to get up but I can't simply hang about in bed all day. You wouldn't come along to the lounge with me, would you?'

The old man gripped Erlendur's arm as he helped him into the corridor and together they went in the direction he indicated. They sat down in the lounge where the radio was on and a familiar voice was reading a serial.

'Do you happen to remember a friend of your son's called Gilbert who moved to Denmark around the time Davíd went missing?' Erlendur asked, deciding to come straight to the point.

'Gilbert?' the old man whispered thoughtfully. 'I can barely remember him.'

'They were at sixth-form college together. He lived in Copenhagen for years. He spoke to Davíd just before he vanished.'

'And could he tell you anything?'

'No, nothing concrete,' Erlendur said. 'Your son hinted to Gilbert that he had formed a relationship with a girl. I remember that you didn't think this was likely; we discussed it specifically. What Gilbert says may indicate something different.'

'Davíd wasn't in any relationship,' the old man said. 'He would have told us.'

'It hadn't necessarily got very far; it might only have been in the early stages. Your son hinted as much to Gilbert. Did no girl ever get in touch with you after he vanished? Did no one who you didn't know call and ask after him? It need only have been a voice on the phone.'

The old man stared at Erlendur, trying to remember all that had happened during the days and weeks after it became clear that his son had vanished. The family gathered, the police took statements, friends offered their help, the press needed pictures. Davíd's parents hardly had time to come to terms with what had happened before they collapsed exhausted into bed each night and tried to catch up on some sleep. Not that they got any rest. At night their minds would present them with vivid images of their son and they were filled with dread at the thought of never seeing him again.

The old man continued to gaze at Erlendur, trying to recollect anything unfamiliar or unexpected, a visitor or a phone call, a voice he didn't recognise, an odd question: *'Is Davíd home?'*

'Did he chase after girls at all?' Erlendur asked.

'Very little. He was so young.'

'Did no one who you didn't know very well ask after him – a girl of his own age, for instance?' Erlendur rephrased his earlier question.

'No, not that I can remember, not that I can remember at all,' the old man said. 'I, we, would have known if he'd met a girl. Anything else is out of the question. Although . . . I'm so old now that I may have missed something. Gunnthórunn would have been able to help you.'

'Kids are often shy when it comes to talking about that sort of thing.'

'That may well be true; it must have been a very new relationship. I don't remember him ever having a girlfriend. Not once.'

'Do you think his brother would have known?'

'Elmar? No. He would have told us. He wouldn't have forgotten something important like that.'

The old man began to cough, an ugly, rattling noise that grew steadily worse until he couldn't stop. Blood spurted from his nostrils and he collapsed on the sofa in the lounge. Erlendur rushed out and called for help, then tried to tend to him until it arrived.

'I haven't got as long as they thought,' the old man groaned.

The nurses shooed Erlendur away and he watched them move the old man back to the ward. They closed the door and he walked away down the corridor, not knowing if he would ever see him again.

*

Erlendur lay awake that night, thinking about his mother. His thoughts often strayed to her at this time of year. He pictured her as she'd been when they had lived out east, standing in the yard, gazing at Mount Hardskafi, then looking back at him encouragingly. They would find him. All hope was not yet lost. He no longer knew whether the image of her in the yard was a memory or a dream. Perhaps it didn't matter.

She died three days after being admitted to hospital. He sat at her bedside throughout. The staff offered him the chance to rest in an empty room if he wanted but he declined politely, unable to bring himself to leave his mother. The doctors said she could go at any minute. Although she regained consciousness from time to time, she was delirious and did not know him. He tried to talk to her but it was useless.

So the hours passed, one by one, as his mother slowly drew near the end. His mind was flooded with memories of his childhood when she had seemed to be everywhere in a strangely circumscribed world; a watchful protector, a gentle teacher and a good friend.

In the end she appeared to regain her senses slightly. She smiled at him.

'Erlendur,' she whispered.

He held her hand.

'I'm here with you,' he said.

'Erlendur?'

'Yes.'

'Have you found your brother?'

13

It was shortly before curtain-up when Erlendur parked at the stage door. He knew he was late but he wanted to finish what he had set out to do before calling it a day. A friendly caretaker showed him the way to the dressing rooms but was anxious on his behalf, warning him he would have very little time. Erlendur sought to reassure him by explaining that he had called ahead and Orri was expecting him. It shouldn't take long.

Pandemonium reigned behind the scenes. Actors were pacing the corridors in full costume. Others were still being made up. Stagehands were dashing about. Out in the audience a few scattered figures were beginning to take their seats. A disembodied voice announced that it was half an hour till the performance began. Erlendur knew that the play was *Othello*. According to Valgerdur the critics had described the production as ambitious and original in its way, but incoherent.

Orri Fjeldsted was alone in his dressing room, going over his lines, when Erlendur eventually tracked him down. He was playing Iago in a 1940s-style suit, because the director, a young go-getter recently returned from his studies in Italy, according to Valgerdur, had decided to set the production in Reykjavík during the Second World War. Othello was black, a colonel in the occupying American army; Desdemona was a Reykjavík girl involved with the GIs. The colonel had just returned from a mission to Europe when he met Desdemona. Meanwhile, Iago was plotting his downfall.

'Are you the policeman?' Orri asked when he opened the door to Erlendur. 'Couldn't you have found a better time?'

'I'm sorry, I meant to get here ages ago – it won't take a moment,' Erlendur said.

'At least you're not a bloody critic!' the actor exclaimed. He was small and scrawny, almost wizened, with thick greasepaint on his face, an unconvincing Clark Gable moustache glued to his upper lip and his hair slicked back from his forehead. He reminded Erlendur of a gangster in an American movie.

'Do you read the reviews?' Orri Fjeldsted asked. He had a powerful voice despite his diminutive size.

'Never,' Erlendur said.

'They've really gone to town with their bullshit on this one,' Orri said, and Erlendur remembered that Valgerdur had quoted the critics as saying that Orri Fjeldsted appeared lost in the role of Iago.

'I haven't followed them,' Erlendur said.

'You haven't seen the production?'

'I don't go to the theatre much.'

'Bunch of bloody charlatans! Scum! Do you think we do this for fun?'

'Er, no, it . . . they're . . .'

'Year in, year out, the same crowd with the same pig-ignorant bullshit! What was it you wanted?'

'It's about Baldvin . . .'

'Oh yes, you mentioned that on the phone. I heard he'd lost his wife. All very sudden. We don't keep in touch any longer. Haven't for years.'

'You were at drama school together, if I've understood correctly.'

'That's right. He was a very promising actor. Then he went into medicine. Wise move. At least he's free of the bloody critics! And makes a sight more money, of course. What's the point of being a famous actor if you don't have two pence to rub together? Actors are paid a pittance in this country – almost as little as teachers!'

'I think he's doing all right,' Erlendur said, trying his best to pacify the actor.

'He was forever having money troubles. I do remember that. Used to tap us for cash and so on and took his time paying it back. You really had to chase him and sometimes he didn't pay up at all. Apart from that he was a good bloke.'

'There was a group of you at the drama school?'

'Yes, that's right,' Orri said, stroking a finger over his thin moustache to make sure it was firmly attached. 'A bloody good gang.'

'Fifteen minutes to curtain-up,' a voice announced over the tannoy.

'He met his wife when he had just given up his drama studies,' Erlendur said.

'Yes, I remember it well, a sweet girl from the university. Tell me, why are the police asking questions about Baldvin?'

Erlendur chose his words with care, mindful of what Valgerdur had said about actors being dreadful gossips.

'We're collaborating in a Swedish study . . .'

Orri Fjeldsted's interest seemed to cool abruptly.

'They were a resourceful bunch, those kids,' he said, 'I'll give them that. I gather a friend of his drove some guy called Tryggvi round the bend with his experiments.'

'Acting experiments?'

'Acting . . .? No, this was when Baldvin was studying medicine. Was there anything else? I've got to go; it's only five minutes till I'm due on stage. Was there anyone in the audience? They've completely destroyed this production. The critics. Ruined it. They haven't a fucking clue about the theatre. Not a fucking clue! That people even listen to those imbeciles! The public have been calling the theatre and cancelling their tickets in droves.'

Orri opened the door.

'What about this Tryggvi?' Erlendur asked.

'Tryggvi? I think that was his name. They described him as a burn-out. You must have heard of the type. An outstanding student who lost the plot. Quit his studies. I've no idea where he is today.'

'Was Baldvin involved?'

'That's what they always said: him and his friend the medic. I have a feeling the medic might have been Tryggvi's cousin; they were related somehow. They used to be great mates.'

'What happened?'

'You haven't heard?'

'No.'

'Tryggvi's supposed to have asked his cousin to—'

Othello came storming down the corridor with Desdemona on his heels. He was dressed as an American colonel, she in a light blue summer suit and bouffant blonde wig. Othello's head was shaven and sweat was already breaking out on his scalp.

'Let's get this bloody nightmare over,' Othello boomed, dragging Iago off towards the stage. Desdemona smiled sweetly at Erlendur.

'What did Tryggvi ask him to do?' Erlendur called after them.

Orri stopped and looked back at Erlendur.

'I don't know if there's any truth in it but it's what I heard years ago.'

'What? What did you hear?'

'Tryggvi asked him to kill him.'

'Kill him? Is he dead?'

'No, full of beans but weird in the head.'

'What are you trying to tell me? I don't under—'

'It was an experiment that the cousin carried out on Tryggvi.'

'What kind of experiment?'

'The way I heard it, he stopped Tryggvi's heart for several minutes before resuscitating him. They said Tryggvi was never the same again.'

And with that the trio stormed on stage.

Next day, Erlendur dug up the old reports in the police archives about the incident on Lake Thingvallavatn. He read the statement by María's mother Leonóra, as well as the expert witness's verdict on the boat and outboard motor. He found a post-mortem report in the files indicating that Magnús had drowned in the cold water. Apparently, no statement had been taken from the little girl. The case was treated as an accident. Erlendur checked who had led the investigation. It was an officer called Níels. He sighed. He had never had any time for Níels. They had been working for the CID for an equal length of time but, unlike Erlendur, Níels was dilatory; his cases had a tendency to become drawn out to the point of invalidation, and were almost invariably sloppily handled.

Níels was on his coffee break. He was joking with the women in the cafeteria when Erlendur asked if he could have a word.

'What was it you wanted, Erlendur old chap?' Níels asked, with his habitual air of empty condescension. 'Friend' and 'chap', 'chum' and 'my old mate' were words he appended to every sentence, insignificant in themselves but deeply meaningful in the mouth of Níels who had full confidence in his own superiority, despite the lack of any foundation for this.

Erlendur drew him aside and sat down with him in the cafeteria before asking if he remembered the accident on Lake Thingvallavatn, and Leonóra and her daughter María.

'It was an open-and-shut case, wasn't it?'

'Yes, I expect so. You don't happen to remember anything unusual about the circumstances: the people involved or the accident itself?'

Níels adopted an expression intended to convey the idea that he was racking his brains in an effort to recall the events at Lake Thingvallavatn.

'You're not trying to uncover a crime after all these years?' he asked.

'No, far from it. The little girl you saw at the scene with her mother died the other day. It was her father who drowned.'

'I don't recall anything unusual in connection with that investigation,' Níels said.

'How did the propeller come loose from the engine?'

'Well, naturally I don't have the exact details on the tip of my tongue,' Níels answered warily. He regarded Erlendur with suspicion. Not everyone at the police station appreciated it when Erlendur started digging up old cases.

'Do you remember what forensics said?'

'Wear and tear, wasn't it?' Níels asked.

'Something like that,' Erlendur replied. 'Not that that

explains much. The engine was old and clapped out and hadn't received any particular maintenance. What did they tell you that didn't go in the report?'

'Gudfinnur was in charge of the examination. But he's dead now.'

'So we can't ask him. You know that not everything goes into the reports.'

'What is it with you and the past?'

Erlendur shrugged.

'What are you trying to get at, old chap?'

'Nothing,' Erlendur said, controlling his impatience.

'What exactly do you need to know?' Níels asked.

'How did they react, the wife and daughter? Can you remember?'

'There was nothing unnatural about their reactions. It was a tragic accident. Everyone could see that. The woman almost had a breakdown.'

'The propeller was never found.'

'No.'

'And there was no way of establishing exactly how it had come loose?'

'No. The man was alone in the boat and probably started tinkering with the engine, fell overboard and drowned. His wife didn't see what happened, nor did the girl. The wife suddenly noticed that the boat was empty. Then she heard the man cry out briefly but by then it was too late.'

'Do you remember . . .?'

'We talked to the retailer,' Níels said. 'Or Gudfinnur did. Talked to someone at the company that sold the outboard motors.'

'Yes, it's in the report.'

'He said the propeller wouldn't come off that easily. It required some effort.'

'Could it have gone aground?'

'There was no evidence of that. But the wife told us that her husband had been messing around with the engine the day before. She didn't ask him about it and didn't know what he was doing. He might have loosened the propeller accidentally.'

'Her husband?'

'Yes.'

Erlendur recalled Ingvar telling him that Magnús did not have the first clue about engines.

'Do you remember the girl's reaction when you arrived on the scene?' he asked.

'Wasn't she only about ten or so?'

'Yes.'

'Well, of course she was like any child who suffers a shock. She clung to her mother. Never left her side.'

'I can't see from the reports that you spoke to her at all.'

'No, we didn't, or at least not to any extent. We didn't see any reason to. Children aren't the most reliable witnesses.'

Erlendur was on the point of objecting when he was interrupted by two uniformed officers entering the cafeteria and hailing Níels.

'Where are you going with this?' Níels asked. 'What's it all about?'

'Fear of the dark,' Erlendur replied. 'Simple fear of the dark.'

14

María's friend Karen met Erlendur at the door of her home, a spacious flat in a block situated in the west end of Reykjavík. She had been expecting him and invited him inside. When he had called her after their meeting at the police station she had given him a list of names of people connected with María, as well as discussing their friendship that had begun when they were eleven and had shared a desk at their new school. Leonóra had recently moved María to a different school due to her dissatisfaction with the governors and teachers at her previous one where she had been subjected to minor bullying. Given little say in the matter, María was trying her best to find her feet among the unfamiliar faces at her new school. Karen meanwhile had just moved to the neighbourhood and knew no one. Leonóra used to drive María to school every morning and fetch her in the afternoons, and once María asked if Karen would like to come home with her. Leonóra welcomed Karen as her daughter's new friend, and from then on their friendship quickly blossomed under her protection.

'Actually her mother was a bit overbearing,' Karen told Erlendur. 'She enrolled us for ballet, which neither of us could stand, took us to the cinema, arranged for me to come for sleep-overs with them in Grafarvogur, though my mum never let me go for sleepovers with any other friends. She organised cinema tickets, made popcorn for us when we were watching TV. We hardly had a moment to play by ourselves. Leonóra was very kind, don't get me wrong, but sometimes you'd just had enough of her. She wrapped María in cotton wool. But although she was spoilt to death in my opinion, María never lorded it over other people: she was always polite and dutiful and good – it was her nature.'

Karen and María's friendship grew closer by the year. They graduated from sixth-form college together, Karen embarked on a teaching degree and María read history, they travelled abroad together, formed a sewing circle that eventually fizzled out, took holidays together, spent weekends in the country and went out on the town together.

Erlendur now had a better appreciation of why Karen had come to see him at the police station after her close friend's suicide and had claimed that there must have been something more to it than bottomless despair.

'What did you think of the seance?' Karen asked.

'Did you know about her going to this seance?' he asked, evading the question.

'I drove her there,' Karen said. 'The medium's called Andersen.'

'Apparently Leonóra was going to let María know if she found herself in some sort of afterlife,' Erlendur said.

'I don't see anything odd about that,' Karen said. 'We often discussed it, María and I. She told me about Proust. How do you explain something like that?'

'Well, there are a number of possible explanations,' Erlendur said.

'You don't believe in that sort of thing, do you?' Karen said.

'No,' Erlendur replied. 'But I understand María. I can well understand why she chose to speak to a medium.'

'A lot of people do believe in life after death.'

'Yes,' Erlendur said, 'but I'm not one of them. What people on the point of death describe as a bright light and tunnel are to my mind nothing more than the brain sending out its final messages before shutting down.'

'María thought differently.'

'Did she tell anyone else apart from you about the Proust business?'

'I don't know.'

Karen sat staring at Erlendur as if wondering whether he was the right man to talk to, whether she had made a mistake. Erlendur met her gaze. The light in the room was fading.

'There's probably no point telling you what María told me only a short while ago.'

'You needn't tell me anything unless you want to. The fact of the matter is that your friend took her own life. You may find it hard to face up to – but then, a lot of things happen in this world that we find it hard to reconcile ourselves to.'

'I'm perfectly well aware of that and I know how María felt after Leonóra died but I still find it a bit odd.'

'What?'

'María said she'd seen her mother.'

'You mean after Leonóra died?'

'Yes.'

'Saw her at a seance?'

'No.'

'I gather María used to see a lot of things and was petrified of the dark.'

'I know all that,' Karen said. 'This was slightly different.'

'How?'

'María woke up one night several weeks ago to find Leonóra standing at the bedroom door, dressed in summer clothes with a ribbon in her hair and wearing a yellow jumper. She beckoned her to follow her out of the room. Then she vanished round the doorpost and when María came out she was nowhere to be seen.'

'You can see what a strain the poor woman was under,' Erlendur commented.

'I would be wary of judging her,' Karen said. 'You heard on the tape how Leonóra meant to make contact?'

'Yes,' Erlendur said.

'And?'

'And nothing. The book must have fallen on the floor. It happens.'

'Precisely that book?'

'Perhaps she had taken it out herself and forgotten. Perhaps she told Baldvin about the book and he took it out and then forgot. Perhaps she told some visitor and they fiddled with the book. She told *you* about it.'

'Yes, but I would never have dropped the book on the floor and left it there,' Karen pointed out.

'I believe in coincidence,' Erlendur said. 'Anyway, Leonóra's apparition seems to have been prowling round the house, large as life. I'd have thought that would have been more than sufficient as proof of life after death. María's old boyfriend said she was forever seeing things in some kind of dream state; people she knew and so on.'

There was a long silence.

'Anyway, so you know the identity of the medium on the tape?' Erlendur said at last.

'Yes. He's not very well known. I directed María to him. I heard about him from another friend of mine who went to see him.'

'How did the recording end up with you?'

'María lent it to me the other day. I was curious to listen to a seance because I've never been to a medium myself.'

'Do you know if she went to see any other psychics?'

'Apart from this one, there was another whom she saw very recently. Just before she died.'

'Who was that?'

'María said the medium knew everything about her. Literally everything. She said it was unbelievable. It was one of my last conversations with her. I knew she wasn't in a good way but I didn't know she was that far gone.'

'Do you know who the psychic was?'

'No, she didn't tell me but I got the impression that María liked and trusted her.'

'So it was a woman?'

'Yes.'

Karen sat in silence, staring out of the large sitting-room window into the dusk.

'Have you heard what happened at Lake Thingvallavatn?' she asked out of the blue.

'Yes, I've heard.'

'I've always had the feeling that something went on at the lake that has never come to light,' Karen said.

'Such as?' Erlendur asked.

'María never referred to it explicitly but she was haunted by something. Something from her past that she would never talk about, connected to that terrible accident.'

'Do you know Thorgerdur who studied history with her?'

'Yes, I know who she is.'

'She spoke along similar lines and thinks it might have been linked to María's father. As if he was meant to die. Does that sound familiar?'

'No. "As if he was meant to die"?'

'It was something that María let slip; it could mean anything.'

'As if his time had come?'

'Possibly. In the sense that it was his fate to die that day and that nothing could have changed it.'

'I never heard her say anything like that.'

'One could also put another construction on her words,' Erlendur said.

'You mean . . . as if he had deserved it?'

'Possibly, but why?' Erlendur asked.

'That it wasn't an accident? That . . .'

Karen stared at Erlendur.

'That it wasn't an accident?'

'I really couldn't say,' Erlendur answered. 'The case was investigated at the time. We didn't find anything out of the ordinary. Then years later someone quotes this remark of María's. Did she ever say anything of the sort in your hearing?'

'No, never,' Karen said.

'There's a voice that comes through on the recording of the seance,' Erlendur went on.

'Yes?'

'A deep masculine voice that tells María to be careful, that she doesn't know what she's doing.'

'Yes.'

'Did she have any explanation for that?'

'The voice reminded her of her father.'

'Yes, that's clear on the tape.'

'All I know is that something happened at the lake. I sensed it so often from her behaviour. Something connected to her father Magnús – that she couldn't bring herself to tell anyone.'

'Tell me something else: have you ever heard of a man called Tryggvi who studied medicine at the same time as Baldvin?'

Karen thought, then shook her head.

'No,' she said. 'I don't know of any Tryggvi.'

'Did María never mention the name?'

'I don't think so. Who is he?'

'All I know is that he was at university with Baldvin,' Erlendur said, deciding not to reveal what Orri Fjeldsted had told him about Tryggvi.

Erlendur left shortly afterwards. Karen watched him get into his car, an old black model with round rear lights in the parking lot. She didn't recognise the make. But instead of starting the engine and driving away, he sat tight. Before long cigarette smoke began to curl out of the driver's window. It was forty minutes before the round lights finally came on and the car moved slowly away.

He used to long to dream about his brother when he was younger. He would find something that had belonged to Bergur – a small toy or a jumper that his mother had carefully folded away, because she never threw out any of his things – and put the object under his pillow before going to sleep; something different each time. At first he wanted to know if Bergur would appear to him in a dream and help him in his search. Later he simply wanted to see him, to remember him as he had been when he went missing.

But he never dreamed of Bergur.

It was not until many years later, alone in a chilly hotel room, that he finally dreamed of his brother. His dream lingered with him after he awoke and, in the liminal state between waking and sleeping, he saw his brother huddled shivering in a corner of the room. He felt as if he could touch him. Then the vision disappeared and he was left alone once more with an old yearning for the reunion that would never be.

After she found Swann's Way *lying on the floor by the bookcase María's anxiety diminished and she began to feel better. Her dreams were no longer as dark. Nights of dreamless sleep became increasingly frequent and she felt better rested than ever before.*

Baldvin was even more understanding. She didn't know whether it was because he was afraid she would cross the line into the world of insanity, or because the sign from Leonóra had shaken him more than he cared to admit.

'Might it be worth talking to a medium?' he asked one evening.

María cast him an astonished look. She hadn't expected this from Baldvin who had never expressed anything but antipathy for psychics. That was why she had kept quiet about her visit to Andersen. She hadn't wanted to cause friction, and anyway she still felt that matters concerning herself and her mother were private.

'I thought you were anti that sort of thing,' she said.

'Well, I . . . if there was something that could help you, I wouldn't care what it was or where it came from.'

'Do you know any psychics?' she asked.

'N-no,' Baldvin said hesitantly.

'What?' she asked.

'It's something they were discussing at work. The heart surgeons.'

'What?'

'Life after death. A recent incident. They had a man die for two minutes on the operating table. They were performing a bypass and the patient experienced cardiac arrest. They had to administer several shocks to resuscitate him. Afterwards he claimed he'd had a near-death experience.'

'Who did he tell?'

'Everyone. The nurses. The doctors. He hadn't been religious before but he said this experience had converted him into a believer.'

Neither of them spoke.

'He said he'd crossed over into the next world,' Baldvin said.

'I've never asked you, but are they common in hospitals – stories like this?'

'You hear similar stuff from time to time. People have even experimented on themselves to try to find answers to questions about the afterlife.'

'How?'

'By manufacturing a near-death experience. It's not unknown. I once saw a bad movie on the subject. Anyway, the doctors started talking about psychics and mediums, and someone knew a good one that his wife had been to see. It occurred to me that . . . it might be something for you.'

'What's his name?'

'It's a woman. Her name's Magdalena. I wondered if you'd like to talk to her. If it might help you in some way.'

15

Tryggvi's last known abode had been a dirty, stinking mattress in a dump near Raudarárstígur, not far from the Hlemmur bus station, where he sometimes stayed with three other homeless men, all ex-prisoners and down-and-outs. It was a condemned building, clad in corrugated iron, with broken windows and a leaky roof, reeking of cats' pee and crammed with rubbish. The house had been left in a will to its present owners who were embroiled in a bitter dispute over their inheritance and had let the property go to rack and ruin in the meantime. The four men could hardly be described as squatters since they lacked the initiative even for that. Tryggvi had been picked up by the police a few times for drunkenness or vagrancy, but from what Erlendur could discover he was a peaceable loner who took no more notice of other people than they did of him. Sometimes, when it was bitterly cold on the streets of Reykjavík, he would seek shelter in the police cells or at the Salvation Army hostel.

The second time Erlendur walked the short distance from his office on Hverfisgata to the condemned house just off Raudarárstígur in an attempt to track Tryggvi down, he encountered a man who could by a stretch of the imagination be called his housemate, a semi-conscious alcoholic who lay propped up on a filthy mattress that had at some stage been

123

placed on the concrete floor for comfort. It was raining and a puddle had formed on the floor beside the man. Empty *brennivín* bottles lay strewn beside the mattress, along with small bottles that had once contained vanilla essence or some other alcoholic substance used in baking, as well as meths bottles and two hypodermics with short needles. The man squinted up at Erlendur from his mattress. One of his eyes was swollen shut.

'Who are you?' he slurred in a hoarse, almost unintelligible voice.

'I'm looking for Tryggvi,' Erlendur said. 'I understand that he stays here sometimes.'

'Tryggvi? He's not here.'

'I can see that. Can you tell me where he would be at this time of day?'

'I haven't seen him for ages.'

'I gather he sometimes sleeps here.'

'He used to,' the man said, sitting up. 'But he hasn't stayed with us for ages. What day is it today?'

'Does it matter?' Erlendur asked.

'Have you got anything to drink?' the man asked, a note of hope entering his voice. He was wearing a thick jacket over a jumper, brown trousers and tattered boots that reached up to his bony white calves. Erlendur noticed that his lip was split. He looked as if he had recently been in a fight.

'No.'

'What about Tryggvi?' the man asked.

'Nothing important,' Erlendur said. 'I just wanted to see him.'

'Are you, what . . . his brother?'

'No. How is Tryggvi?'

Erlendur knew that if he stayed too long in this tip his clothes would stink of urine for the rest of the day.

'I don't know how he is,' the tramp snarled, suddenly filled with indignant rage. 'How do you think he is? Could his life be anything but shit? What, you think you can rescue him from the gutter? They come here and beat you up, the bloody bastards. Threaten to set you alight.'

'Who?'

'Fucking kids! Won't leave you alone.'

'Was this recently?'

'A few days ago. They get worse every year, the little shits.'

'Did they have a go at Tryggvi?'

'I haven't seen Tryggvi for . . .'

'. . . ages. Okay.' Erlendur finished the sentence.

'Try the pubs. That's where I saw him last. At the Napoleon. He must have got his hands on some cash or they'd have chucked him out.'

'Thank you,' Erlendur said.

'Have you got any money?' the man asked.

'Won't it just go on booze?'

'Does it matter?' the man said, giving Erlendur a crooked glance.

'No, I don't suppose it does,' Erlendur replied, digging in his trouser pocket for some notes.

The Napoleon pub had changed little since Erlendur's last visit. Men sat hunched over the odd rickety table; the bartender, sporting a black waistcoat and red shirt, was solving a crossword, while the radio over the bar broadcast the afternoon serial, *A Place to Call My Own*.

Erlendur knew next to nothing about the man he was looking for. He had spoken to the actor Orri Fjeldsted again on the phone. Orri was garrulous now that he had time on his hands following the premature closure of *Othello*. He didn't know any more than he had already told Erlendur about the incident in which Tryggvi had been caused to die and then brought back to life. Although he was sure that Baldvin had been involved he couldn't remember the name of Tryggvi's cousin who had been in charge of the operation. He referred Erlendur to the Faculty of Theology at the university, where Erlendur was informed that Tryggvi had dropped out after his first year. From there the trail led to the Faculty of Medicine, where Tryggvi had studied for only two years before leaving to get a job. On enquiry, it turned out that he had gone to sea and worked on both trawlers and merchant vessels until he returned to dry land and became a labourer on the docks. An old co-worker from the docks said that he had already been well on his way to becoming a wino back then, a terrible drunk who missed so many days that he was eventually given the boot. After that Tryggvi began to turn up in police reports, generally as a vagrant occupying squats like the one near Hlemmur or else found lying in the street in an alcoholic stupor. But he had no criminal record, as far as Erlendur could ascertain.

He interrupted the bartender's crossword.

'I'm looking for Tryggvi,' he said. 'I gather he sometimes drinks here.'

'Tryggvi?' the bartender repeated. 'You think I know these blokes by name?'

'I haven't a clue. *Do* you know them by name?'

'Talk to the guy in the green anorak,' the bartender said. 'He's here every day.'

Erlendur peered across the dimly lit room in the direction the bartender pointed and glimpsed a man in a green anorak sitting over a half-empty beer glass. There were three shot glasses on the table in front of him. A middle-aged woman sat at the same table with a similar ration lined up in front of her.

Erlendur went over.

'I'm looking for a man called Tryggvi,' he announced. He fetched a chair from the next table and sat down beside them.

The couple looked up, surprised at the disturbance.

'Who are you?' the man asked.

'A friend of his,' Erlendur said. 'From school. I heard he sometimes came here and I wanted to see him.'

'And . . . what . . .?' the woman asked.

It was hard to guess the couple's ages; both had swollen faces and bloodshot eyes, and were smoking roll-ups. Erlendur had interrupted their cottage industry; they were rolling little cigarettes from tobacco and Rizlas. She carefully placed a pinch of tobacco in each Rizla, making sure that nothing went to waste, then he rolled them up and licked them.

'Nothing,' Erlendur said. 'I wanted to see him, that's all. Do you know where he is?'

'Tryggvi's dead, isn't he?' the man in the green anorak said, looking at the woman.

'I haven't seen him for ages. Maybe he is dead.'

'You know him, then?'

'I've stumbled across him from time to time,' the man said, licking a new roll-up that the woman handed him.

'Is it long since you last saw him?'

'Yes.'

'Do you remember when that was?'

'It was probably . . . wasn't it? . . . I don't remember. Talk to Rúdólf. He's over there.'

The man gestured towards the door where another man in a

blue ski jacket was sitting alone smoking, with a beer glass in front of him. He was staring down at the table and seemed completely absorbed in a world of his own when Erlendur took a chair opposite him. He glanced up.

'Do you know where I can find Tryggvi?' Erlendur asked.

'Who are you?'

'A friend of his. From university.'

'Was Tryggvi at university?'

Erlendur nodded.

'Do you know where I can get hold of him? They thought he might be dead,' he said, nodding towards the couple with the roll-ups.

'Tryggvi's not dead,' the man said. 'I met him two or three days ago. If it's the same Tryggvi. I don't know any other. Was he at university?'

'Where did you meet him?'

'He said he was going to get a job, try to go on the wagon.'

'Really?' Erlendur said.

'I've heard it all before,' the man continued. 'He was down at the central bus station. Shaving in the gents.'

'He hangs out at the bus station, does he?'

'Sometimes, yes. Watching the buses. Sits there all day, watching the buses come and go.'

16

Later that day Erlendur walked in out of the rain and stood in the entrance to Skúlakaffi, glancing round for the woman he had come to meet. He saw her sitting with her back to him, hunched over a cup of bad coffee and with a smoked-down cigarette between her fingers. He hesitated for a moment. Only the odd table was occupied, by lorry drivers reading the paper or labourers taking a late coffee break, men who had finished their pastries but still had a few minutes to themselves before they had to go back to work. The worn lino and shabby seats matched their weathered faces and the dried calluses on their hands. The place was more like a workers' cafeteria than a restaurant and had not been painted in all the years Erlendur had been going there. Nowhere in town could you get better salted lamb with a sweet white sauce. Skúlakaffi had been his choice for their meeting and she had agreed without protest, according to Eva Lind.

'Hello,' Erlendur said when he reached the table.

Halldóra looked up from her coffee cup.

'Hello,' she said, her tone unreadable.

He held out his hand to her and she raised her own, but only to pick up her cup. She took a mouthful of coffee.

He stuck his hand in his coat pocket and sat down facing her.

'You sure know how to choose a venue,' she said, stubbing out her cigarette.

'They do good salted lamb here,' Erlendur replied.

'Same old country boy,' Halldóra said.

'I suppose I am,' he said. 'How are you?'

'You needn't be polite for my sake,' Halldóra said, raising her gaze from the table.

'All right,' Erlendur said.

'Eva told me you were living with some woman.'

'We don't live together,' Erlendur said.

'Really? What, then?'

'We're good friends; her name's Valgerdur.'

'Oh.'

Neither of them spoke.

'This is just bullshit,' Halldóra said all of a sudden, grabbing the packet of cigarettes and a disposable lighter from the table and stuffing them in her coat pocket. 'I don't know what I was thinking of,' she added, rising from her seat.

'Don't go,' Erlendur said.

'I must,' Halldóra said. 'I don't know what Eva thought she would get out of this but . . . it's just bullshit . . .'

Reaching over the table, Erlendur grabbed her arm.

'Don't go,' he repeated.

Their eyes met. Halldóra jerked her arm away, then sank back into her seat.

'I only came because Eva wanted me to,' she said.

'Me too,' Erlendur said. 'Shouldn't we try to do this for her?'

Halldóra took out another cigarette and lit it. Erlendur thought it said 'Mallorca' on the lighter. He wasn't aware that she had ever been on a holiday to the Med. Perhaps she had bought it to conjure up memories of sunshine. Or to keep alive the dream of hot sand on a beach somewhere. Once he had refused to take her on a package holiday to the sun, saying he couldn't see the point of going to places like that. 'The point!' she had retorted. 'The point is that people go there to do nothing!'

'Eva's doing well,' Halldóra said.

'We should try to emulate her,' Erlendur said. 'I think it would help her if we could find some way of offering her our mutual support.'

'There's just one problem with that,' Halldóra said. 'I don't want anything to do with you. I told her and she knows it. I've told her over and over again.'

'I can well understand that,' Erlendur said.

'Understand?' Halldóra spat out. 'Do you think I care what you do or don't understand? You destroyed our family. You have that on your conscience. You just walked out as if your children had nothing to do with you. What do you understand?'

'I didn't just walk out – you're wrong about that and it was not nice of you to tell the children that.'

'Not nice of me!'

'Can we skip the row?' Erlendur asked.

'You dare to judge me!'

'I'm not judging you.'

'No, that's right,' Halldóra snorted. 'You never want to argue about anything. You've got your own way, so everyone else can shut up. Isn't that how you want it?'

Erlendur didn't answer. He had been dreading this meeting because he'd known that Halldóra would launch into him like this. For her, what had happened in the past was neither buried nor forgotten. He looked at her and saw how she had aged, how the muscles of her face had slackened, her lower lip jutted slightly, the skin on her nose and under her eyes had reddened. She used to wear make-up in the old days but it seemed that she could no longer be bothered. He supposed he presented the same depressing sight himself.

'We made a mistake,' he said. 'I made a mistake. I have to live with that. I should have behaved differently, I should have insisted on getting access to the children. I should have explained things better to you. I tried but probably not hard enough. I'm sorry about what happened but I can't change anything. It's no longer about us but about Sindri and Eva; perhaps it was always about them. I could have done better but I let you take charge. You kept the children.'

Halldóra finished her cigarette and ground it into the ashtray. She immediately took out another and lit it with the Mallorca lighter, then inhaled the blue smoke, expelling it slowly through her nostrils.

'So, you want to blame me for everything?'

'I don't want to blame anyone for anything,' Erlendur said.

'Naturally you get off scot-free. I kept the children! Isn't that just how you wanted it?'

'I didn't mean that. And I'm not getting off—'

'Do you think my life has been a bed of roses? A divorced single mother with two children. You think there was nothing to it?'

'No. If you're looking for a scapegoat, then it's me. No one else. I know that. I've always known that.'

'Good.'

'But you're not exactly innocent either,' Erlendur said. 'You wouldn't give me access to the kids. You told lies about me. That was your revenge. I could have pushed harder to get access to them. That was my mistake.'

Halldóra glared at him without speaking. Erlendur met her gaze.

'Your mistake, my revenge,' she said at last.

He did not reply.

'You haven't changed,' she said.

'I don't want to quarrel with you.'

'No, but you are anyway.'

'Couldn't you see what was happening? Couldn't you have intervened? Couldn't you have looked up from your own self-pity for one minute and seen what was happening? I know my own responsibility and I know it's my fault for not having made sure that they were all right. Ever since Eva sought me out and I saw what had happened, I've blamed myself, because I know I failed them. But what about you, Halldóra? Couldn't you have done something?'

Halldóra did not answer him straight away. She looked out at the rain, twiddling the lighter between her fingers. Erlendur waited for a hail of angry recriminations, but Halldóra simply gazed calmly at the rain and smoked. Her voice sounded weary when she finally answered.

'Dad was a labourer, as you know,' she said. 'He was born poor and died even poorer. Mum, too. We never had anything. Not a damned thing. I imagined another life. I wanted to escape the poverty. Get a nice flat. Nice things. A good man. I thought you were him. I thought we were embarking on a life that would bring us a bit of happiness. It didn't work out like that. You . . . walked out. I started drinking. I don't know what Eva and Sindri have told you. I don't know how much you know about my life – our life – but it hasn't exactly been fun. I've been unlucky with men. Some of them were real bastards. I've worked my fingers to the bone. I've lived in a series of rented flats, some of them

133

total dumps. Sometimes the children and I were thrown out. Sometimes I went on long benders. I probably didn't look after them like I should have done. They've probably had an even worse life than I have, especially Eva – she was always more sensitive than Sindri when it came to strangers and bad conditions.'

Halldóra sucked in the smoke.

'That's what happened. I've tried not to give way to self-pity. I . . . I can't help it if I have a tendency to blame you for some of it.'

'May I?' he asked, reaching for her cigarettes.

She shoved the packet towards him, together with the Mallorca lighter. They sat and smoked, each absorbed in their own thoughts.

'She was always asking about you,' Halldóra said, 'and I usually told her you were like one of those bums I used to go out with. I know it wasn't nice of me but what was I to say? What would you have liked me to say?'

'I don't know,' Erlendur said. 'It can't have been an easy life.'

'You brought it on us.'

Erlendur did not reply. The rain fell silently from the dark winter sky. Three men in checked shirts stood up and walked out, calling their thanks to the cook in the kitchen on the way.

'The odds were against me from the beginning,' Halldóra said.

'Maybe,' Erlendur replied.

'There's no "maybe" about it.'

'No.'

'Do you know why?'

'I think so.'

'They were against me because I gave the relationship a hundred per cent,' Halldóra said.

'Yes.'

'But you never did.'

Erlendur did not speak.

'Never,' Halldóra said again, exhaling smoke.

'I expect you're right,' Erlendur said.

Halldóra snorted. She avoided meeting his gaze. They sat a good while in silence until she coughed. Reaching for the ashtray, she ground out her cigarette stub.

'Do you think that was fair?' she asked.

'I'm sorry it wasn't reciprocated,' Erlendur said.

'"I'm sorry"!' Halldóra mimicked him. 'How do you think that helps? What on earth were you thinking of?'

'I don't know.'

'It didn't take me long to realise,' Halldóra continued. 'To realise I didn't matter. But I kept on trying anyway. Like an idiot. The better I knew you, the harder I tried. I would have done anything for you. If you'd given us time and . . . Why did you let things go so far? When you weren't the slightest bloody bit interested?'

Halldóra lowered her gaze to her coffee cup, fighting back the tears. Her shoulders drooped and her lower lip quivered.

'I made a mistake,' Erlendur said. 'I . . . I didn't know how to behave, didn't know what I was doing. I don't know what happened. I've tried not to dwell on it. Tried to avoid thinking about that chapter of my life. Perhaps it's cowardice.'

'I never understood you.'

'I think we're very different, Halldóra.'

'Maybe.'

'My mother had died,' Erlendur said. 'I felt rather alone in the world. I thought . . .'

'You'd find yourself a new mother?'

'I'm trying to tell you what sort of state I was in.'

'Don't bother,' Halldóra said. 'It doesn't matter any more.'

'I think we should concentrate on the future instead,' Erlendur said.

'Yes, I suppose so.'

'I thought we could talk about Eva,' he said. 'This is not about us. Not any more. It hasn't been for a long time, Halldóra. You must understand that.'

Neither of them spoke. There was a clatter of dishes from the kitchen. Two men in denim jackets came in and walked over to the counter. They helped themselves to coffee and pastries and sat down with them in the corner. A man in an anorak sat alone at another table, looking through the paper. There was no one else in the room.

'You were bad news,' Halldóra said in a low voice. 'That's what Dad always said. Bad news.'

'Things could have been different,' Erlendur said. 'If you'd shown the slightest understanding for how I felt. But it was too painful and you became bitter and full of hate and you still are. You wouldn't let me near the children. Don't you think it's gone far enough? Don't you think you could let up on the recriminations?'

'Go ahead – blame it all on me!'

'I'm not.'

'Sure you are.'

'Can't we do something for Eva?'

'I don't see how. I have no interest in salving your conscience.'

'Can't we even try?'

'It's too late.'

'It wasn't supposed to be like this,' Erlendur said.

'What do I know about that? It was your doing.'

Halldóra took her packet of cigarettes and lighter and stood up.

'The whole thing was your doing,' she hissed and stormed out.

17

Every now and then over the next few days Erlendur dropped into the Central Bus Station in search of Tryggvi. All he had to go on was the rather vague description given to him by Rúdólf at the Napoleon, which he hoped would be sufficient. The third time he arrived at the long-distance coach station, passengers were being called for the bus to Akureyri. A small group of people began to gather up their belongings in the departure lounge. The lunchtime rush hour was over and the cafeteria, which served hot meals, soft drinks and sandwiches, was quiet. Smoking was permitted at tables over by the windows facing the bus stands behind the terminal. A man was sitting there alone, clutching a yellow plastic bag that he had placed on the table. He was watching the passengers boarding the Akureyri bus. His hair was rough, there was a big scar on his chin from an old accident or knife wound, and his hands were large and dirty, the nails black on his index and middle fingers.

'Excuse me,' Erlendur said, approaching him, 'you're not Tryggvi, by any chance?'

The man eyed him suspiciously.

'Who are you?'

'My name's Erlendur.'

'Huh . . .' the man grunted, apparently uninterested in strangers who addressed him out of the blue.

'Can I offer you a coffee or something to eat?' Erlendur asked.

'What do you want?'

'I just wanted a bit of a chat with you. I hope that's all right.'

The man gave him a calculating look.

'A bit of a chat?'

'If that's all right.'

'What do you want from me?'

'Can I get you something?'

The man gave Erlendur a long look, uncertain how to react to this interruption.

'You can buy me a schnapps,' he said at last.

Erlendur gave him a chilly smile and, after a moment's hesitation, went over to the counter. He asked for a double *brennivín* and two coffees. The man waited for him by the window, watching the Akureyri bus pull slowly away. Erlendur asked the bartender if he knew anything about the man who was sitting over by the window in the smoking area.

'You mean the tramp over there?' the bartender asked, nodding towards the man.

'Yes. Does he come here often?'

'He's been coming here on and off for years,' the bartender said.

'What does he do?'

'Nothing. He never does anything and is never any trouble. I don't know why he comes here. I sometimes see him shaving in the gents. He sits where he's sitting now for hours on end, watching the buses leaving. Do you know him?'

'Not really,' Erlendur said. 'Hardly at all. Does he never go anywhere on the buses?'

'No, never. I've never seen him board a bus,' the bartender said.

Erlendur took the change and thanked him. Then he returned to the man by the window and sat down facing him.

'Who did you say you were?' the man asked.

'Is your name Tryggvi?' Erlendur countered.

'Yes, I'm Tryggvi. And you? Who are you?'

'My name's Erlendur,' he repeated. 'I'm from the police.'

Tryggvi slowly moved his plastic bag off the table.

'What do you want with me? I haven't done anything.'

'I don't want anything with you,' Erlendur said. 'And I don't care what you've got in that bag. The fact is that I heard a strange story about your time at university and I wanted to know if there was any truth in it.'

'What story?'

'Er . . . how shall I put it? . . . About your death.'

Tryggvi stared at Erlendur for a long time without saying a word. He had downed the large shot of *brennivín* in one and now pushed the glass back across the table. He had colourless eyes set deep under bristly brows, a fleshy face that made an odd contrast with his emaciated body, a big nose that had been broken at some point, and thick lips. His face had succumbed to gravity, which made it appear unusually long and drawn.

'How did you find me here?'

'By various means,' Erlendur said. 'Including a visit to the Napoleon.'

'What do you mean, "about my death"?'

'I don't know if there's anything in it but I heard about an experiment performed by some medical students or a medical student at the university. You yourself were studying theology or medicine, I'm not sure which. You agreed to take part in the

140

experiment. It consisted of temporarily stopping your heart, then reviving you. Is it true?'

'Why do you want to know?' the man asked in his hoarse, rough drinker's voice. He delved into his breast pocket in search of cigarettes and brought out a half-empty packet.

'I'm curious.'

Tryggvi looked pointedly at the shot glass and then at Erlendur. Erlendur stood up and went back to the counter where he purchased half a bottle of Icelandic *brennivín* and brought it over to the table. Having filled the shot glass, he placed the bottle on his side of the table.

'Where did you hear this story?' Tryggvi asked. He emptied the glass and slid it back across.

Erlendur refilled it.

'Is it true?'

'What about it? What are you planning to do about it?'

'Nothing,' Erlendur said.

'Are you a cop?' the man asked, sipping from the glass.

'Yes. Are you the right Tryggvi?'

'My name's Tryggvi,' the man said, looking round. 'I don't know what you want from me.'

'Can you tell me what happened?'

'Nothing happened. Nothing. Nothing at all. Why are you asking about this now? What's it got to do with you? What's it got to do with anyone?'

Erlendur didn't want to scare him off. He could have told him, filthy down-and-out stinking of the gutter that he was, that it was none of his business. But then he wouldn't get to hear what he wanted to know. He tried to be conciliatory instead, addressing Tryggvi as an equal, refilling the shot glass and lighting his cigarette for him. He made some general chit-chat

141

about the place where they were sitting, which still sold singed sheep's head with mashed swede like in the old days when the boys used to cruise around the block with their girlfriends and drop into the bus station for its speciality dish. The schnapps worked its magic too. Tryggvi fairly knocked it back, one shot after another, and his tongue began to loosen. Slowly but surely Erlendur manipulated the conversation back to what had happened when Tryggvi had been at university and some of his fellow students had wanted to conduct an unusual experiment.

'Would you like something to eat?' Erlendur asked once they had got chatting.

'I thought I could be a vicar,' Tryggvi said, waving his hand to indicate that food would not agree with him. He seized the bottle instead and took a long swig, then wiped his lips on his sleeve. 'But theology was boring,' he continued. 'So I tried medicine. Most of my friends went in for that. I . . .'

'What?'

'I haven't seen them for years,' Tryggvi said. 'I expect they're all doctors by now. Specialists in this and that. Rich and fat.'

'Was it their idea?'

Tryggvi gave Erlendur a look as if he was getting ahead of himself. This was *his* story and if Erlendur didn't like it he could always leave.

'I still don't know why you're digging this up,' he said.

Erlendur sighed heavily.

'It may be relevant to a case I'm investigating, that's all I can really say.'

Tryggvi shrugged.

'As you like.'

He took another swig from the bottle. Erlendur waited patiently.

'I heard it was you who asked them to do it,' he said finally.

'That's a bloody lie,' Tryggvi said. 'I didn't ask for any of it. They approached me. It was them who came to me.'

Erlendur was silent.

'I should never have listened to that prick,' Tryggvi said.

'What prick?'

'My cousin. Stupid bloody prick!'

Another silence fell but Erlendur did not dare to break it. He didn't want to drop any hints but hoped that the tramp would feel an urge to tell his story, to open up about what had happened, even if only to a stranger at the Central Bus Station.

'Aren't you cold?' Tryggvi asked, pulling his jacket more tightly around himself.

'No, it's not cold in here.'

'I'm always cold.'

'What about your cousin?'

'I don't really remember much about it,' Tryggvi said.

Looking at him, Erlendur had the feeling that, on the contrary, he remembered every last detail of what had happened.

'It was some crazy idea we had during a piss-up that went too far. They needed a guinea pig. "Let's use the theology student," they said. "Let's send him to hell." You see, one of them was . . . he was my cousin, a rich bugger with some stupid bloody fixation with death. I was a bit that way myself and he knew it. He knew it so he paid me what was a whole month's wages back then. And there was a girl in the group too who I . . . who I was a little in love with. Maybe I did it for her. I can't say I didn't. They were senior to me; my cousin was in his final year and so was she. The girl.'

18

Tryggvi had downed half the bottle and was staring blearily out at the bus stands. His account was meandering and repetitive and strangely convoluted, and sometimes he stopped and sat in silence for a long time. But Erlendur didn't dare to interrupt him. Then he lowered his head and stared down at the table as if he were alone in the world, alone with his thoughts, alone in life. Erlendur sensed that Tryggvi had spoken little of these events since they occurred and that they involved various unresolved issues that he had never managed to shake off, that had continued to haunt him ever since.

It had been his cousin's idea. His cousin had been in his final year of medicine and was intending to go on to do postgraduate study in the States in the autumn. He worked in what used to be known as the City Hospital, was top of his year, the life and soul of the party, played the guitar, told amusing stories, organised weekend trips to the mountains. He was at the centre of every-thing, his self-confidence was unshakeable; he was energetic, domineering and determined. Once, bumping into Tryggvi at a family get-together, he asked him if he had read about the French medical students who had recently conducted an interesting, but of course totally illegal, experiment.

'What experiment?' Tryggvi asked. He was his cousin's

opposite in every way: shy and retiring, and liked to keep himself to himself. He never spoke up in company, refused to go on trips to the mountains with the rowdy medical students and was already beginning to have problems with alcohol.

'It was unbelievable,' his cousin said. 'They induced a cardiac arrest in one of their fellow students and kept him dead for three minutes until they resuscitated him. The justice system hasn't a clue what to do with them. They killed him, but.they didn't, if you see what I mean.'

Tryggvi's cousin seemed obsessed with this piece of news. For weeks afterwards he talked of nothing but the French medical students, followed their trial in the news, and started whispering to Tryggvi that he would be interested in doing something similar. He had been contemplating the idea for ages and now this news had brought his enthusiasm to a pitch he couldn't control.

'You studied theology, you must at least be curious,' he said one day when they were sitting in the medical faculty cafeteria.

'I'm not letting anyone kill me,' Tryggvi said. 'Find someone else.'

'There is no one else,' his cousin said. 'You're the perfect person. You're young and strong. There's no heart disease of any kind in our family. Dagmar's going to be in on it, and Baddi, another guy I know who's studying medicine. I've talked to them already. It's watertight. Nothing can happen. I mean, you've often wondered about it – you know, life after death.'

Tryggvi knew who Dagmar was. He had noticed her as soon as he started medicine.

'Dagmar?' he said.

'Yes,' his cousin answered, 'and she's no fool.'

Tryggvi knew that. She was his cousin's friend and had once

talked to him, at the first and only medical faculty party he had attended. She knew they were cousins. He had met her several times since and they had chatted. He thought she was lovely but he didn't have the courage to take the next step.

'Does she want to be in on this?' he asked in surprise.

'Of course,' his cousin said.

Tryggvi shook his head.

'And naturally I'll pay you,' his cousin added.

In the end Tryggvi gave in. He didn't know exactly why he let them persuade him. He was always broke, he yearned to be with Dagmar. His cousin was extremely overbearing and moreover he had reawakened Tryggvi's fascination with life after death. He knew about Tryggvi's interest from when they were younger and used to discuss the existence of God, heaven and hell. They both came from deeply religious families who used to pack them off to Sunday school, were regular churchgoers and did good works in the parish. But the cousins were not particularly devout themselves when they grew up and began to have their doubts about various aspects of doctrine, such as the resurrection and eternal life and the existence of heaven. Tryggvi thought his decision to embark on a theology degree had stemmed from this. From his doubts, combined with the urgent questions that had pursued him all his life: what if? What if God existed? What if eternal life was true?

'We've discussed it so often,' his cousin said.

'It's one thing to talk about it . . .'

'We've got this one minute. You'll have one minute to go over to the other side.'

'But I . . .'

'You went into theology in search of answers to these questions,' his cousin pointed out.

'What about you?' Tryggvi asked. 'What do you want to prove by this?'

His cousin smiled.

'Nothing ever happens around here and no one ever does anything,' he said. 'At least, not like this. It would be exciting to test those stories about the bright light and the tunnel, because we can do it without taking too great a risk. We can do it.'

'Why don't you do it yourself? Why don't we put *you* to sleep?'

'Because we need a good doctor and with all due respect, coz, I'm a better doctor than you are.'

Tryggvi read about the trial of the French medical students. They had successfully resuscitated their friend who had made a full recovery and by his own account had suffered no ill effects afterwards.

The evening they put their plan into action was his cousin's twenty-seventh birthday. They all met up at his place: the cousins, Dagmar and Baddi, and from there headed down to the hospital. Tryggvi's cousin had prepared an empty room with a bathtub and brought in a cardiograph and defibrillator. Tryggvi lay down in the bath. It was filled with a constant flow of cold water and they had procured large bags of ice which they added to the tub.

Gradually Tryggvi's heartbeat slowed and he lost consciousness.

'All I remember is coming round,' Tryggvi said, watching an empty coach pulling up to the terminal. It had started to rain and the sky was overcast in the south. Rainwater streamed down the windows.

'What happened?' Erlendur asked.

'Nothing,' Tryggvi said. 'Nothing happened. I felt nothing,

147

saw nothing. No tunnel, no light. No nothing. I fell asleep and woke up again. That was it.'

'The experiment worked, then – they managed to . . . managed to put you to death?'

'That's what my cousin said.'

'Where is he now?'

'He went to do postgraduate study in the States and has lived there ever since.'

'And Dagmar?'

'I don't know where she is. I haven't seen her since . . . since then. I quit medicine. Quit university. Went to sea. I felt happier there.'

'Were you unhappy?'

Tryggvi didn't answer.

'Did they ever try it again?' Erlendur asked.

'I wouldn't know.'

'Did you make a full recovery?'

'There was nothing to recover from,' Tryggvi said.

'And no God?'

'No God. No heaven. No hell. Nothing. My cousin was very disappointed in me.'

'Were you expecting some answers?'

'Maybe. We were all a bit high on the excitement.'

'But nothing happened?'

'No.'

'And there's no more to tell?'

'No. No more to tell.'

'Are you sure? You're not hiding something?'

'No,' Tryggvi said.

They sat without talking for a while. The cafeteria was beginning to fill up with customers. They sat down with their trays or cups of coffee at the empty tables and picked up a paper to look at before going on their way. From time to time announcements were made over the tannoy.

'Since then it's been downhill all the way,' Erlendur commented.

'What do you mean?'

'Your life,' Erlendur said. 'It hasn't exactly been easy.'

'That has nothing to do with the stupid experiment, if that's what you're implying.'

Erlendur shrugged.

'You've been coming here for years, I gather. Sitting here by the window.'

Tryggvi looked silently out through the glass and rain at something beyond the fading outline of the Reykjanes peninsula and Mount Keilir on the horizon.

'Why do you sit here?' Erlendur asked, so quietly as to be barely audible.

Tryggvi looked at him.

'Do you want to know what I felt?'

'Yes.'

'Peace. I felt at peace. Sometimes I feel as if I should never have come back.'

There was a crash as someone dropped a glass over by the counter and fragments scattered all over the floor.

'I experienced a strange sense of peace that I can't describe, not to you or anyone else. Not even to myself. After that nothing mattered any more; not other people, not my studies, not my surroundings. Somehow life stopped mattering. I didn't feel connected to it any longer.'

Tryggvi paused. Erlendur listened to the rain mercilessly lashing the window.

'And since that peace . . .'

'Yes?' Erlendur said.

'To tell the truth I haven't experienced a moment's peace since,' Tryggvi said, watching the Keflavík bus pulling out of the forecourt. 'I feel this constant need to be on the move, as if I'm waiting for something or someone's waiting for me but I don't know where and I don't know who it is and I don't know where I'm going.'

'Who do you think you're waiting for?'

'I don't know. You think I'm mad. People think I'm weird.'

'I've met weirder people,' Erlendur said.

Tryggvi continued to watch the Keflavík bus.

'Aren't you cold?' he asked again.

'No,' Erlendur said.

'It's a strange feeling, watching people leave,' Tryggvi continued after a lengthy silence. 'Watching them climb on to the buses and the buses driving away. People leaving, all day long.'

'Do you never want to take a trip on them?'

'No, I'd never go anywhere,' Tryggvi said. 'Not in a million years. I'd never go anywhere. I wouldn't let myself be taken anywhere by bus. Where are those people going? Tell me that. Where are all those people going?'

Afraid that Tryggvi was losing the plot, Erlendur tried to keep him on track a little longer. He looked at the dirty hands and elongated face and it occurred to him that this was probably the closest he would ever come to meeting a ghost.

'So it was your cousin who now lives in America, a girl called Dagmar and another bloke you called Baddi. Who was he?'

'I didn't know him,' Tryggvi said. 'He was a friend of my cousin's. I don't even remember his proper name. He studied drama before he took up medicine. He was known as Baddi.'

'Might his name have been Baldvin?'

'Yes, that was it,' Tryggvi said. 'That was the name.'

'Are you sure?'

Tryggvi nodded, an unlit cigarette drooping from the corner of his mouth.

'And he'd been at drama school before?'

Tryggvi nodded again.

'He was a friend of my cousin's,' he said. 'He was a real actor type. I trusted him least of the lot.'

19

The woman looked surprised when she opened the door to Erlendur. A gale had blown up, blasting cold, dry air from the north. Erlendur hugged his coat more tightly around him as he stood on the doorstep. He had not called ahead and the woman, whose name was Kristín, stood blocking the doorway, wearing an obstinate expression as if she had no intention of accepting this unannounced visit. Erlendur explained that he was trying to find some information about what had happened when María's father had died. Kristín said she couldn't help at all in that case.

'Why are the police digging this up now?' she asked.

'Because of the suicide,' Erlendur said. 'We're taking part in a joint Nordic study on the causes of suicide.'

The woman stood in the doorway without speaking further. María's father Magnús had been her brother. His friend Ingvar had suggested that Erlendur talk to her, since he thought it not unlikely that Leonóra might have told her something about Magnús's fatal accident on Lake Thingvallavatn. Kristín lived alone. Ingvar said she had never married, had always lived alone and probably wasn't that keen on visitors.

'If I could just come in for a moment,' Erlendur said, stamping his feet. He was cold. 'It won't take long,' he added.

After an awkward pause Kristín finally gave in. She closed the door behind them, with a shiver.

'It's unusually cold today,' she remarked.

'Yes, I suppose it is,' Erlendur replied.

'I don't know why you're digging it up after all this time,' she said again, seeming far from happy as she took a seat with him in the sitting room.

'I've been talking to people who knew María well and some information has emerged that I wanted to run past you.'

'Why are the police investigating María? Is it usual in cases like this?'

'We're not investigating her,' Erlendur said. 'We're merely processing the information we've received. The incident at Lake Thingvallavatn was investigated at the time and the series of events is perfectly clear. I'm not going to look into that any further. The verdict of accidental death will stand unchanged.'

'What are you after, then?'

'Let me emphasise what I said: the verdict will not be changed.'

Kristín still did not cotton on. She was in her sixties, pretty and rather fragile, with short, wavy hair. She stared at Erlendur with a suspicious gaze that indicated she was on her guard.

'Then what do you want from me?' she asked.

'Nothing you say to me now or later will change the verdict that your brother's death was accidental. I hope you understand that.'

Kristín took a deep breath. Perhaps she had begun to grasp what Erlendur was hinting at, but she didn't show it.

'I don't know what you're insinuating,' she said.

'I'm not insinuating anything,' Erlendur said. 'I have no interest in reopening a case that has been dormant all this time.

If Leonóra told you something we don't know, it won't change anything. You got on well, I gather.'

'We did,' Kristín said.

'Did she ever talk to you about what happened?'

Erlendur knew he was taking a risk. All he had to go on was a faint suspicion, a tiny inconsistency between what Ingvar had said and a badly written report, and a bond between mother and daughter that was deeper and more powerful than any he had ever encountered before. Kristín might conceivably know more if she had been Leonóra's confidante. In the unlikely event that she had been keeping quiet about something all these years, she might, under certain circumstances, reveal it. She came across as an honest and scrupulous woman, a witness who might have done the only right thing in a difficult situation.

A silence fell in the room.

'What do you want to know?' Kristín asked at last.

'Anything you can tell me,' Erlendur said.

Kristín stared at him.

'I don't know what you're talking about,' she said, but her voice did not carry the same conviction.

'I was told that your brother Magnús had never gone near an engine in his life and didn't have the first clue about them. But the police report states that he had been tinkering with the motor the day before the accident. Is that correct?'

Kristín did not answer.

'His friend Ingvar – actually, he was the one who suggested I talk to you – said Magnús didn't know a thing about engines and had never touched one in his life.'

'That's right.'

'Leonóra told the police he had been repairing the outboard motor.'

154

Kristín shrugged.

'I know nothing about that.'

'I spoke to an old friend of María's who says she always had the feeling that something happened up at the lake that never came out, that Magnús's death was not just a simple accident,' Erlendur said. 'She doesn't have much to base her hunch on, only María's comment that perhaps he was meant to die.'

'Meant to die?'

'Yes. That's what María said. About her own father.'

'What did she mean by that?' Kristín asked.

'Her friend didn't know but perhaps she meant it was his fate to die that day. Though there's another possible interpretation.'

'Which is what?'

'Perhaps he deserved to die.'

Erlendur studied Kristín. She closed her eyes and her shoulders drooped.

'Can you tell me something we don't know about what happened at the lake?' he asked carefully.

'When you say that the verdict won't be changed now . . .'

'You can tell me whatever you like, it won't change the original verdict.'

'I've never spoken of this,' Kristín said, so quietly that Erlendur could barely hear her. 'Except when Leonóra was on her deathbed.'

Erlendur could tell that she was finding this very difficult. She thought for a long time and he tried to put himself in her shoes. She hadn't been expecting this visit, let alone the offer with which Erlendur had confronted her. But apparently she didn't see any reason to distrust him.

'I think I've got a little Aalborg left in the cupboard,' she said at last, rising to her feet. 'Would you like some?'

Erlendur accepted the offer. She fetched two shot glasses, placed them on the table and filled them to the brim with the aquavit. She downed the first shot in one while Erlendur was still raising his to his mouth. Then she refilled her glass and promptly downed half of it.

'Of course they're both dead now,' she said.

'Yes.'

'So perhaps it won't change anything.'

'I don't think so.'

'I know nothing about any propeller,' Kristín said. She sat in silence for a moment, then asked:

'Why did María do it?'

'I don't know,' Erlendur said.

'Poor girl,' Kristín said with a sigh. 'I remember her so well before Magnús died. She was their little ray of sunshine. They didn't have any more children and she grew up with boundless parental love. Then when my brother died on Lake Thingvallavatn it was as if the ground had been snatched from under her feet. From under both of them, both María and Leonóra. Leonóra was terribly in love with Magnús; he meant the world to her. And the girl was very attached to him too. That's why I can't understand it. I can't understand what he was thinking of.'

'He? You mean Magnús?'

'After the accident they were inseparable. Leonóra was so protective of María that I felt she went too far. I felt she became overprotective. Hardly anyone else was allowed near María, least of all us, Magnús's family. Our relationship with them gradually dwindled to nothing. In fact, Leonóra broke off all contact with us, the girl's father's family, after what happened at Thingvellir. I always found it very strange. But then I didn't learn the truth until shortly before Leonóra died. She summoned me to meet her before she passed away; she was in the last stages by then, bed-bound and very weak, and knew that she had only a few days left to live. We hadn't been in touch for . . . for quite a long time. She was in her room and asked me to shut the door and sit down beside her. She said she had something to tell me before she died. I didn't know what to think. Then she started talking about Magnús.'

'Did she tell you what happened at the lake?'

'No, but she was angry with Magnús.'

Kristín charged her glass with another shot of aquavit. Erlendur declined. She tipped the drink down her throat, before replacing the glass calmly on the table.

'Now they've both gone, mother and daughter,' she said.

'Yes,' Erlendur replied.

'They were almost like one person.'

'What did Leonóra tell you?'

'She told me that Magnús was going to leave her. He'd met another woman. I knew already. Magnús had told me at the time. That was why Leonóra summoned me. It was as if I had taken part in a conspiracy against her. She didn't say it straight out but she made sure I felt it.'

Erlendur hesitated.

'So he was having an affair?'

Kristín nodded.

'It started a few months before he died. He confided in me. I don't think he told anyone else and I haven't told anyone either. It's nobody else's business. Magnús told Leonóra that he wanted to end the marriage. It came as a terrible shock to her, from what she told me. She'd had absolutely no idea. She had loved my brother and given him everything . . .'

'So he told her about it, at Thingvellir?'

'Yes. Magnús died and I never mentioned the affair. To Leonóra or anyone else. Magnús was dead and I didn't think it was anyone else's business.'

Kristín took a deep breath.

'Leonóra blamed me for not having told her about the affair as soon as I found out. Magnús must have told her that I knew. But I thought it was right for her to hear it from him. She was very stubborn and prone to holding grudges. It was as if she felt I had betrayed her, even after all these years. When she died . . . I simply couldn't bring myself to go to the funeral. I regret it now. For María's sake.'

'Did you ever talk to María about the accident?'

'No.'

'Can you tell me the identity of the woman that Magnús was involved with?'

Kristín took a sip of aquavit.

'Does it matter?' she asked.

'I don't know,' Erlendur said.

'I think that was one reason why Magnús was so hesitant. Because of who she was.'

'Why?'

'The woman Magnús was involved with was a good friend of Leonóra's.'

'I see.'

'They never spoke again after that.'

'Have you ever connected this with the accident?'

Kristín looked at Erlendur gravely.

'No. What do you mean?'

'I . . .'

'Why are you investigating the accident now?'

'I heard about the incident at—'

'Did any of this come out in connection with María's death?'

'No,' Erlendur said.

'But María told some friend of hers that maybe Magnús was meant to die?'

'Yes.'

'I've always considered what happened at the lake as a ghastly accident. It never occurred to me that it could have been anything else.'

'But . . .?'

'No, no buts. It's too late to change it now.'

The taxi company was located downtown in a low-rise building that had seen better days. It had once been a community centre, in the days when young men wore their hair in Brylcreemed quiffs and their girlfriends sported perms and they used to go crazy on the dance floor to the new American rock 'n' roll, before they eventually vanished into oblivion. One half of the building had been converted into the premises of a taxi company where peace and quiet now reigned. Two older men were playing rummy. The yellow lino on the floor was full of holes, the shiny white paint on the walls had long ago succumbed to the grime, and the air freshener had not yet been invented that could overcome the stench of mould rising from the floor and wooden walls. It was like stepping back fifty years in time. Erlendur savoured the sensation. He stood for a moment in the middle of the room, breathing in its history.

The woman operating the radio looked up and, when she saw that the rummy players weren't about to stir, asked if he needed a cab. Erlendur went over and enquired about a driver with the company who was called Elmar.

'Elmar on 32?' the woman said. She had been in her prime at about the same time as the building.

'Yes, probably,' Erlendur replied.

'He's on his way in. Would you like to wait for him? He won't be long. He always eats here in the evenings.'

'Yes, so I gather,' Erlendur said.

He thanked her and sat down at a table. One of the rummy players glanced up in his direction. Erlendur nodded but received no response. It was as if the pair's existence was completely defined by the card game.

Erlendur was leafing through an old magazine when a taxi driver appeared at the door.

'He was asking for you,' the woman operating the radio called, pointing at Erlendur who stood up and greeted him. The man shook his hand, introducing himself as Elmar. He was the brother of Davíd, the young man who had gone missing. He was in his fifties, plump, with a round face, thinning hair and no arse as a result of a lifetime spent sitting behind the wheel. Erlendur explained his business in a lowered voice. He noticed out of the corner of his eye that the rummy players had pricked up their ears.

'You're not still picking over that?' Elmar asked.

'We're wrapping up the case,' Erlendur said, without elaborating.

'Do you mind if I get stuck in while we're talking?' Elmar asked, sitting down at the table furthest from the rummy players. He had his supper in a plastic container: sausage and onion hash from the supermarket hot-food counter. Erlendur sat down with him.

'There wasn't much of an age gap between you brothers,' Erlendur began.

160

'Two years,' Elmar said. 'I'm two years older. Have you discovered anything new?'

'No,' Erlendur said.

'Davíd and I weren't really that close. You could say I wasn't very interested in my younger brother; I thought of him as just a kid. I tended to hang out more with my friends, people my own age.'

'Have you come to any conclusion about what might have happened?'

'Only that he might have topped himself,' Elmar said. 'He didn't mix with the sort of people – wasn't involved in anything, you know – where someone might have wanted to hurt him. Davíd was a good kid. Shame he had to go like that.'

'When was the last time you saw him?'

'The last? I asked him to lend me some money for the pictures. I never had any cash in those days. Any more than I do now. Davíd sometimes worked alongside his studies and scraped a bit of money together. I've already told the police all this.'

'And . . .?'

'And nothing: he lent it to me. I didn't know he was going to disappear that evening, you know, so there weren't any fond farewells, just the usual "Thanks, see you." '

'So you were never close?'

'No, you couldn't really say that.'

'You didn't confide in each other at all?'

'No. I mean, he was my brother and all that, but we were very different and . . . you know . . .'

Elmar wolfed down his food. He added that he generally only took half an hour for supper.

'Do you know if your brother had got himself a girlfriend before he went missing?' Erlendur asked.

'No,' Elmar said. 'I don't know of any girlfriend.'

'His friend says he had met a girl but it's all very vague.'

'Davíd never had any girlfriend,' Elmar said, taking out a packet of Camel cigarettes. He offered it to Erlendur who declined. 'Or at least not that I was aware of,' he added, glancing over at the rummy table.

'No, that's the thing,' Erlendur said. 'Your parents clung for a long time to the hope that he'd come back.'

'Yes, they . . . they thought about nothing but Davíd. He was all they ever thought about.'

Erlendur detected a note of bitterness in the man's voice.

'Are we done, then?' Elmar asked. 'I'd quite like to join them for a hand.'

'Yes, I'm sorry,' Erlendur said, standing up. 'I didn't mean to ruin your supper.'

20

Eva Lind came round that evening. She had seen her mother and heard about the encounter with Erlendur. He said it had been a mistake to try to bring them together. Eva shook her head.

'You're not going to meet again?' she asked.

'You've done everything possible,' Erlendur said. 'We simply don't get on. There's too much awkwardness between your mother and me that we just can't overcome.'

'Awkwardness?'

'It was a very acrimonious meeting.'

'She said she stormed out.'

'Yes.'

'But you still met up.'

Erlendur was sitting in his chair with a book in his hand. Eva Lind had taken a seat on the sofa facing him. They had often sat there opposite one another. Sometimes they quarrelled bitterly and Eva Lind rushed out, hurling abuse at her father. At other times they managed to talk and show each other affection. Eva Lind would sometimes fall asleep on the sofa while he read her the story of an ordeal in the wilderness or else some Icelandic folklore. She used to visit him in a variety of states, either so high that Erlendur couldn't make any sense of what she was saying or so low that he was afraid she would do something stupid.

He hesitated to ask if Halldóra had relayed their conversation to her in detail but Eva spared him the trouble.

'Mum told me you never loved her,' she began warily.

Erlendur turned the pages of his book.

'But she was crazy about you.'

Erlendur didn't say anything.

'Maybe it goes some way to explaining your weird relationship,' Eva Lind said.

Still Erlendur did not speak, he merely gazed down at the book he was holding.

'She said there was no point talking to you,' Eva Lind continued.

'I don't know what we can do for you, Eva. We can't agree on anything. I've already told you that.'

'Mum said the same.'

'I know what you're trying to do but . . . We're difficult parents, Eva.'

'She says that you two should never have met.'

'It would probably have been better,' Erlendur said.

'So it's completely hopeless?'

'I think so.'

'It was worth trying.'

'Of course.'

Eva stared at her father.

'Is that all you're going to say?' she demanded.

'Can't we just try and forget it?' he said, looking up from the book. 'I tried. So did she. It didn't work. Not this time.'

'But maybe another time, you mean?'

'I don't know, Eva.'

Eva Lind sighed heavily. She took out a cigarette and lit it.

'Bloody ridiculous. I thought maybe . . . I thought it was

possible to make things a bit better between you. It's probably pointless. You're both completely hopeless cases.'

'Yes, I suppose we are.'

Neither of them spoke.

'I've always tried to see us four as a family,' Eva Lind said. 'I still do. Pretend we're a family, which of course we're not and never have been. I thought we could establish some kind of harmonious atmosphere around us. Felt it might help all of us, me and Sindri and you and Mum. Christ!'

'We tried, Eva. We won't get anywhere. Not now. I think we would have made our peace by now if the will was there.'

'I told her about your brother. She knew nothing about him.'

'No, I never told her. Any more than anyone else. I've never talked about him to anyone.'

'She was very surprised. She didn't know your parents either, granny and grandad. She seemed to know very little about you.'

'It was your grandmother's birthday the day before yester-day,' Erlendur said. 'Not a major anniversary, but her birthday all the same. I always used to try and visit her on her birthday.'

'I'd have liked to have met her,' Eva Lind said.

Erlendur looked up from his book again.

'And she'd have liked to have known you,' he said. 'Things would probably have been rather different if she'd lived.'

'What are you reading?'

'A tragedy.'

'Is it the one about your brother?'

'Yes. I'd like . . . can I read it to you?'

'You don't need to make it up to me,' Eva Lind said.

'For what?'

'For the way you and Mum behave.'

'No, I want you to hear it. I want to read it to you.'

Lifting the book, Erlendur leafed back a few pages and started to read in a low but steady voice about the violent blizzard that had shaped his entire life.

Tragedy on Eskifjördur Moor
By Dagbjartur Audunsson

For centuries the main inland route from Eskifjördur to the Fljótsdalshérad district used to pass across Eskifjördur Moor. There was an old bridleway that ran north of the Eskifjördur River, inland along the Langihryggur ridge, up the near side of the Innri-Steinsá River, through the Vínárdalur valley and over the Vínárbrekkur slopes to Midheidarendi, then up on to Urdarflöt and along the Urdarklettur crags until it left the Eskifjördur area. To the north of this is the Thverárdalur valley flanked by the mountains Andri and Hardskafi, with Hólafjall and Selheidi beyond them to the north.

There used to be a farm called Bakkasel Croft, which stood on the old route over to the Fljótsdalshérad district at the head of Eskifjördur fjord. The farm is now derelict but around the middle of the century Bakkasel was home to the farmer Sveinn Erlendsson, his wife Áslaug Bergsdóttir and their two sons, Bergur and Erlendur, aged eight and ten. Sveinn kept a few sheep and also taught at the primary school in Eskifjördur. Saturday 24th November 1956 dawned cold and bright, with a fairly deep covering of snow on the ground. Sveinn was planning to round up a few sheep that had wandered off. The weather at that time of year was very unpredictable and there was little bare ground. Sveinn and his two sons set out on foot from Bakkasel at first light, intending to be home before dark.

At first they made their way inland towards the Thverárdalur valley and Mount Hardskafi without finding any sheep. Then they headed south, ascending on to Eskifjördur Moor. They had made slow progress inland over Langihryggur to the Urdarklettur crags when the weather abruptly took a turn for the worse. Sveinn was concerned enough to consider heading straight for home but before they knew it a violent storm had blown up with a northerly gale and blizzard. Conditions continued to deteriorate until they could no longer see their way and before they knew it they were groping blindly through a complete white-out. The boys became separated from their father. He searched for them for a long time, shouting and calling in vain, before finally making his painful way down from the moor, following the Eskifjördur River home to Bakkasel. The conditions were so extreme by now that he could no longer stand upright and was forced to crawl the last stretch. He was in a desperate state when he reached home, hatless, coated in ice and barely in his right mind.

They phoned for help from Eskifjördur and the news soon spread around the district that the two boys were fighting for their lives in the violent storm that had now hit the village as well. A volunteer search party gathered at Bakkasel that evening but deemed it impossible to start the search until the wind dropped a little and daylight returned. These were difficult hours for the parents, knowing that their two sons were out there on the moor, caught in the blizzard. The boys' father in particular was distraught and barely in a fit state to talk to anyone, overwhelmed – beside himself, almost – with grief. He considered the boys beyond all aid and refused to take part in organising the search party, whereas his wife, Áslaug was tireless in looking after the helpers and at the head of the company when they finally set out at first light next day.

By then search parties had been called out from the villages of Reydarfjördur, Neskaupstadur and Seydisfjördur, and quite a crowd had gathered. Although the wind had lost much of its force the searchers were hindered by deep drifts. They made first for Eskifjördur Moor, armed with long poles to poke into the snow, and tried to find the brothers' tracks. But with no luck. It had been snowing heavily all night. It was thought that the brothers were together and had probably dug themselves into a drift. They had been missing for some eighteen hours by the time the rescue operation commenced and, given the freezing temperatures on the mountainsides, it was clear that the searchers were involved in a race against time.

The brothers had been warmly kitted out when they left home, in winter coats, scarves and woollen hats. After about four hours of searching a scarf was found, which Áslaug said belonged to the elder boy, and the search was intensified in the area where it was discovered. A volunteer by the name of Halldór Brjánsson from Seydisfjördur thought he met resistance when he stuck his pole into the snow and when people began to dig there they discovered the elder brother. He was lying as if he had fallen face down. Although he was showing signs of life, he was very cold and frostbite had started to form on his hands and feet. He was barely conscious and could give the searchers no clue as to his brother's whereabouts. The man who could travel fastest was sent to fetch hot milk, then people took it in turns to carry the boy down from the moor and home to Bakkasel. A doctor was waiting there to examine him and issued instructions for restoring warmth to the boy. He dressed his frostbite and in time the boy began to recover, though it was obvious that he had had a narrow escape. He had come very close to dying of hypothermia.

The search was intensified again in the area where the elder boy had been found but without success. It seemed as if he had been forced by the wind back towards the Thverárdalur valley and Mount Hardskafi. The area of the search was widened again when news came from Bakkasel that the brothers had become separated in the storm and the elder boy did not know what had happened to his brother. He said that they had stuck together for a long time but then he had lost him in the blizzard. He had hunted for him and shouted out his name until he was exhausted and fell again and again into the snow. The boy was said to be inconsolable and barely capable of human interaction. He was frantic to return to the mountains and look for his brother and in the end the doctor had to give him a sedative.

Dusk began to fall again and the weather worsened, so the searchers were forced to retreat to the inhabited area. By then reinforcements had arrived from Egilsstadir. A headquarters was set up in Eskifjördur. At dawn next day a large number of people set out to comb both the moor and the Thverárdalur valley, and the slopes of the mountains Andri and Hardskafi. They tried to work out the boy's movements after he had become separated from his brother. When the search in that area proved unsuccessful, it was

169

extended both to the north and south but the boy was not found. So the day passed until evening fell.

The organised search lasted for more than a week but, to cut a long story short, the boy was never found. There were a great many conjectures about his fate because it was as if the earth had simply swallowed him up. Some thought he had drowned in the Eskifjördur River and been carried down to the sea, others that he had been driven by the weather higher up into the mountains than anyone had envisaged. Others still thought he must have been lost in the bogs above the head of Eskifjördur fjord as he was making his way home.

Sveinn Erlendsson's grief at the fate of his sons was said to be terrible to behold. Later the rumour arose in the neighbourhood that his wife Áslaug had warned her husband against taking both boys with him on to the moor that day but that he had ignored her warning.

The elder brother recovered from his frostbite but was said to have been left gloomy and withdrawn by his ordeal. He was reputed to have continued searching for his brother's remains for as long as the family lived at Bakkasel.

Two years after these events, the family left the district and moved to Reykjavík and Bakkasel was left derelict, as we have said.

Erlendur closed the book and ran his hand over the worn cover. Eva Lind sat silently facing him on the sofa. A long moment passed before she reached for the packet of cigarettes on the table.

'Gloomy and withdrawn?' she asked.

'Old Dagbjartur didn't mince his words,' Erlendur said. 'He

needn't have been so blunt. He didn't know if I was gloomy or withdrawn. He never met me. He was barely acquainted with your grandparents. He learnt his information from members of the search party. People have no business printing gossip and rumour and dressing it up as the truth. He hurt my mother in a way that was quite uncalled-for.'

'And you as well.'

Erlendur shrugged.

'It was a long time ago. I haven't been keen to advertise the existence of this account, probably out of respect for my mother. She wasn't happy with it.'

'Was it true? Didn't she want you to go with your father?'

'She was against it. But later on she didn't blame him for what happened. Of course she was grief-stricken and angry but she knew it wasn't a question of guilt or innocence. It was a question of survival, survival in the battle against nature. The journey had to be made. There was no way of knowing beforehand that it would turn out to be so dangerous.'

'What happened to your father? Why didn't he do anything?'

'I never really understood that. He came down from the moor in a state of shock, convinced that Bergur and I were both dead. It was as if he'd lost the will to live. He himself only survived by the skin of his teeth after we were separated, and when it grew dark and night fell and the storm intensified your grandmother said it was as if he simply gave up. He sat on the edge of his bed in his room and took no further interest in what was going on. Admittedly he was exhausted and suffering from frostbite. When he heard I'd been rescued he revived a little. I crept into his room and he took me in his arms.'

'He must have been glad.'

'He was, of course, but I . . . I felt oddly guilty. I couldn't understand why I was spared while Bergur died. I still don't really understand. I felt as if I must have caused it in some way, as if it was my fault. Little by little I shut myself in with those thoughts. Gloomy and withdrawn. Maybe he was right after all.'

They sat in silence until finally Erlendur laid the book aside.

'Your grandmother left everything in good order when we moved. I've been to derelict farms where it seems as if people have walked out in a hurry and never looked back. Plates on the table, crockery in the cupboards, furniture in the living room, beds in the bedrooms. Your grandmother emptied our house and left nothing behind, took our furniture to Reykjavík and gave the rest of the stuff away. No one cared to live there after we left. Our home fell derelict. That's a peculiar feeling. On the last day we walked from room to room and I felt a strange emptiness that has stayed with me ever since. As if we were leaving our life behind in that place, behind those old doors and blank windows. As if we no longer had a life. Some power had taken it away from us.'

'Like it took Bergur?'

'Sometimes I wish he'd leave me in peace. That a whole day would pass without him entering my thoughts.'

'But it doesn't?'

'No. It doesn't.'

21

Erlendur sat in his car outside the church, smoking and brooding on coincidences. He had long pondered the way simple coincidence could decide a person's fate, decide their life and death. He knew examples of such coincidence from his work. More than once he had surveyed the scene of a murder that was committed for no motive whatsoever, without any warning or any connection between murderer and victim.

One of the cruellest examples of such a coincidence was that of a woman who was murdered on her way home from the supermarket in one of the city suburbs. The shop was one of a handful in those days that opened in the evenings. She encountered two men who were well known to the police. They meant to rob her but she clung on to her bag with a peculiar obstinacy. One of the repeat offenders had a small crowbar with him and struck her two heavy blows on the head. She was already dead by the time she was brought in to Accident and Emergency.

Why her? Erlendur had asked himself as he stood over the woman's body one summer's evening twenty years ago.

He knew that the two men who had attacked her were walking time bombs; in his view it had been inevitable that they would commit a serious crime one day, but it was by complete coincidence that their paths had crossed that of the woman. It could have been someone else that evening, or a week, a month, a year later. Why her, in that place, at that time? And why did she react as she did when she encountered them? When did the sequence of events begin that was to end with this murder? he asked himself. He was not for a moment trying to absolve the criminals of blame, only to examine the life that had ended in a pool of blood on a Reykjavík pavement.

He discovered that the woman was from the countryside and had lived in the city for more than seven years. Because of redundancies in the fisheries she had moved there with her two daughters and her husband from the fishing village where she'd been born. The trawler that their community relied on had been sold to another district, the prawn catch failed. Perhaps her final journey really began there. The family settled in the suburbs. She had wanted to move closer to the town centre but the same kind of flat would have been considerably more expensive there. That was another nail in her coffin.

Her husband found work in the construction business and she became a service rep for a phone company. The company moved their headquarters, making it harder for her to travel to work by public transport, so she handed in her notice. She was taken on as a caretaker at the local elementary school and liked the job; she got on well with the children. She went to work on foot every day and became a keen walker, dragging her husband out every evening, walking around the neighbourhood and only missing her breather if the weather was really bad. Their daughters were growing up. The eldest was nearing her twentieth birthday.

Her time was running out. That fateful evening the family were all at home and the elder daughter asked her mother for home-made ice cream. With that she set the chain of events in motion. They were out of cream and one or two other minor ingredients. The mother went out to the shop.

The younger daughter offered to run over for her but her mother said no, thanks. She fancied an evening stroll and caught her husband's eye. He said he didn't feel like it. There was a repeat on television of an Icelandic documentary featuring interviews with people from the countryside, some of them real oddballs, and he didn't want to miss it. Perhaps that was one of the coincidences. If the programme hadn't been on, he would have gone with her.

The mother went out and never came back.

The man who inflicted her death blow said that she wouldn't let go of her handbag, no matter what they did. It turned out that the woman had withdrawn a large amount of cash earlier that day for the birthday present she planned to buy her daughter, and was carrying it in her bag. That was why she held on to it so tightly. She never normally carried so much money around.

That too was a coincidence.

She lost her life that summer's evening with her daughter's birthday present on her mind; all she had done wrong was to live her ordinary life and take loving care of her family.

Erlendur stubbed out his cigarette and stepped out of the car. He looked up at the church, a cold, grey lump of concrete, and thought to himself that the architect must have been an atheist. At any rate, he couldn't see how the building could have been raised to the glory of God; if anything, it would have been to the glory of the company that supplied the concrete.

The vicar Eyvör was sitting in her office, talking on the phone. She gestured at a chair. He waited for her to finish her conversation. There was a cupboard containing a cassock, ruff and other vestments standing half-open in the office.

'Back again?' Eyvör said, having finished her conversation. 'Is it still about María?'

'I read somewhere that cremations are becoming increasingly popular,' he said, hoping to avoid giving her a direct answer.

'There are always people who choose that course and leave strict instructions to that effect. People who don't want their body to rot in the ground.'

'It has nothing to do with the Christian faith, then?'

'No, not really.'

'I understand Baldvin had María cremated,' Erlendur said.

'Yes.'

'That it was her wish.'

'I wouldn't know.'

'She never discussed it with you?'

'No.'

'Did Baldvin discuss her wishes with you?'

'No. He didn't. He simply told me that it was what she would have wanted. We don't require any proof of that sort of thing.'

'No, of course not.'

'Her death seems to be preying on you,' Eyvör commented.

'Maybe,' Erlendur said.

'What do you think happened?'

'I think she must have been suffering very badly,' he said. 'Very badly, for a long time.'

'I think so too. Perhaps that's why I wasn't as surprised as many other people about what happened.'

'Did she talk to you at all about her visions, hallucinations or anything like that?'

176

'No.'

'Nothing about believing she had seen her mother?'

'No.'

'Visits to mediums?'

'No, she didn't.'

'What did you talk about, if I may ask?'

'Naturally it's confidential,' Eyvör said. 'I can't tell you in any detail, and anyway I don't think it had any direct bearing on the way she chose to leave this world. We generally discussed religion.'

'Any aspect in particular?'

'Yes. Sometimes.'

'What?'

'Forgiveness. Absolution. Truth. How it sets people free.'

'Did she ever talk to you about what happened at Lake Thingvallavatn when she was a child?'

'No,' Eyvör said. 'Not that I remember.'

'About her father's death?'

'No. I'm sorry I can't help you at all.'

'That's all right,' Erlendur said, standing up.

'Though I can perhaps tell you one thing. We often discussed life after death, as I think I mentioned to you when we last talked. She was . . . what can I say . . . she became increasingly fascinated by the subject as the years went by, especially, of course, after her mother died. What she really wanted was proof of something of the kind and I had the feeling she was prepared to go quite a long way if necessary to obtain that proof.'

'What do you mean?'

Eyvör leant forward over the desk. Out of the corner of his eye Erlendur glimpsed her vicar's ruff in the cupboard.

'I think she was ready to go all the way. But that's just my opinion and I wouldn't want you to spread it any further. Let's keep it between ourselves.'

'Why do you think that?'

'I just got that impression.'

'So her suicide was . . .?'

'Her search for answers. I think. I know I shouldn't talk like this but from my knowledge of her over the last few years I could well believe that she was quite simply searching for answers.'

When Erlendur was back in his car, driving away from the church, his mobile phone rang. It was Sigurdur Óli. Erlendur had asked him to run a check on María's mobile phone and Baldvin had willingly given his consent. In the days leading up to her death she had been in contact with people about her academic work, with Karen about the holiday cottage and with her husband, both at the hospital and on his mobile.

'Her last call from the mobile was made the evening she hanged herself,' Sigurdur Óli said, without beating about the bush.

'What time was that?'

'At twenty to nine.'

'So she must have been alive then?'

'Apparently. The call lasted ten minutes.'

'Her husband said she called him from the cottage that evening.'

'What are you thinking?' Sigurdur Óli asked.

'What do you mean?'

'What is it with this case? The woman killed herself; is there any more to it than that?'

'I don't know.'

'Do you realise you're investigating it as if it was murder?'

'No, I'm not,' Erlendur said. 'I don't think she was murdered. I want to know why she committed suicide, that's all there is to it.'

'What's it to you?'

'Nothing,' Erlendur said. 'Absolutely nothing.'

'I thought you were only interested in missing-person cases.'

'Suicide is a missing-person case too,' Erlendur said and hung up on him.

The medium greeted María at the door and invited her in. They had a lengthy chat before the seance proper began. Magdalena made a good impression on María. She was warm and understanding and solicitous, just as Andersen had been, but María found it different talking to a woman. She wasn't as shy with Magdalena. And it seemed that Magdalena's psychic powers were stronger. She was more receptive, knew more, could see more and further than Andersen.

They sat down in the living room and Magdalena gradually eased them into the seance proper. María took in little of the flat or its furnishings. Baldvin had obtained the number from his colleague at the hospital and she had immediately called Magdalena who said she could meet her straight away. María received the impression that the psychic lived alone.

'I sense a strong presence,' Magdalena said. She closed her eyes and opened them again. 'A woman has made contact,' she continued. 'Ingibjörg. Does that sound familiar?'

'My grandmother's name was Ingibjörg,' María said. 'She died a long time ago.'

'She's very distant. You weren't close.'

'No, I hardly knew her. She was my father's mother.'

'She's terribly sad.'

'Yes.'

'She says it wasn't your fault what happened.'

'No.'

'She's talking about an accident,' Magdalena said.

'Yes.'

'There's water. Someone who drowned.'

'Yes.'

'A tragic accident, the old woman says.'

'Yes.'

'Are you familiar with . . . There's a painting, is it a painting of water? It's a picture of Lake Thingvallavatn. Does that sound familiar?'

'Yes.'

'Thank you. There's . . . there's a man who . . . It's unclear, a picture or painting . . . There's a woman who calls herself Lovísa, does that ring any bells?'

'Yes.'

'She's related to you.'

'Yes.'

'Thank you. She's young . . . I . . . hardly more than twenty.'

'Yes.'

'She's smiling. There's so much light around her. There's a radiance around her. She's smiling. She says that Leonóra's with her and is content.'

'Yes.'

'She says you're not to worry. . . . She says Leonóra's feeling wonderful. She says . . .'

'Yes?'

'She says she's looking forward to seeing you again.'

'Yes.'

'She wants you to know that she's happy. It'll be wonderful when you come. Wonderful.'

'Yes?'

'She says you mustn't be afraid. She says you're not to worry. Everything will be fine. Whatever you do. She says that whatever you decide to do . . . it'll . . . she says it'll turn out well. You mustn't worry. Everything will turn out fine.'

'Yes.'

'There's a beautiful aura around this woman. She . . . There's a radiance coming from her. . . . She's telling you . . . are you familiar with . . . there's a writer?'

'Yes.'

'A French writer?'

'Yes.'

'She's smiling. It's . . . the woman with her . . . she's . . . she says she's feeling better now. All the . . . all the pain . . .'

Magdalena squeezed her eyes shut.

'They're fading . . .'

She opened her eyes but it took her a while to recover her bearings.

'Was . . . was that all right?' she asked.

María nodded.

'Yes,' she said quietly. 'Thank you.'

When María got home she told Baldvin what had happened at the seance. She was in an emotional state, declaring that she had not expected such unequivocal messages and was surprised at who had made contact during the seance. She hadn't thought about her maternal grandmother since she was a little girl and she had only ever heard people talk about her great-aunt Lovísa. She was her maternal grandmother's sister, who had died young of typhoid fever.

María had difficulty getting to sleep that night. She was alone in the house because Baldvin had had to pop down to the hospital and the autumn wind was howling outside.

Finally she managed to drop off.

She started awake a moment later at the sound of the garden gate banging against the fence. It was pouring with rain. She listened to the banging of the gate and knew it would keep her awake.

Getting out of bed, she put on her dressing gown and slippers and went into the kitchen. There was a back door to the garden that opened on to the sun deck they'd added on a few years ago. She tied the belt of her dressing gown tightly around her and opened the door. As she did so she smelled a strong smell of cigar smoke in the air.

She stepped cautiously on to the sun deck, feeling the cold rain stinging her face.

Has Baldvin been smoking? she wondered.

She saw the gate banging but instead of hurrying to close it and running back inside she stood as if frozen to the spot, staring into the darkness of the garden. She saw a man standing there, drenched from head to foot: a heavily built figure with a paunch and a deathly white face. The water was pouring off him and he opened his mouth and closed it several times as if trying to gasp for air before shouting at her:

'Be careful! . . . You don't know what you're doing!'

22

The medium Andersen was suspicious and unwilling to disclose any information over the phone, refusing even to believe that Erlendur was from the police. Erlendur recognised his voice immediately from the recording. The man said that if Erlendur wanted to talk to him he would have to make an appointment like anyone else. Erlendur objected that his business wouldn't take long and wasn't anything very important, but the man would not budge.

'Are you going to charge me?' Erlendur asked at the end of the phone call.

'We'll see,' the man said.

One evening not long afterwards Erlendur rang a bell on the entryphone panel of a block of flats in the Vogar neighbourhood and asked to speak to Andersen.

The medium buzzed him in and Erlendur climbed slowly up to the second-floor landing where Andersen was waiting. They shook hands and the man showed him into the sitting room. As he entered the flat Erlendur was met by the faint aroma of incense and by soothing music flowing from invisible speakers.

Erlendur had postponed this visit until he felt it could no longer be avoided. He had no particular interest in the work of psychics or their ability to make contact with the dead, and was afraid this might lead to unpleasantness. He was determined to behave himself, however, and hoped that the medium Andersen would do the same.

Andersen offered him a seat at a small round table and sat down opposite him.

'Do you live here alone?' Erlendur asked, surveying his surroundings. It looked like a perfectly ordinary Icelandic home. There was a large television, a collection of films on video and DVD, three stands full of CDs, parquet on the floor, family photos on the walls. No veils or crystal balls, he noted.

No ectoplasm.

'Do you need to know that for your investigation?' the medium asked.

'No,' Erlendur admitted. 'I'm . . . What can you tell me about María? The woman I asked you about on the phone. The one who committed suicide.'

'Can I ask why you're investigating her?'

Erlendur began his speech about the Swedish survey on suicide and its causes but was not sure if he could lie convincingly to a man who made his living from being clairvoyant; wouldn't Andersen see straight through him? He gave a hasty explanation and hoped for the best.

'I really don't know how I can help you,' Andersen said. 'A strong bond of confidentiality often forms between me and the people who seek me out, and I find it hard to break that.'

He smiled apologetically. Erlendur smiled back. Andersen was a tall man of about sixty, greying at the temples, with a bright countenance, a pure expression and an unusually serene manner.

'Are you kept busy?' Erlendur asked, trying to lighten the atmosphere a little.

'I can't complain. Icelanders are very interested in matters of the soul.'

'You mean in life after death?'

Andersen nodded.

'Isn't it just the old peasant superstition?' Erlendur asked. 'It's not so long since we emerged from our turf huts and the Dark Ages.'

'The life of the soul has nothing to do with turf huts,' Andersen retorted. 'That sort of prejudice may help some people but I've always found it ridiculous myself. Though I understand when someone is sceptical about people like me. I would be sceptical myself, of course, if I hadn't been born with this power – or insight, as I prefer to call it.'

'How often did you see María?'

'She came to see me twice after her mother died.'

'She tried to make contact with her, did she?'

'Yes. That was her aim.'

'And . . . how did it go?'

'I think she went away satisfied.'

'I needn't ask whether you believe in the afterlife,' Erlendur said.

'It's the basic tenet of my life.'

'And she did too?'

'Without a shadow of doubt. Quite without doubt.'

'Did she talk to you about her fear of the dark?'

'Only a little. We discussed the fact that fear of the dark is a psychological fear like any other and that it is possible to overcome it with cognitive therapy and self-discipline.'

'She didn't tell you what caused her fear?'

'No. But then, I'm not a psychologist. Judging from our conversations, I could well believe it was connected somehow to her father's death in an accident. It's not hard to imagine that it must have had a huge impact on her as a child.'

'Has she . . . what do you say . . . appeared to you – María, I mean – since she took her life?'

'No,' Andersen said, smiling. 'It's not that simple. I think you have some rather odd notions about psychics. Do you know anything about our work?'

Erlendur shook his head.

'I gather María had a special fascination with life after death,' he said.

'That's self-evident; she wouldn't have come to me otherwise,' Andersen replied.

'Yes, but more of a fascination than is quite normal, more like a mania. I understand she was completely obsessed with curiosity about death. About what comes afterwards.'

Erlendur wanted, if possible, to avoid having to refer to the recording that Karen had lent him and hoped the medium would oblige him. Andersen gave him a long look as if weighing up what he could or should say.

'She was a seeker,' he said. 'Like so many of us. I'm sure you are, too.'

'What was María searching for?'

'Her mother. She missed her. Her mother was going to provide her with an answer to the question of whether there is life after death. María thought she'd received that answer and came to me. We talked. I think it did her some good.'

'Did her mother ever make contact during your meetings?'

'No, she didn't. Though that's not necessarily significant.'

'What did María think about that?'

'She went away satisfied.'

'I gather she suffered from delusions,' Erlendur said.

'Call them what you like.'

'That she had seen her mother.'

'Yes, she told me about that.'

'And?'

'And nothing. She was unusually receptive.'

'Do you know if she went to see anyone else, talked to any other mediums?'

'Naturally she wouldn't tell me something that was none of my business. But she did phone me one day to ask about another medium, a woman I didn't know and had never heard of. She must be new. One tends to know most people in this business.'

'You don't know who this woman was?'

'No. Except her name. As I said, I don't know of any psychic by that name.'

'And what was her name?'

'María didn't give any second name – she just referred to her as Magdalena.'

'Magdalena?'

'I've never heard of her.'

'What does that mean? That you haven't heard of her?'

'Nothing. It doesn't necessarily mean anything. But I called a few places and no one knows this Magdalena.'

'Mightn't she just be new, as you say?'

Andersen shrugged.

'I assume that must be it.'

'Are there many of you in this business?'

'No, not so many. I can't give an exact number.'

'How did María find out about her, this Magdalena?'

'I don't know.'

'Isn't what you said about fear of the dark rather a strange attitude for someone who makes a living from making contact with ghosts?'

'What do you mean?'

'That fear of the dark is a psychological fear, not caused by a belief in ghosts.'

'There's nothing malign about the spirit world,' Andersen said. 'We all have our ghosts. You not least.'

'Me?' Erlendur said.

Andersen nodded.

'A whole crowd,' he said. 'But don't worry. Keep looking. You'll find them.'

'You mean him,' Erlendur said.

'No,' Andersen said, contradicting him and standing up. 'I mean them.'

23

Erlendur had once developed a condition known as cardiac arrhythmia. At times it was as if his heart took an extra beat, which was very uncomfortable; at others as if his heart rate was slowing down. When, instead of improving, the condition grew worse, he leafed through the Yellow Pages, stopping at a name that caught his fancy in the 'Heart Specialists' column: Dagóbert. Erlendur took an immediate liking to the name and decided to make him his doctor. He had hardly been in the doctor's surgery five minutes before his curiosity got the better of him and he enquired about his moniker.

'I'm from the West Fjords,' the cardiologist said, apparently used to the question. 'I'm fairly resigned to it. My cousin envies me. He got landed with Dósótheus.'

The waiting room in the medical centre was packed with people suffering from a whole range of ailments. A variety of specialists worked there, including ear, nose and throat doctors, a vascular surgeon, three cardiologists, two nephrologists and one eye specialist. Erlendur stood by the entrance to the waiting room, thinking that each of these specialists should be able to find something to suit them in there. He was worried about barging in on his doctor without having made an appointment months in advance. He knew the cardiologist was extremely busy and was presumably booked up far into next year, and that his visit would increase the waiting time of some of the people in here by at least a quarter of an hour, depending when the doctor could fit him in. He had already been standing here for around twenty minutes.

The doctors' surgeries were on a long corridor off the waiting room, and after forty-five minutes had passed since Erlendur had announced his presence a door opened and Dagóbert came out into the waiting area and beckoned to him. Erlendur followed him into his surgery and the doctor closed the door behind them.

'Has the problem come back?' Dagóbert asked, inviting Erlendur to lie down on the bed. His file was open on the desk.

'No,' Erlendur said. 'I'm fine. I'm sort of here on official business.'

'Really?' the doctor said. He was a fat, humorous man, dressed in a white shirt, a tie and jeans. He might not have worn a white coat but he did have a stethoscope slung round his neck. 'Won't you lie down anyway and let me listen to your chest?'

'No need,' Erlendur said, taking a chair in front of the desk. Dagóbert sat down on the bed. Erlendur remembered their previous meetings when the doctor had explained how the electrical impulses that controlled his heartbeat had been disrupted. The problem was generally caused by stress. Erlendur understood little of what he had said beyond the fact that the condition was not life-threatening and would get better in time.

'Then what can I . . .?' Dagóbert asked.

'It's a medical matter,' Erlendur said.

He had been struggling with the wording ever since it had first occurred to him to consult the cardiologist. He didn't want to talk to anyone involved with the police, such as a pathologist, because he didn't want to have to explain anything.

'Well, fire away.'

'If one wanted to kill a person, but only for a couple of minutes, how would one go about it?' Erlendur asked. 'If one wanted to revive him immediately so that nobody could see any sign of what had happened?'

The doctor gave him a long look.

'Do you know of such a case?' he asked.

'Actually, I was going to ask you that,' Erlendur said. 'I don't know of any myself.'

'I'm not aware of anyone having done it deliberately, if that's what you mean,' Dagóbert replied.

'How would one go about it?'

'That depends on a number of factors. What are the circumstances?'

'I'm not sure. Let's say, for example, that it was done at home.'

Dagóbert looked at Erlendur gravely.

'Has someone you know been messing around with that sort of thing?' he asked. Dagóbert knew that Erlendur worked for the CID and thought it obvious that his irregular heartbeat was occupational, as he put it. Otherwise he didn't often slip into jargon, much to Erlendur's relief.

'No,' Erlendur said. 'And it's not a police matter. I'm just curious because of an old report I came across.'

'You're talking about how to achieve cardiac arrest without its being discovered and in such a way that the victim would survive?'

'Possibly,' Erlendur said.

'Why on earth would anybody want to do something like that?'

'I have no idea,' Erlendur replied.

'I assume you have some further criteria.'

'Not really.'

'I don't quite follow. As I said: why would anyone want to bring about cardiac arrest?'

'I don't know,' Erlendur said. 'I was hoping you'd be able to tell me.'

'The first consideration would be the prevention of damage to the organs,' Dagóbert said. 'As soon as the heart stops beating, decomposition begins, immediately endangering the tissues and organs. I expect there are a number of drugs that would do the trick by inducing a coma but, from the way you describe it, this might be a case of hypothermia. Otherwise I'm not really sure.'

'Hypothermia?'

'Extreme cold,' the doctor said. 'It achieves two goals. The heart stops beating when the body temperature drops below a certain level and you experience clinical death, while at the same time the cold has the effect of preserving the body and organs. Cold slows down all metabolic processes.'

'How would the person be resuscitated?'

'Probably with a defibrillator, followed by rapid rewarming.'

'And you'd need specialist knowledge to do that?'

'Unquestionably. I can't imagine any other scenario. There would have to be a doctor present, even a cardiologist. And it goes without saying that no one should meddle with this sort of thing.'

'How long is it possible to keep someone in a state like that before it becomes irreversible?'

'Well, I'm no expert when it comes to inducing clinical death by hypothermia,' Dagóbert said, with a smile. 'But it's a question of a few short minutes after cardiac arrest – four to five, tops. I don't know. You'd have to factor in the facilities available to you. If you're in hospital with access to all the best technology, it might be possible to go even further. Hypothermia has been used in recent years to keep people in a coma while their wounds are healing. It's also a good method of protecting the organs of people who have experienced cardiac arrest, for example. In that case the body temperature is held at thirty-one degrees Celsius or thereabouts.'

'If it was done at home, what equipment would you need?'

The doctor stopped and thought.

'I can't . . .' he began, before breaking off again.

'What's the first thing that comes to mind?'

'A good-sized bathtub. Ice. A defibrillator and easy access to electricity. A blanket.'

'Would it leave any trace? If the person in question was successfully resuscitated?'

'Signs that it had taken place? I don't think so,' Dagóbert said. 'I should think it's like getting caught in a blizzard. The cold gradually slows the metabolic processes; the person would become drowsy initially, then fall into a stupor and finally experience cardiac arrest and death.'

'Isn't that exactly what happens when people die of exposure?' Erlendur asked.

'Exactly the same.'

The woman who had last spoken to the student Gudrún, as far as could be established with any certainty, now worked as a departmental manager at the National Museum of Iceland. They had been cousins and Gudrún's parents had asked her to keep an eye on their daughter while they were on their extended trip through Asia. She was three years older than Gudrún, short, with thick blonde hair tied back in a ponytail. Her name was Elísabet and she called herself Beta.

'I find it very uncomfortable raking this up,' she said once she and Erlendur had taken a seat in the museum café. 'I was sort of responsible for Dúna, or at least I felt I was, though of course, you know, I couldn't have prevented anything. She just vanished. It was absolutely unbelievable. Why are you investigating this now?'

'We're closing the file,' Erlendur said, hoping it would do as an explanation.

'So you're sure she'll never be found now?' Beta said.

'It's been a long time,' Erlendur said, without answering her directly.

'I just can't imagine what could have happened,' Beta said. 'One day she drives away and – poof! – she vanishes. Her car's never found, nor any trace of her. She doesn't seem to have stopped off at any shops or villages, either on the way north or in the Reykjavík area.'

'People have mentioned suicide,' Erlendur said.

'She just wasn't the type,' Beta said immediately.

'What is the type?' Erlendur asked.

'No, I mean, she wasn't like that.'

'I don't know anyone who is,' Erlendur said.

'You know what I mean,' Beta said. 'And what happened to her car? *It* can hardly have committed suicide!'

Erlendur smiled.

'We dragged the harbours all round the country. Sent divers to search along the docks in case she'd lost control of the car. We didn't find anything.'

'She was incredibly fond of her little yellow Mini,' Beta said. 'I've never been able to picture her driving it off some jetty. I've always found the idea absurd. Ludicrous.'

'She didn't reveal anything about her plans in your last conversation?'

'Nothing. If I'd known what was going to happen it would have been different. She rang to ask me about a hairdresser's on Laugavegur I'd recommended to her. She was intending to go there. That's why I've never believed in suicide. There was nothing to point to it.'

'Was there some reason, some special occasion?'

'For the hairdresser's appointment? No, it was just time for a haircut, I think.'

'And you didn't discuss anything else?'

'No, not really. I didn't hear from her again. I assumed she'd gone up north; I called a couple of times but she was never in, or at least that's what I thought. By then, of course, she had gone missing. I find it so hard to imagine what could have happened. Why should a girl like her, in the prime of life, vanish like that without any reason or warning? What does it tell you? How can you ever be expected to understand?'

'She'd never been in a relationship, lived with a boyfriend or . . . ?'

'No, never – she had all that to look forward to.'

'Where did she go when she used to take trips in the car? I know it's in the files but one can never ask too often.'

'Up north, of course. She missed Akureyri at times and used to go there whenever she could. Then there was the area around Reykjavík. The Reykjanes peninsula. Over the mountains to the east. An outing to Hveragerdi for an ice cream. The usual. You know about her passion for lakes.'

'Yes.'

'Lake Thingvallavatn was a great favourite.'

'Thingvallavatn?'

'She knew it like the back of her hand. Was forever going there and had her favourite spots by the lake. Our uncle down here in Reykjavík had a holiday cottage in Lundarreykjadalur in the Borgarfjördur area, which we used a lot, and she often took the mountain road over Uxahryggir and down to Thingvellir on her way back to town. She'd drive round the eastern shore of the lake and then home. She used to camp at Thingvellir sometimes with her girlfriends. And sometimes alone. She'd drive out of town and stay alone by the lake. She quite liked being alone – she was self-sufficient in so many ways.'

'There was no sign that she'd visited your uncle's holiday cottage?' Erlendur asked, trying to recall the files on Gudrún's disappearance.

'No, she hadn't been there,' Beta said.

'Where did this fascination with lakes come from?'

'No one knew, not even her. Dúna had always been like that, ever since we were small. She once told me that lakes had a strange power, a wonderful tranquillity. That you could commune best with nature beside lakes, with all the birds and the life of the shore. Of course she was studying biology. It wasn't a coincidence.'

'Did she ever go out on the lake? Did she own a boat?'

'No, that was the strange thing about Dúna. She was afraid of water when she was a girl. It was difficult to get her to take swimming lessons and she never much enjoyed trips to the pool. She had no interest in being in the water, only in being near lakes. That was the nature lover in her.'

'There aren't many places as beautiful as Lake Thingvallavatn,' Erlendur commented.

'That's true.'

24

Two days later Erlendur was sitting in the home of an ageing drama teacher called Jóhannes while the man poured him a fruit tea. It was not the sort of thing that Erlendur usually drank, but the man had been rather uncooperative, failing to understand what the police wanted with him and extremely unwilling to let him in. However, when he heard that the matter involved gossip about other people rather than him personally he calmed down and opened the door. He said he had just made himself some fruit tea and asked if Erlendur would like to join him.

Orri Fjeldsted had suggested the teacher when Erlendur asked him who would be the best person to ask about old students at the Drama School. Orri didn't even stop to think. He said that Jóhannes had taught him in his time and was a great guy, though a terrible old gossip with a nose for information, and anything he said about Orri himself, should he crop up in conversation, was a lie.

Jóhannes lived alone in a terraced house in the east of town. He was quite tall, with a booming voice, a bald head, a twinkle in his eye and unusually large ears. Orri said he was divorced; his wife had left him years ago. They had no children. Jóhannes had been a hell of an actor himself in his youth but as he grew older the roles had begun to dry up and he had started teaching at the drama school in between taking the odd part in professional and amateur productions. Occasional cameos in films had also kept his face in the public eye and he sometimes took part in radio and TV chat shows, reminiscing about the old days.

'I remember Baldvin well,' Jóhannes said once he was seated in his study with two cups of fruit tea. Erlendur sipped his and thought it tasted vile. He had explained his business to Jóhannes and asked him not to mention to anyone that he was asking questions about one of his old students. From what Orri had said, there was little point in insisting on confidentiality but Erlendur hoped for the best.

'He wasn't good actor material; quit in his second year, from what I recall,' Jóhannes continued. 'Though he had a reasonable talent for comedy. That was it, though. He quit in the middle of the course – mid-performance, you might say. Seemed to think he'd discovered a vocation for medicine. I've hardly seen him since.'

'Were they a good group, his year?'

'Yes, they were,' Jóhannes said, sipping his tea. 'They were indeed. Well, there was Orri Fjeldsted, a decent actor, though he can be a bit one-note. I saw that appalling production of *Othello*. He was a disaster in that. Svala was in the group as well, and Sigríður who was a real actress, born to play the Scandinavian giants, Ibsen and Strindberg. And of course Heimir, who I personally have always felt deserved bigger roles. He became rather bitter and disillusioned with age. Took to the bottle. I got him to play Jimmy in my production of *Look Back in Anger* and thought he did it very well, though not everyone agreed. I don't actually know where he is today, though I did catch him in a small role in a radio play the other day. They're all middle-aged now – Lilja, Saebjörn, Einar. Then there was Karólína. She was never much of an actress, poor dear.'

'Do you remember anything about the time when Baldvin dropped out?' Erlendur asked, realising that he wouldn't exactly have to resort to torture to extract information from the old thespian.

'Baldvin? Well, he just quit. He didn't give any particular reason, didn't need to. Though it was very difficult to get into drama school in those days and places were highly sought after, so people didn't usually drop out in mid-performance, let me tell you. In mid-performance.'

'You don't mean literally?'

'No, it's just a figure of speech, you know; I just mean that he did it, he dropped out. Very suddenly, I thought, given what those kids went through to get into the school. Young people used to dream of becoming actors in those days. That was the dream. To make the big time, be famous and admired. Acting can give you that if that's what you're after. But it gives so much more to serious actors. It gave me culture, literature and theatre, opened the door to life itself.'

The old actor broke off and smiled.

'Excuse me if I'm getting pompous. We actors have a tendency to be bombastic. Especially when we're on stage.'

He laughed loudly at himself.

'I gather Baldvin met the woman he later married shortly after he quit,' Erlendur said, with a smile.

'Yes, she was a historian, wasn't she? I heard she died the other day. Killed herself. Perhaps that's why you're here, or . . .'

'No,' Erlendur said. 'Did you know her at all?'

'Not in the slightest. Was there something suspicious about it? About how she died?'

'No,' Erlendur said. 'Was he completely resigned to giving up acting? Baldvin, I mean. Do you remember?'

'I always thought Baldvin did just as he pleased,' Jóhannes said. 'That's the impression he made on me. As if he wouldn't let anyone push him around: a headstrong boy who did his own thing. But then the kids said that this girl had got such a strong hold over him that he completely changed gear. And anyway, he was no good as an actor. He must have realised that himself, thought better of it.'

'Did they get involved with each other at all?' Erlendur asked, putting down his fruit tea. 'The drama students?'

'Well, you know how it is,' Jóhannes said. 'A bit of that sort of thing is inevitable, but it doesn't always last. Some of them have got married since, people from the same year. It's always happening.'

'What about Baldvin?'

'You mean before he met his wife? I can't really help you much with that. Though I did hear something about him falling for Karólína who was in his year. She was pretty enough but had no real talent as an actress and never played any major roles. In fact, I have no idea on what grounds we let her into the school. I never did know.'

'Did she ever become an actress?' Erlendur asked, regretting his ignorance of the theatre.

'Oh, her career didn't last long; it was a complete non-event. I don't think she's acted for years. She generally played very minor roles. Her biggest part got such bad reviews that it must have utterly destroyed her.'

'What role was that?' Erlendur asked.

'It was a Swedish problem play that used to do all right in the old days. Not great but not a stinker either. It was known as

Flame of Hope in Icelandic. I don't know why they put it on; kitchen-sink drama was going out of fashion by then.'

'Mm,' Erlendur said, in complete ignorance of Swedish theatre.

'The author was quite popular in those days.'

Erlendur nodded, still none the wiser.

'There was one thing that was a bit unusual about Karólína. No one wanted fame more than her: to be the star, the diva. I think it was the only reason she went to the school, whereas the other students were probably more interested in the actual drama and what it can teach you. Karólína was a bit daft in that way. But then, she didn't have what it takes, didn't have the talent. No matter what we tried at the school, it just didn't work.'

'But she got the role anyway?'

'The role in *Flame of Hope* wasn't that bad,' Jóhannes said, finishing his fruit tea. 'But she was a disaster in it. Utterly wooden, poor darling. After that I think she more or less retired. Anyway, she and Baldvin were seeing each other before he married and had . . . no, they never did have children, did they?'

'No,' Erlendur said, surprised at how well informed the drama teacher was. Apparently there wasn't much that those big ears missed.

'Perhaps it affected the woman that way,' he said. 'Being childless.'

Erlendur shrugged.

'I wouldn't know.'

'Hanged herself, didn't she?'

Erlendur nodded.

'And Baldvin? How did he take it?'

'How anyone would, I imagine.'

'Yes, how do people cope with something like that? I don't know. I met Baldvin a few years ago. He was standing in for my GP at the local surgery. A very dear boy, Baldvin. Always had money troubles, from what I remember. Left a trail of debts everywhere. He used to cadge loans from me until I stopped lending him money. He spent way beyond his income, but doesn't everyone these days?'

'Yes,' Erlendur said, getting to his feet.

'It's as if it's in fashion to run up as large a debt as possible,' Jóhannes said, accompanying him to the door.

Erlendur shook him by the hand.

'She actually made rather a lovely Magdalena,' the actor said. 'A pretty girl.'

Erlendur stopped in the doorway.

'Magdalena?' he said.

'Yes, a lovely Magdalena. Karólína, I mean. Hang on, am I talking rubbish? It's all getting mixed up in my head, actors and roles and all that.'

'Who was Magdalena?' Erlendur asked.

'Karólína's part in the Swedish play. She played a young woman called Magdalena.'

'Magdalena?'

'Does that help you at all?'

'I don't know,' Erlendur said. 'Possibly.'

Erlendur sat in his car, still brooding on coincidences. He had smoked four cigarettes and was aware of a touch of heartburn. He hadn't eaten properly since that morning and had been assuaging his hunger pangs by smoking. Most of the smoke escaped via a narrow gap at the top of the driver's window. It was evening. He had watched the autumn sun disappear behind a bank of cloud. The car was parked at a discreet distance from an old detached house in the west of Kópavogur, the town immediately to the south of Reykjavík, and he had been keeping an intermittent eye on the house while watching the sunset. He knew the woman lived there alone and presumably didn't have much money or else some of it would surely have been spent on maintenance. The place was in a pretty bad state of repair; hadn't been painted for a long time and brown streaks of rust ran down beside the windows. He hadn't seen anyone coming or going. A battered little Japanese car was parked in the road in front. The people who lived in the surrounding houses had trickled home from work or school or shopping trips or whatever people did in their daily grind, and, feeling rather ashamed of himself, Erlendur spied on the typical family life going on behind the two kitchen windows that were visible from his car.

He was there because of a coincidence in a case which he had no idea why he was investigating so assiduously. There was no indication of anything other than the tragic death of a woman who had been on the brink. This was indicated by her past, certainly by the loss of her mother, her obsession with the afterlife. He had found no evidence of foul play until recently when he had heard a name that had come up before. The name sparked off odd ideas about connections, both known and unknown, between the people that the unhappy woman at Thingvellir had known or not known. Magdalena was the name of the medium that María had visited. Erlendur knew that coincidences were rarely anything other than life itself playing nasty tricks on people or giving them a nice surprise. They were like the rain that fell on both the just and the unjust. They could be good and they could be bad. They shaped people's so-called fate to a greater or lesser degree. They originated from nowhere: unexpected, odd and inexplicable.

Erlendur was careful to avoid confusing coincidences with something else. But from his job he knew better than anyone that they could sometimes be manipulated. They could be skilfully planted in the lives of unsuspecting individuals. In that case the incidents could no longer be described as coincidence. It varied as to how one referred to them but in Erlendur's line of work there was only one name: crime.

He was going over and over these thoughts when a light came on by the entrance to the house, the door opened and a woman stepped out. She closed the door behind her, went over to the car that was parked in front, got in and drove away. She had to try the ignition three times before the engine coughed into life, and the car disappeared down the road with a considerable racket. Erlendur thought that part of the exhaust must have gone.

He watched the car drive away, then started his old Ford and followed at a slight distance. He knew little about the woman he was spying on. After his visit to the drama teacher he had given himself a quick briefing on the career of Karólína Franklín. Her patronymic was Franklínsdóttir but she used the Franklín part as a surname, a show of pretension which her old teacher found very telling: 'Utterly superficial, that girl,' he said, adding, 'nothing up here,' and tapped his forehead with his finger. Erlendur discovered that Karólína worked as a secretary at a large finance company in the city. She was single, childless and had not acted in public for years. The part of Magdalena in *Flame of Hope* had been her last role. In it she had played a working-class Swedish girl, according to Jóhannes, who discovered that her husband was committing adultery and plotted her revenge on him.

He followed Karólína to a kiosk and video-rental shop in the neighbourhood, and watched her choose a film and buy some snacks before driving back home.

Erlendur sat in his car outside her house for an hour or so, smoked two more cigarettes, then drove away down the street and towards home.

25

The bank manager did not keep Erlendur waiting. He came out and greeted him with a firm handshake before inviting him into his office. He was in his forties, smartly dressed in a pinstriped suit with a tastefully chosen tie and gleaming patent-leather shoes. The same height as Erlendur, he was a smiling, friendly man who said he had just been to London with a select group of clients to watch a major football match. Erlendur recognised the names of the teams but that was about it. The bank manager was accustomed to dealing with rich customers whose primary requirement was swift, efficient service. Erlendur knew he had worked his way up to his position through diligence, tenacity and an innate desire to please. Their paths had often crossed, ever since the manager had been a humble cashier at the bank. They had always got on well, especially after Erlendur had discovered that the cashier was not a native of Reykjavík but had grown up on a small farm in the remote south-eastern district of Öraefasveit until his family abandoned the attempt to scratch a living from the land and moved to the city.

The manager poured a coffee for Erlendur and they sat down on the leather sofas in his spacious office. They discussed horse breeding in the east and news of Reykjavík's escalating crime rate, which was directly linked to the rise in drug use. When the conversation seemed to have run its course and Erlendur was worried that the manager would have to return to the business of making millions for the bank, although he showed no sign of impatience, he cleared his throat and came round in a circuitous way to the point of his visit.

'Of course, you'll have stopped helping out the police long ago,' he said, surveying the office.

'Other people take care of that side of things nowadays,' the bank manager said, smoothing his tie. 'Would you like to speak to them?'

'No, no. It's you I want to talk to.'

'What is it? Do you need a loan?'

'No.'

'Was it about an overdraft?'

Erlendur shook his head. He had never had any particular money troubles. His salary had been perfectly adequate to cover his needs, except when he'd been setting himself up in his flat, and he had never had an overdraft or any other loan apart from his mortgage, which he had long since paid off in full.

'No, nothing like that,' Erlendur said. 'Though it is a personal matter. This is strictly between the two of us. Unless you want to get me thrown out of the police.'

The bank manager smiled.

'You're exaggerating, surely? Why would they want to fire you?'

'You never know with that lot. Anyway. Do you believe in ghosts? People used to in Öraefasveit, didn't they?'

'They certainly did. My father could tell you a story or two about that. He said the spooks were so active that they should have been made to pay council tax.'

Erlendur smiled.

'Are you investigating ghosts?' the bank manager asked.

'Maybe.'

'Ghosts who have business with the bank?'

'I have a name,' Erlendur said. 'I have an ID number. I know he banks here. This was also his late wife's bank.'

'Is she the ghost?'

Erlendur nodded.

'And you need to look this man up?'

Erlendur nodded again.

'Why don't you take the usual route? Do you have a warrant?'

Erlendur shook his head.

'Is he a criminal?'

'No. Possibly.'

'Possibly? Is he someone you're investigating?'

Erlendur nodded.

'What's going on? What are you looking for?'

'I can't tell you, I'm afraid.'

'Who is it?'

Erlendur shook his head.

'Aren't I allowed to know?'

'No. Look, I know this is highly irregular, and no doubt incomprehensible to an honest man like you, but I want to look at this man's account and I can't do it through the system, unfortunately. I would if I could but I can't.'

The bank manager stared at him.

'You're asking me to break the law.'

'Yes and no,' Erlendur said.

'So this is not an official investigation?'

Erlendur shook his head.

'Erlendur,' the bank manager said, 'are you out of your mind?'

'This case, which I can't discuss with you, is turning into a complete nightmare. I know next to nothing about what has happened but the information I'm asking you for could conceivably help me get a better handle on it.'

'Why isn't this a normal inquiry?'

'Because I'm undertaking a private investigation,' Erlendur said. 'No one knows what I'm up to or what I've uncovered. I'm completely alone on this. What happens here with you will go no further. I don't have enough evidence yet to turn it into an official inquiry. The people I'm investigating are not aware of the fact – or at least I hope they aren't. I don't know exactly what information I need but I'm hoping to find out something here at the bank. You'll have to trust me.'

'Why are you doing this? Aren't you putting your career on the line?'

'It's one of those cases where you have nothing tangible, just a whole heap of suspicions. All I've got to go on is fragments. I need simple connections, some kind of background to the events that later took place. I need to fill in the gaps in these people's story, including their financial history. I wouldn't ask you if I didn't think . . . if I didn't think a crime had been committed. A sordid crime that no one knows about and that . . . the person in question . . . seems likely to get away with.'

The bank manager stared at Erlendur for a long time in meaningful silence.

'Can you call up the bank's customers on that computer?' Erlendur asked at last, nodding towards three flat screens on the bank manager's large desk.

'Yes.'

'Are you going to help me?'

'Erlendur, I . . . I'm afraid I can't get involved in this. I can't do it.'

Their eyes met for a long moment.

'Can you tell me if the person in question is badly in debt? A simple yes or no?' Erlendur asked.

The bank manager thought for a moment.

'I can't do it, Erlendur. Please don't ask me.'

'What about his wife? She's dead. A query about her account shouldn't hurt anyone.'

'Erlendur . . .'

'All right. I understand.'

The bank manager was on his feet. He tapped a finger on the desk.

'Do you have her ID number?'

'Yes.'

The manager typed in the number, pressed several keys on the keyboard, clicked with the mouse and stared at the screen.

'She was rolling in it,' he said.

The old man lay in his hospital bed, apparently asleep. The corridor was quiet after the evening meal. The two men who shared his ward lay in their beds too, taking no notice of Erlendur. One was reading a book, the other was dozing.

Erlendur sat down by the bed and looked at his watch. He had been on his way home when he'd decided to call in. At that moment the old man woke up and saw him.

'I went to see your son Elmar,' Erlendur said.

He came straight to the point, unsure how much time he had.

'Oh?'

The man who had been reading put down his book on the bedside table and turned to face the wall. Erlendur had the feeling that he could hear every word they said. The man dozing in the bed between them now began to snore quietly. Erlendur knew these were not ideal circumstances under which to conduct a police inquiry but there was little that he could do about it, and anyway his visits to the old man hardly deserved to be called an investigation.

'Their relationship was always okay, wasn't it?' Erlendur asked, attempting to sound as if he wasn't trying to sow unnecessary seeds of suspicion. He thought perhaps he had asked this before.

'The boys were very different, if that's what you mean.'

'Not very close, perhaps?' Erlendur suggested.

The old man shook his head.

'No, they weren't close. Elmar never comes here. Never visits me. Says he can't stand nursing homes, hospitals, old people's homes or whatever you like to call them. He's a taxi driver. Did you know that?'

'Yes,' Erlendur said.

'Divorced, like so many of them nowadays,' the old man said. 'Always been a bit of a misfit.'

'Yes, well, some people are like that,' Erlendur replied, for the sake of saying something.

'Did you find that girl you were asking about?'

'No. Your son Elmar said Davíd had never been involved with any girls.'

'He's right.'

The snores from the middle bed grew louder.

'Perhaps you should give up the search,' the old man said.

'It's hardly a search,' Erlendur said. 'Anyway, there's not much to do down at the station at the moment, so don't you worry about me.'

'Do you really think you'll ever find him?'

'I have no idea,' Erlendur said. 'People go missing. Sometimes they're found, sometimes not.'

'It's too long ago. We stopped picturing him alive a long time ago. It was actually something of a relief, despite the fact that we were never able to mourn him properly.'

'No, of course,' Erlendur said.

'And soon I'll be gone myself,' the old man said.

'Does the thought worry you?'

'No. I'm not afraid.'

'Do you worry about what will come next?' Erlendur asked.

'Not at all. I expect to meet my Davíd again. And Gunnthórunn. That'll be good.'

'You believe that?'

'I've always believed it.'

'In life after death?'

'Yes, of course.'

Neither of them spoke for a moment.

'I'd like to have known what became of the boy,' the old man said. 'Strange how these things happen. He told his mother he was going to the bookshop and then to his friend's house, and that was the end of his short life.'

'No one recognised him in any of the bookshops. Not here in Reykjavík, or in any of the neighbouring towns. The police checked up on that specifically at the time. Nor had he arranged to meet any of his friends.'

'Perhaps his mother misunderstood him. The whole thing was incomprehensible. Utterly incomprehensible.'

The man who had been reading was now asleep.

'What did he want from the bookshop? Can you remember?'

'He mentioned it to Gunnthórunn. He was going to buy a book about lakes.'

'A book about lakes?'

'Yes, some lake book.'

'What kind of lakes? What did he mean by that?'

'It was a new book, his mother said. A book of photographs of the lakes around Reykjavík.'

'Was he interested in that sort of thing? In the Icelandic countryside?'

'Not that I was ever aware. I seem to remember that his mother thought he was planning to give it to someone. But she wasn't sure. She thought it might have been a misunderstanding on her part because he had never mentioned anything like that before.'

'Did you know who it was? Who the book was intended for?'

'No.'

'And his friends knew nothing about it?'

'No, no one.'

'Could it have for been the girl that Gilbert mentioned? The one he thought your son had met?'

'There was no girl,' the old man said. 'Davíd would have told us. And anyway, she would have come forward when he went missing. Anything else would be unthinkable. That's why there can't have been any girl. It's out of the question.'

The old man waved his hand dismissively.

'Out of the question,' he repeated.

26

Erlendur drove into the cul-de-sac in Grafarvogur as evening fell the following day and parked in front of the doctor's house. They had an appointment. Erlendur had called after lunch, saying that he needed to see him. Baldvin wanted to know why and Erlendur said he had received information from a third party that he would like to discuss with him. The doctor seemed surprised and wanted to know who the third party was and whether he, Baldvin was under some sort of police scrutiny. Erlendur placated him as he had before, saying it would take no time to deal with his questions. He was on the point of adding that it was nothing serious but knew this would be a lie.

He remained sitting in the car for some time after turning off the engine. The impending meeting with Baldvin was not a prospect he relished. He was on his own with this case. Neither Elínborg nor Sigurdur Óli knew exactly what he was up to, nor did his superiors at the CID. Erlendur had no idea how long he could persevere in this inquiry without its becoming official. The future of the investigation would probably depend on Baldvin's reaction to his questions.

Baldvin greeted Erlendur at the door and invited him into the living room. The doctor was alone in the house. Erlendur had expected nothing else. They sat down. The atmosphere was more strained than during their previous meetings. Baldvin was civil but very formal. He had not asked if he would need a lawyer when they spoke on the phone. Erlendur was relieved. He would not have known how to answer. In the circumstances, he reckoned that it would be best to talk to Baldvin privately.

'As I told you on the phone—' Erlendur began, launching into the preamble that he had rehearsed in the car. Baldvin stopped him.

'Can't you just get to the point?' he said. 'I'm hoping this meeting won't take long. What is it that you want to know?'

'I was going to tell you that there are three things but . . .'

'What do you want to know?' the doctor asked again.

'Magnús, your father-in-law—'

'I never met him,' Baldvin replied, cutting Erlendur off once more.

'No, I'm aware of that. What did he do?'

'What did he do?'

'How did he make a living, I mean?'

'I have the feeling that you already know.'

'It would be simplest if you just answered the question,' Erlendur said sternly.

'He was an estate agent.'

'Was he successful?'

'No, extremely *un*successful. He was facing bankruptcy when he died, from what María told me. Leonóra mentioned the fact too.'

'But he didn't go bankrupt?'

'No.'

'And they were his beneficiaries? Leonóra and María?'

'Yes.'

'What did they inherit?'

'It didn't amount to much at the time,' Baldvin said. 'They managed to hold on to this house because Leonóra was shrewd and tough.'

'Anything else?'

'A plot of land in Kópavogur. Magnús had accepted it in some settlement, as a down payment or something, and ended up owning it. That was two years before he died.'

'And Leonóra held on to it over the years? Even when she needed to save the house?'

'Where are you going with this?'

'Since then Kópavogur has grown faster than any other community in Iceland and more people have moved here than anywhere else in the country, including Reykjavík. When Magnús acquired the land it was so far out of town that people could hardly be bothered to drive there. Now it's almost in the centre. Whoever would have believed it?'

'Yes, it is incredible.'

'I checked the price at the time Leonóra sold it – what, three or four years ago now? She got a very decent sum for it. According to the calculations of Kópavogur Council it was around three hundred million krónur. Leonóra was good with money, wasn't she? She didn't boast about the fact, probably wasn't particularly interested in money as a rule. So the bulk of it sat in her bank account, accumulating interest. María was her mother's heir. You were María's heir. No one else. Just you.'

'There's not much I can do about it,' Baldvin said. 'I would have told you about it if I'd thought it had the slightest bearing.'

'What was María's attitude to the money?'

'Attitude? I . . . no particular attitude. She wasn't very interested in money.'

'For example, did she want you both to use the money to get

more out of life? Did she want to spend it on luxuries? Or was she like her mother and preferred to avoid thinking about it?'

'She was well aware of the existence of the money,' Baldvin said.

'But didn't spend it?'

'No. Neither she nor Leonóra did. You're right. I think I know why, but that's another matter. Who have you been talking to, if I may ask?'

'That probably has no bearing at this stage. I imagine that *you* would have preferred to enjoy the good things in life. All that money just sitting there, no one using it.'

Baldvin took a deep breath.

'I have no interest in talking about the money,' he said.

'What sort of financial arrangement did you and María have? Did you have a prenuptial agreement?'

'Yes, we did, as it happens.'

'What kind of agreement?'

'She would keep the land or any money raised from its sale.'

'So it was in her name?'

'Yes. She would keep the lot if we divorced.'

'Right,' Erlendur said. 'Then there's question number two. Do you know a man by the name of Tryggvi?'

'Tryggvi? No.'

'Of course, it's a long time since you met but you ought to remember the circumstances. He has a cousin by the name of Sigvaldi who lives in the States. His girlfriend was called Dagmar. She's on holiday in Florida at the moment but she'll be back in a week or so. I'm going to try and catch up with her then. Do those names ring any bells?'

'Sort of . . . What . . . ?'

'Did you study medicine with them?'

'Yes, if we're talking about the same people.'

'Did you take part in an experiment on Tryggvi, during which his heart was stopped for several minutes?'

'I don't know what—'

'You and your mate Sigvaldi and his girlfriend Dagmar?'

Baldvin stared at Erlendur for a long time without answering. Then, apparently unable to sit still any longer, he sprang to his feet.

'Nothing happened,' he said. 'How did you dig that up? What are you trying to do? I was only an onlooker, it was Sigvaldi who was in charge. I . . . nothing happened. I just stood there, didn't even know the bloke. Was his name Tryggvi?'

'So you do know what I'm referring to?'

'It was a stupid experiment. It wasn't meant to prove anything.'

'But Tryggvi died briefly?'

'I don't even know. I left the room. Sigvaldi had wangled some ward at the hospital and we went over there. That guy Tryggvi was a bit of a weirdo. Sigvaldi was always making fun of him, long before this happened. I'd just started medicine. Sigvaldi was very bright but a bit wild. It was his responsibility, his alone. Well, and maybe Dagmar's. Most of the time I wasn't even in on what they were planning.'

'I haven't spoken to them yet but I intend to,' Erlendur said. 'How did Sigvaldi go about stopping Tryggvi's heart?'

'He lowered his body temperature and gave him some drug. I don't remember what it's called, or if it's still on the market. The drug caused his heart to slow down gradually until it stopped. Sigvaldi timed the cardiac arrest and after a minute he used the defibrillator. It worked immediately. His heart started beating again.'

'And?'

'And what?'

'What did Tryggvi say?'

'Nothing. He didn't say anything. He didn't feel anything, didn't feel any pain. He described it as being like a deep sleep. I don't know why you're digging this up. How far back are you looking? Why are you investigating me and my life so thoroughly? Just what do you think I've done? Is it normal for the police to investigate suicide in this way? Are you persecuting me?'

'Just one more thing,' Erlendur said, without answering. 'Then I'll be on my way.'

'Has this become an official inquiry?'

'No,' Erlendur said.

'What, then? Do I actually need to answer these questions?'

'Not really. I'm only trying to find out what happened when María took her life. Whether anything unnatural occurred.'

'Unnatural? Isn't suicide unnatural enough for you? What do you want from me?'

'María went to see a medium before she died. She referred to the medium as Magdalena. Know anything about that?'

'No,' Baldvin said. 'I know nothing about that. We've discussed this. I didn't know she'd been to a psychic. I don't know any medium called Magdalena.'

'She went to a medium because she thought she saw her mother here in the house, quite some time after Leonóra died.'

'I know nothing about that,' Baldvin said. 'She may have been more receptive than other people; she thought she saw things as she was waking up. It's not uncommon. And not unnatural, if that's what you're driving at.'

'No, of course not.'

Baldvin hesitated. He had taken a seat opposite Erlendur again.

'Maybe I should have a word with your superiors,' he said.

'Of course,' Erlendur said. 'If you think it'll make you feel better.'

'It's . . . speaking of ghosts. There's one thing I haven't told you,' Baldvin said, suddenly burying his face in his hands. 'You might understand María better if you knew. What she did. It might allay your suspicions. I hope you understand that I didn't do anything to her. That what she did, she did alone.'

Erlendur remained silent.

'It's connected with the accident at Thingvellir.'

'The accident? You mean when Magnús died?'

'Yes. I thought I wouldn't need to bring it up but since you seem to think something shady has happened it's probably best if I tell you. I promised María not to tell anyone but I don't like your visits and I want them to stop. I don't want you coming round here with your hints and insinuations. I want you to stop this and let us . . . let *me* mourn my wife in peace.'

'What are you talking about?'

'Something María told me after Leonóra died. About her father and Lake Thingvallavatn.'

'Which was?'

Baldvin took a deep breath.

'Leonóra and María's description of what happened when he drowned is correct on all the main points apart from one. You may have examined the case; you seem incapable of leaving any of our affairs alone.'

'I know something about it,' Erlendur said.

'I only knew the official version, like everyone else. The propeller came loose, Magnús probably tried to fiddle with the motor and fell overboard, the water was freezing cold and he drowned.'

'Yes.'

'Well, according to María, he wasn't alone in the boat. I know I shouldn't be telling you this but I don't know how else to get rid of you.'

'Who was with him in the boat?'

'Leonóra.'

'Leonóra?'

'Yes. Leonóra and . . .'

'And who?'

'María.'

'María was in the boat as well?'

'Magnús went behind Leonóra's back; he was having an affair. I gather he told her at Thingvellir. At the holiday cottage. Leonóra was shattered. She'd had no idea. Then Magnús, Leonóra and María went out in the boat. María didn't tell me what happened there but we know that Magnús fell overboard. The end came very quickly. No one survives long in Lake Thingvallavatn in autumn.'

'And María?'

'María witnessed it,' Baldvin said. 'She said nothing when the police arrived, simply confirmed the story that Magnús had been alone in the boat.'

'Didn't she tell you what happened on board?'

'No. She didn't want to.'

'And you believed her?'

'Of course.'

'Did it affect her badly?'

'Yes, all her life. It wasn't until after Leonóra had died, after the harrowing period when she'd lain dying here in the house, that María told me. I promised not to tell a soul. I hope you'll honour that promise.'

'Was that why they didn't touch his money? Because of a guilty conscience?'

'The land was completely worthless until the suburbs around Reykjavík started to grow. They forgot all about it until a big building contractor tracked them down and made them an offer. Three hundred million. They were flabbergasted.'

Baldvin looked at the photograph of María that stood on the table beside them.

'She'd quite simply had enough,' he said. 'She'd never been able to talk to anyone about what happened and Leonóra somehow managed to make her complicit in her guilt, secured her silence. María couldn't live alone with the truth and . . . chose this way out.'

'You mean that the suicide was connected to this business with her father?'

'It seems obvious to me,' Baldvin said. 'I wasn't going to tell you but . . .'

Erlendur rose to his feet.

'I won't bother you any more,' he said. 'That's enough for today.'

'Are you going to use this knowledge? About what happened at Thingvellir?'

'I see no reason to reopen the case. It was a long time ago and both Leonóra and María are dead.'

Baldvin escorted Erlendur to the door. He had already stepped out on to the pavement when he turned back.

'Just one more thing,' Erlendur said. 'Do you have a shower at Thingvellir?'

'A shower?' Baldvin said, perplexed.

'Yes, or a bathtub?'

'We have both. A shower and a hot tub. I expect you mean the hot tub. It's out on the veranda. Why do you ask?'

'No reason. Of course, a hot tub. Doesn't everyone have one at their holiday home?'

'Goodbye.'

'Yes, goodbye.'

María had not had any problems with hallucinations for a long time until her father appeared to her in the garden and shouted at her to be careful. No one else had seen him. No one else had heard him shouting. Her father vanished as suddenly as he had appeared and all María could hear afterwards was the moaning of the wind and the slamming of the gate. Fleeing inside, she locked the door to the veranda, retreated into her bedroom and buried her face in the pillow.

She had heard that voice before during the seance with Andersen, exactly the same words of warning, but did not know what they were supposed to mean, why they had been said and how much notice she should take of them. She did not know what she was supposed to be careful of.

She was still awake when Baldvin came home late that night and they returned to the topic of the seance with Magdalena that María had told him about. She described the meeting and its effect on her more fully, saying she not only believed what had emerged there but wanted to believe it too. Wanted to believe that there was another life after this one. That our time on Earth was not the end of it all.

Baldvin lay listening to her in silence.

'Have I ever told you about a guy I knew when I was studying medicine? His name was Tryggvi,' he said.

'No,' María said.

'He wanted to try and find out if there was an afterlife. He persuaded his cousin who was a doctor to help him. He had read something about a French experiment on near-death experience. We studied medicine together. There was a girl with us. The four of us took part in the experiment.'

María listened attentively to Baldvin's account of how they had stopped Tryggvi's heart, then revived him, and how it had worked perfectly except that Tryggvi had had nothing to tell.

'What became of him?' María asked.

'I don't know,' Baldvin said. 'I haven't seen him since.'

A long silence descended on the room where Leonóra's final struggle had taken place.

'Do you think . . . ?'

María broke off.

'What?' Baldvin asked.

'Do you think you could do something like that?'

'It's perfectly possible.'

'Could you do it to me? For me?'

'For *you*?'

'Yes, I . . . I've read so much about near-death experiences.'

'I know.'

'Is the experiment risky?'

'It could be,' Baldvin said. 'I'm not going to—'

'Could we do it here?' María asked. 'Here at home?'

'María . . .'

'Is it very dangerous?'

'María, I can't—'

'Is it very dangerous?'

'That . . . that depends. Are you seriously considering it?'

'Why not?' María said. 'What have I got to lose?'

'Are you sure?' Baldvin said.

'Did you lock the gate?' María asked.

'Yes, I locked it when I came in.'

'He looked horrible,' María said. 'Horrible.'

'Who?'

'Dad. I know he's not happy. He can't be happy. I know that. He wasn't meant to go like that. He wasn't meant to die like that. It should never have happened.'

'What are you talking about?'

'Tell me more about this Tryggvi,' María said. 'What happened exactly? How would you go about something like that? What would you need to make it work?'

27

Erlendur called his daughter early on Sunday morning and asked if she would like to come for a drive. He wanted to spend the day driving around the Reykjavík area, looking at lakes. Eva Lind was asleep when he rang and it took her a while to grasp what he was saying. She was unenthusiastic but Erlendur would not accept no for an answer. Surely she didn't have much to do that Sunday, any more than she ever did. It was not as if she went to church, after all. Finally she gave in. Erlendur tried to get hold of Sindri Snaer but received a message saying that either his phone was switched off or he was out of range. Valgerdur was working all weekend.

Under normal circumstances he would have made the trip alone and been happy to do so, but this time he wanted Eva's company; naturally he was fed up with his own, as she was quick to point out during their phone conversation. He smiled. Eva Lind was in a better humour than usual, even though her idea of bringing Erlendur and Halldóra together had led nowhere and her dream of establishing a better relationship between her parents seemed doomed to failure.

Neither mentioned the subject as they drove out of town together. It was a beautiful autumnal day. The sun shone low over the Bláfjöll range and the weather was still but cold. They stopped off at a kiosk where Erlendur bought them some sandwiches and cigarettes. He had made a thermos of coffee before leaving home. There was a blanket in the boot. It occurred to him as he drove away from the shop that he had never been for a Sunday outing with Eva Lind before.

They began with a small circuit of the city. He had studied detailed maps of Reykjavík and its vicinity, and was surprised at the vast number of lakes that were to be found in a relatively small area. They were almost uncountable. He and Eva Lind started at Lake Ellidavatn where a new suburb had sprung up, then did a circuit of Raudavatn on a decent road, before continuing to Reynisvatn which had now disappeared behind the new suburb of Grafarholt. From there they drove past Langavatn and had a view of numerous little lakes on Middalsheidi Moor before slowly proceeding to Mosfellsheidi. They inspected Leirvogsvatn beside the road to Thingvellir, followed by Stíflisdalsvatn and Mjóavatn. It was late by the time they descended to Thingvellir, turned north and passed Sandkluftavatn which lay beside the road north of Hofmannaflöt on the route over the pass at Uxahryggir and down the Lundarreykjadalur valley. They picnicked beside Litla-Brunnavatn, just off the road to Biskupsbrekka.

Erlendur spread out the blanket and they stretched their legs and tucked into the sandwiches from the kiosk. He took out some chocolate biscuits and poured them two cups of coffee, then gazed across the treeless landscape to Thingvellir and Hofmannaflöt beneath Mount Ármannsfell, where people in the Middle Ages used to entertain themselves with horse fights. He had visited various second-hand bookshops in search of the lake book that Davíd might conceivably have been intending to buy. The only one that seemed to fit the bill had been published just before Davíd had gone missing and was called simply *Lakes in the Reykjavík Area*. It was a handsome volume, lavishly illustrated with photographs of lakes and their surroundings, taken in different seasons. Eva Lind leafed through the book, studying the pictures.

'If you think she fell in one of these lakes then all I can say is good luck finding her,' she remarked, sipping her coffee.

Erlendur had told her about Gudrún, or Dúna, who had disappeared thirty years ago without anyone knowing exactly when. He told her about Gudrún's fascination with lakes and said that he did not think it was completely far-fetched to link her disappearance to another missing-person case, that of a young man called Davíd. Eva Lind was intrigued by the idea that Davíd might have met the girl shortly before he vanished. Erlendur imagined that the book might have been intended for Gudrún. She and Davíd would only just have met at that point, so recently that no one except Davíd's friend Gilbert would have had any inkling of it. Information about their budding relationship had not emerged until many years later when Gilbert moved home to Iceland from Denmark.

Eva Lind found her father's theory rather implausible and said as much. Erlendur nodded but pointed out that the one important detail that these two cases had in common was that there was so little information to go on. Nothing was known about Davíd's disappearance. And all that was known about Gudrún was that her car had vanished with her and had never been found.

'What if they knew each other?' Erlendur said, gazing out over Litla-Brunnavatn. 'What if Davíd bought the lake book for her? What if they went for that last drive together? We know when Davíd went missing. The report of Gudrún's disappearance reached the police just over a fortnight later. That's why we never connected the two cases, but she might well have gone missing at the same time as him.'

'Then good luck finding them,' Eva Lind repeated. 'There must be a thousand lakes that fit the bill if you think that's what they went to look at. It's like fucking Finland. Wouldn't it be simpler to assume that they drove into the sea, drove off the docks somewhere?'

'We dragged all the main harbours for her car,' Erlendur said.

'Couldn't they both have just committed suicide separately?'

'Yes, of course. That's what we've thought up to now. I . . . It's a completely new idea to link them. I'm rather taken with it. There's been no progress on these cases for decades, then suddenly it emerges that she was fascinated by lakes and that he mentioned buying a book about lakes, a subject he had never shown the slightest interest in before.'

Erlendur took a sip of coffee.

'And on top of that his father is dying and will probably never receive any sort of answer to his questions. Any more than the boy's mother – who is already dead. I'm thinking of that, too. Of answers. They should have some kind of answer. People don't just walk out of their homes and disappear. They always leave some trace. Except in these two cases. That's what they have in common. There's no trace. We have nothing to go on. In either case.'

'Granny never got any answers,' Eva Lind said, lying back on the blanket and staring up at the sky.

'No, she never got any answers,' Erlendur agreed.

'Yet you never give up,' Eva said. 'You keep on looking. You go out east.'

'Yes, I do. I go out east. I walk over to Hardskafi and up on to Eskifjördur Moor. I camp there sometimes.'

'But you never find anything.'

'No. Nothing but memories.'

'Aren't they enough?'

'I don't know.'

'Hardskafi? What's that?'

'It's a mountain. Your grandmother thought Bergur had died up there. I don't know why she thought that. It was some intuition. He would have had to have been carried quite a way off course if so, but the wind was blowing in that direction and obviously we both sought shelter from the wind. She often went over there, right up until we moved away from the countryside.'

'Have you climbed the mountain?'

'Yes – it's easy enough to climb, in spite of its forbidding name.'

'Have you stopped going there, then?'

'I hardly ever climb up there any more, I content myself with looking.'

Eva Lind reflected on his words.

'Of course, you're bloody past it now.'

Erlendur smiled.

'Have you given up, then?' Eva Lind asked.

'The last thing your grandmother asked was whether I had found my brother. That was the last thing that passed through her mind before she died. I've sometimes wondered if she found him . . . if she found him in the next life. Not that I myself believe in the afterlife at all – I don't believe in God or hell – but your grandmother believed in all that. It was part of her upbringing. She was convinced that the life of toil here on Earth was neither the beginning nor the end. In that sense she was reconciled to dying and she talked of Bergur's being in good hands. With his people.'

'Old people talk like that,' Eva Lind said.

'She wasn't old. She died in her prime.'

'Don't they say that those whom the gods love die young?'

Erlendur looked at his daughter.

'I don't think the gods have ever loved me,' she continued. 'Or at least I can't imagine it. I don't know why they should, either.'

'I'm not sure that people should place their fates in the hands of the gods, whoever they are,' Erlendur said. 'You make your own fate.'

'You can talk. Who made your fate? Didn't your father take you into the mountains in crazy weather? What was he doing taking his children up there? Have you never asked yourself that? Don't you ever get angry when you think about it?'

'He didn't know any better. He didn't arrange for us to be caught in the storm.'

'But he could have acted differently. If he'd thought about his kids.'

'He always took great care of us boys.'

Neither of them spoke. Erlendur watched a car head east over Uxahryggir and turn off towards Thingvellir.

'I always hated myself,' Eva Lind said at last. 'And I was angry. Sometimes so angry I could have burst. Angry with Mum and with you and with school and with the scum who bullied me. I wanted to be free of myself. I didn't want to be me. I loathed myself. I abused myself and let other people abuse me too.'

'Eva . . .'

Eva Lind stared up at the cloudless sky.

'No, that's how it was,' she said. 'Anger and self-loathing. Not

233

a good combination. I've thought about it a lot since I discovered that what I did was only the natural consequence of something that had begun before I was born. Something I had absolutely no control over. Most of all I was angry with you and Mum. Why did you ever have me? What were you thinking of? What did I bring into the world? What was my inheritance? Nothing but the mistakes of people who never knew each other and never wanted to get to know each other.'

Erlendur grimaced.

'That wasn't your only inheritance, Eva,' he said.

'No, maybe not.'

They were silent.

'Isn't this turning out to be a great Sunday drive?' Eva Lind said at last, with a glance at her father.

Another car drove at a leisurely pace along the road over Biskupsbrekka and turned off towards Lundarreykjadalur. It contained a couple with two children; a little dark-haired girl waved at them from the child seat in the back. Neither of them waved back and the little girl watched them, crestfallen, until she vanished from sight.

'Do you think you can ever forgive me?' Erlendur asked, looking at his daughter.

She didn't answer him but stared up at the sky with her arms behind her head and her legs crossed.

'I know people are responsible for their own fates,' she said at last. 'Someone stronger and cleverer than me would have made a different fate for herself. Wouldn't have given a shit about you two – which is the only answer, I think, instead of ending up hating oneself.'

'I never intended you to hate yourself. I didn't know.'

'Your dad probably didn't mean to lose his son.'

'No. He didn't.'

By the time they left Uxahryggir and drove down Lundarreykjadalur to Borgarfjördur it was growing dark. They didn't stop to picnic by any more lakes and sat largely without talking on their drive home through the Hvalfjördur tunnel and around the Kjalarnes peninsula. Erlendur drove his daughter to her door. It was dark by the time they said their goodbyes.

It had been a good day by the lakes and he told her so. She nodded and said they should do it more often.

'If they disappeared in one of the lakes around here you've got as much chance of finding them as you have of winning the lottery.'

'I expect you're right,' Erlendur said.

Neither of them spoke for a while. Erlendur ran his hand over the steering wheel of the Ford.

'We're so alike, Eva,' he said, listening to the quiet hum of the engine. 'You and me. We're chips off the same block.'

'You reckon?' Eva Lind said, getting out of the car.

'Yes, I'm afraid so,' Erlendur said.

With that he drove off down the street and towards home, reflecting on all the unresolved issues between his daughter and himself. He fell asleep with the thought that she had not answered his question about whether she would forgive him. It had remained unspoken between them all day as they drove among the lakes, in search of lost souls.

28

The following afternoon Erlendur drove once more to the house in Kópavogur and parked at a discreet distance. Since there were no lights in the windows and he could see no sign of Karólína's car, he assumed that she hadn't come home from work yet. He lit a cigarette and settled in patiently to wait. He wasn't sure how he was going to question the woman. He assumed that Karólína and Baldvin would have talked after his last visit to Grafarvogur; they must be involved in some way, though he wasn't sure exactly how. Perhaps they had picked up where they'd left off when they were both at drama school and she'd still had dreams of stardom. After a lengthy wait, the little Japanese car pulled up in front of the house and Karólína stepped out. She hurried into the house without looking to right or left, carrying an overflowing bag of groceries. Erlendur allowed half an hour to pass before going up to the house and knocking at the door.

When Karólína came to open it she had changed out of her working clothes into a comfortable outfit of fleece, grey track-suit bottoms and slippers.

'Are you Karólína?' Erlendur asked.

'Yes,' she said brusquely, as if he were a salesman who was inconveniencing her.

Erlendur introduced himself as a police officer investigating a recent death at Lake Thingvallavatn.

'A death?'

'A woman who killed herself at Thingvellir,' Erlendur said. 'Might I come in for a moment?'

'What's it got to do with me?' Karólína asked.

She was as tall as Erlendur, with short dark hair above a high domed forehead and finely arched brows over dark blue eyes. As far as he could tell through the fleece and baggy tracksuit bottoms, she was slender, with a long neck and good figure. Her expression was determined, however, and there was a stubbornness or hardness about her face that was not encouraging. He thought he could recognise what Baldvin saw in her but he did not have time to dwell on the thought. Karólína's question hung in the air.

'You'll have known her husband,' Erlendur said. 'The woman's name was María. She was married to a man called Baldvin. I gather that you two went out together when you were both at drama school.'

'What of it?'

'I just wanted to have a little chat with you about it.'

Karólína shot a glance down the road at her neighbours' house. Then, looking back at Erlendur, she said that they might be more comfortable indoors. Erlendur stepped into the hall and she closed the door behind them. The house consisted of a single storey, with a sitting room, dining room with adjoining kitchen, a lavatory and two rooms on the left as one entered from the hall. It was furnished with handsome furniture, had pictures on the walls and smelled of a combination of Icelandic cooking and the sweet scent of cosmetics and perfumed bath salts, which was most concentrated around the lavatory and the other two rooms. One seemed to be a junk room, the other was

Karólína's bedroom. Through the open door Erlendur glimpsed a large bed against one wall, a dressing table with a good-sized mirror, a sizeable wardrobe and a chest of drawers.

Karólína darted into the kitchen and removed a saucepan from the stove. Erlendur had disturbed her in the middle of cooking. The house was pervaded by the rich smell from the kitchen; roast lamb, he thought.

'I was just making coffee,' Karólína said when she came back from the kitchen. 'Can I offer you a cup?'

Erlendur accepted. The rule was always to accept coffee if it was offered. Elínborg had been quick to learn this. Sigurdur Óli still hadn't grasped the concept.

Karólína came out with two cups of steaming hot coffee. She drank it black, as did Erlendur.

'Baldvin and I met at drama school in old Jóhannes's class. God, he could be a swine. Jóhannes, I mean. And a rotten actor. Anyway, Baldvin and I split up when he quit acting and went to study medicine. May I ask why you're investigating him?'

'I'm hardly investigating him,' Erlendur said. 'But I heard – you know how people gossip – that you two had known each other before and maybe even renewed your acquaintance recently.'

'Where did you hear that?'

'I've forgotten – I'd have to look it up.'

Karólína smiled.

'Is it any of your business?'

'I really don't know yet,' Erlendur said.

'He told me you might drop by,' she said.

'Baldvin?'

'We did pick up the thread again, you're right. It's not as if there's any need to hide the fact. I told him so and he agreed with me. It began again about five years ago. We met at a drama school graduation reunion. Baldvin turned up even though he didn't graduate with us. He said he was fed up with the old bag – Leonóra, that is, María's mother. She was living with them.'

'Why didn't he end his marriage and move in with you then? It seems as if few things could be easier these days.'

'He was going to,' Karólína said. 'I was so pissed off with the situation that I gave him an ultimatum. But then that bitch Leonóra fell ill and he couldn't bring himself to do that to María. He wanted to stand by her through her ordeal and he did. My main fear was that their relationship would improve after the old bitch died and in fact he did stop coming to see me. Didn't have eyes for anyone but María. But he soon got over it.'

'Is that how Baldvin described Leonóra? As a bitch?'

'He couldn't stand her any longer. It got worse over the years. Maybe I should be grateful to her, if I'm mean. He wanted her out of the house but for some reason María had a problem with that.'

'María and Baldvin didn't have any children?'

'Baldvin can't and María wasn't interested,' Karólína said bluntly.

'When are you two thinking of making your relationship official?' Erlendur asked.

'You sound like a country vicar.'

'I'm sorry, I didn't mean to . . .'

'Baldvin's a considerate person,' Karólína said. 'He wants to wait a whole year. I told him that might be overdoing it a bit. But he won't budge. Not until after a year at the earliest, he says.'

'But you're not happy with that?'

'Oh, I understand him all right. It's such a tragedy and all that. We needn't be in any hurry.'

'Did María know about your relationship?'

239

'Can I ask what you're investigating? What you're looking for? Do you think Baldvin did something to her?'

'Is that what you think?'

'No way. He wouldn't be capable of it. He's a doctor, for Christ's sake! What makes you think it wasn't suicide?'

'I don't think that,' Erlendur said.

'Is this some Swedish survey or . . .?'

'You've heard about that?'

'Baldvin heard something. We've no idea what's going on.'

'I'm just gathering information so that we can close the case,' Erlendur said. 'Did you know that he's inherited three hundred million from his wife?'

'I only found out recently. He told me the other day. Wasn't it from some land speculation of her father's?'

'Yes – he owned a small plot in Kópavogur that shot up in value. Baldvin's the sole beneficiary.'

'Yes, he mentioned something about that. I don't think he knew anything about it until a short time ago. Or at least that's what he told me.'

'I heard that the money came in the nick of time,' Erlendur said.

'Really?'

'He's pretty seriously in debt.'

'Baldvin's been a bit unlucky with some shares he bought, that's all I know. Some unlucky investment in a construction company that went bust, on top of the debts still outstanding from the surgery that didn't work out. We don't talk much about that sort of stuff. At least, we haven't up to now.'

'You've given up acting, haven't you?' Erlendur asked.

'Yes, more or less.'

'May I ask why?'

'I was in a few plays. Not very big, but . . .'

'Unfortunately, I go to the theatre far too rarely.'

'I just felt I wasn't getting good enough roles. At the big theatres, that is. And of course the competition's really tough. It's a pretty ruthless world. You find that out straight away at drama school. And age doesn't help. A middle-aged actress like me isn't as sought after. I got a good job at a finance company but the odd small part still comes my way if the director happens to remember me.'

'I gather your biggest role was as Magdalena in that Swedish play, whatever it was called . . .' Erlendur said, pretending not to remember the title.

'Who told you that? Someone who remembered me?'

'Yes, it was, actually. A woman I know called Valgerdur. She's a regular theatre-goer.'

'And she remembered me?'

Erlendur nodded, realising that he needn't worry about having to answer any awkward questions about why he had been discussing Karólína with other people. She seemed to take it as recognition, regardless of the circumstances. He remembered what the drama teacher had said about Karólína's ambition, the fame she had dreamed of achieving. What was it he'd said? She'd wanted to be a diva.

'*Flame of Hope*,' Karólína said. 'It was a really good play and you're right, it was my biggest role – when I hit the heights, as they say.'

She smiled.

'Not that the critics were particularly impressed; they dismissed it as old-fashioned kitchen-sink drama. They can be such bastards. They don't even know what they're talking about half the time.'

'My friend thought maybe she was mixing it up with another role, another character called Magdalena.'

'Really?'

'A clairvoyant or medium,' Erlendur said.

He looked for a reaction from Karólína but she didn't seem to notice anything. He thought that either he was barking up the wrong tree or else she was a better actress than people gave her credit for.

'I'm not familiar with it,' Karólína said.

'I don't remember what she said the play was called,' Erlendur said, permitting himself to go a step further. 'It might have been *The Fake* or something like that.'

Karólína hesitated.

'I've never heard of it,' she said. 'Was it on at the National?'

'I don't know,' Erlendur replied. 'Anyway, this Magdalena believed in the spirit world; she believed it was as real as the two of us here in this room.'

'Oh.'

'María believed something similar, as Baldvin will no doubt have told you.'

'I don't remember him mentioning it,' Karólína said. 'I don't believe in ghosts.'

'No, neither do I,' Erlendur said. 'He didn't tell you that she sought help from psychics, from mediums?'

'No, I didn't know. I don't know much about María, to tell the truth. Baldvin and I didn't waste our time talking about her when we met. We had other fish to fry.'

'I bet you did,' Erlendur said.

'Was there anything else?'

'No, thanks. That's it for the moment.'

29

Erlendur had no problem tracking down the woman who had been having an affair with Magnús at the time of his death. Kristín had told him her name and he found her address in the telephone directory. He tried talking to her on the phone but the moment she heard what he wanted she refused to continue the conversation, so he let the matter lie. Later he resumed his attack by announcing that new information about the incident at Lake Thingvallavatn in which Magnús had lost his life had possibly come to light.

'Who have you been talking to?' she asked over the phone.

'I got your name from Kristín, Magnús's sister,' Erlendur said.

'What did she say about me?'

'Actually, it was about you and Magnús,' Erlendur replied.

A long pause followed his words.

'I suppose you'd better come round,' the woman said at last. Her name was Sólveig and she was married with two grown-up children. 'I'm home during the day all this week,' she added.

When he visited her, Erlendur found Sólveig extremely wary and eager to get the matter out of the way as quickly as possible. She seemed in something of a state. They stood in her entrance hall; she did not invite him in.

'I don't know what I can tell you,' she said. 'I don't know why you've come here. What new information are you talking about?'

'It concerns you and Magnús.'

'Yes, you told me that on the phone.'

'And your affair.'

'Did Kristín tell you about that?'

Erlendur nodded.

'Magnús's daughter recently committed suicide,' he said.

'So I heard.'

Sólveig fell silent. She was kind-looking, with a pretty face and tasteful clothes, and she lived in a small terraced house in the suburb of Fossvogur. She worked as a nurse and was on the evening shift this week.

'Perhaps you ought to come in for a moment,' she said at last and led the way into the sitting room. Erlendur sat down on the sofa without removing his coat.

'I don't know what I can tell you,' she said, with a sigh. 'In all these years no one's ever asked what happened. Then the poor child resorts to this and you start asking questions that no one has ever asked before and no one ever should have asked.'

'Perhaps that was the problem,' Erlendur said. 'María's problem. Has that ever occurred to you?'

'Has it occurred to me? What do you think? Leonóra took care of María. No one else was allowed near her.'

'They went out in the boat together: Magnús, Leonóra and María.'

'You've found out, then?'

'Yes.'

'All three of them were in the boat,' Sólveig confirmed.

'What happened?'

'I've spent so much time thinking about the whole thing. My

244

relationship with Magnús. We were going to tell Leonóra about it at Thingvellir. We were going to break it to her as gently as we could. Magnús wanted me to come along. But Leonóra and I were close friends and I couldn't bring myself to. Maybe things would have turned out differently if I'd been there.'

Sólveig looked at Erlendur.

'Of course, you think I'm completely despicable,' she said.

'I don't think anything.'

'Leonóra was always very bossy. Really overbearing. She completely dominated Magnús. Gave him hell if things didn't go her way, even when other people were listening. Magnús turned to me. He was a good man. We started meeting in secret. I don't know what happened but we fell in love. Maybe I felt sorry for him at first. We wanted to move in together, so we had to make Leonóra understand. I didn't want to be involved in a clandestine affair, go behind her back, take part in some sort of conspiracy against her. I wanted things out in the open. I couldn't stand . . . couldn't stand the furtiveness. He wanted to delay telling her but I put pressure on him. We agreed that he would tell her the truth that weekend at Thingvellir.'

'Didn't Leonóra suspect anything?'

'No. She was completely unsuspecting. Leonóra was like that. Trusting. She trusted people. I betrayed that trust. So did Magnús.'

'Did you ever meet Leonóra after the accident?'

Sólveig closed her eyes.

'Will you be any the better for knowing?' she asked. 'The case was investigated at the time. It was perfectly straightforward. No one has asked any questions since. If anyone should have done so it was me but I never did.'

'Did you meet Leonóra?'

'I did. Once. It was awful. Horrible. It was some time after Magnús's funeral. I didn't know if he had told her about us before he died and at the funeral I tried to pretend that nothing had happened. But I noticed immediately that Leonóra wouldn't look at me. Wouldn't speak to me. Pretended I didn't exist. I knew then that Magnús had told her.'

'Did she want to see you or . . .?'

'Yes – she called and asked me to come and see her in Grafarvogur. She greeted me very coldly.'

Sólveig broke off. Erlendur waited patiently. He sensed her discomfort at reopening these old wounds.

'Leonóra told me that María was at school and that she wanted me to know exactly what had happened at the lake. I told her I didn't need to know anything but she laughed and said I wouldn't escape so lightly. I didn't know what she meant.'

'Magnús told me about the two of you,' Leonóra said. 'He told me you were going to move in together and that he wanted to leave me.'

'Leonóra,' Sólveig said, 'I—'

'Shut up,' Leonóra said, without raising her voice. 'I'm going to tell you what happened. But there are two things you must understand. You must understand that I had to protect the girl and you must understand that it was your fault as well. Yours and Magnús's. You brought this on us.'

Sólveig did not speak.

'What were you thinking of?' Leonóra asked.

'I didn't mean to hurt you,' Sólveig said.

'Hurt me? You have no idea what you've done.'

'Magnús was unhappy,' Sólveig said. 'That's why he turned to me. He was unhappy.'

'That's a lie. He wasn't unhappy. You stole him from me – you lured him away.'

Sólveig was silent.

'I don't want to quarrel with you,' she said at last, quietly.

'No, what's done is done,' Leonóra said. 'No one can change it now. But I don't want to bear the burden alone. You're responsible too. And so was Magnús. You both were.'

'No one's responsible for an accident like that. He fell overboard. It was an accident.'

Leonóra smiled a thin, unreadable smile. She looked to be in a strange state. The house was dark and cold and Leonóra didn't seem herself. Sólveig wondered if she had been drinking or was on strong medication.

'He didn't fall in,' Leonóra said.

'What do you mean?'

'He didn't fall.'

'But . . . I read it in the papers . . .'

'Yes, that's what it said in the papers. But it was a lie.'

'A lie?'

'For María's sake.'

'I don't understand you.'

'Why did you have to take him away from me? Why couldn't you leave us alone?'

'He came to me, Leonóra. What lie did you have to tell for María's sake?'

'Don't you understand? We were with Magnús in the boat. María was with us.'

'With you . . .? But . . .'

Sólveig stared at Leonóra.

'Magnús was alone in the boat,' she said. 'It said so in all the news reports.'

'It was a lie,' Leonóra said. 'My lie. I was with him and so was María.'

'Why . . . why did you need to lie . . .? Why . . .?'

'I'm telling you. Magnús didn't fall off the boat.'

'What, then?'

'I pushed him,' Leonóra said. 'I pushed him and he lost his balance.'

A long time passed before Sólveig spoke again. Erlendur listened to her story in silence, sensing her distress at what had happened.

'It was Leonóra who pushed Magnús so he fell in,' she said. 'They watched him drown. Magnús had told Leonóra about me. They'd quarrelled bitterly that morning. María didn't know and asked them to come out in the boat with her. Magnús was really angry. They started quarrelling again. Then the engine suddenly broke down. They quarrelled even more violently. Then Magnús stood up to check on the engine. Leonóra shoved him away from her and it all happened in a flash . . . he went overboard.'

Leonóra regarded Sólveig in silence.

'Couldn't you have saved him?' Sólveig asked.

'There was nothing we could do. The boat was rocking uncontrollably and it was all we could do to stop ourselves falling in. The boat drifted away from Magnús and by the time we had got it back under control he had vanished.'

'Oh my God!' Sólveig gasped.

'See what you've done?' Leonóra said.

'Me?'

'The girl is inconsolable. She blames herself for what

happened to her father. For the quarrel. All of it. She's internalised the whole thing. She imagines that she's somehow responsible for her father's death. How do you think that makes her feel? How do you think she feels? How do you think I feel?'

'You must talk to a doctor, a specialist. She needs help.'

'I'll look after María. And if you take this any further I'll deny the whole thing.'

'Why are you telling me, then?'

'You're not going to get off scot-free. I want you to know that. You're as responsible as I am!'

Erlendur stared at Sólveig for a long time without speaking after she had finished her story.

'Why didn't you go to the police?' he asked finally. 'What stopped you?'

'I felt . . . I felt as if I bore some of the responsibility myself, as Leonóra said. For what happened. She was quick to point it out to me. "It's your fault," she hissed at me. "It's your fault. All of it. You're to blame." All her anger was directed at me. I was out of my mind with fear and grief and a strange kind of concern for Leonóra. The whole thing was just too much for me, much too much. It was such a shock. I was completely unprepared. And then there was poor little María. I couldn't bring myself to tell the truth about her mother. I couldn't do it. She . . .'

'What?'

'It was so unreal that I could hardly believe it, could hardly believe it had happened.'

'You wanted to protect the girl?' Erlendur said.

'I hope you understand my position. I didn't want to punish anyone. It was an accident, however you look at it. It didn't occur to me to doubt what Leonóra said. She told me she never let María leave her side except when she was at school.'

'It can't have been pleasant living with this knowledge,' Erlendur said.

'No, you're right, it hasn't been pleasant. So imagine how it must have been for them, especially for María. When I heard that she'd committed suicide . . . somehow it didn't come as a surprise. I've . . . I've blamed myself for letting it happen. For letting Leonóra get away with what she did. Get away with not telling anyone about this.'

'What were they quarrelling about on the boat?'

'Magnús said he was going to leave her no matter what she said. It was what he'd told me. He'd had enough of the way she rode roughshod over him, couldn't stand her any longer, said all that remained was for them to agree on custody of María. Leonóra said she'd see he never got access to the girl. He could forget it. They fought over María right in front of her. No wonder she thought it was all her fault.'

'Did you ever meet Leonóra or María again after that?'

'No. Never. Neither of them.'

'Were there no witnesses?'

'No. They were completely alone at the lake.'

'No visitors?'

'No.'

'Or tourists?'

'No. No tourists. That was the week before, when Magnús and I were alone at the holiday cottage. We used it twice, as far as I can remember, to meet in secret. That time he bumped into a woman and told me about her afterwards because she was studying the lakes around the city; she was fascinated by lakes. This was right by the cottage. She was looking at a map and was on her way up to Lake Sandkluftavatn. It stuck in my mind because I'd never heard the name before.'

'Was she in a car?' Erlendur asked.

'Yes, I think so.'

'What kind of car?'

'It was yellow.'

'Yellow? Are you sure?'

'Yes. They're called Mini-somethings, aren't they? I saw it driving away through the birch scrub.'

'And you think the person driving this car was the woman that Magnús had met?' Erlendur asked, on the edge of his seat now.

'I think so. It was right by the cottage.'

'A Mini? Do you mean an Austin Mini?'

'Yes, that's it, isn't it? Tiny little cars.'

'A yellow Austin Mini?'

'Yes. Why?'

Erlendur was on his feet.

'On its way to Sandkluftavatn?'

'Yes. Goodness, what's the matter?'

'Was there anyone with her?'

'I don't know. What's the matter? What have I said?'

'Could there have been a young man with her?'

'I don't know. Who are these people? Do you know them? Do you know who these people are?'

'No,' Erlendur said. 'Possibly. No, hardly. Did you say Lake Sandkluftavatn?'

'Yes, Sandkluftavatn.'

30

What did he know about Lake Sandkluftavatn? He had driven past it with Eva Lind without paying it any particular attention. It was about an hour's drive from Reykjavík, beside the road just north of Thingvellir, between the mountains Ármannsfell and Lágafell, before the ascent to Bláskógaheidi Moor. It was overlooked by the unmistakable bulk of Mount Skjaldbreidur to the north-east.

The diver, whose name was Thorbergur, was familiar with the lakes of south-west Iceland, having explored many of them. He had once worked for the fire brigade and had assisted the police with smuggling cases, as well as diving from the country's docks in search of missing people. He had been available when a person was reported missing and search parties were organised to comb the beaches and drag the sea and lakes. But eventually he retired from diving for a living and became a mechanic instead, starting up his own garage, which was now his main occupation. Erlendur had sometimes taken the Ford to him for servicing. Thorbergur was six foot five and had always reminded Erlendur of a giant, with his red hair and beard, long swimmer's arms and strong teeth that often used to gleam through his beard as he was a humorous man and was quick to smile.

'You have divers working for you,' he said. 'Why don't you go to one of them? I've given up. You know that.'

'Yes, I know,' Erlendur said. 'I just thought of talking to you because . . . you still have the equipment, don't you?'

'Yes.'

'And the inflatable?'

'Yes. The little one.'

'And you still go diving sometimes, even though you've stopped working for us?'

'Very occasionally.'

'This is not, how shall I put it, an official investigation,' Erlendur explained. 'More like a spot of private dabbling. I'd pay you out of my own pocket if you could be bothered to do this.'

'Erlendur, I can't go taking your money.'

Thorbergur sighed. Erlendur knew why he had stopped working for the police. The final straw had come one day when he had dived for the body of a woman who'd been found in Reykjavík harbour. She had been missing for three weeks and her body was badly decomposed when Thorbergur found it. He didn't want to run the risk of seeing such horrors again. He didn't want to wake up in the middle of the night gasping because the woman, or some nightmarish figure like her, wouldn't stop invading his dreams.

'It's an old missing-person case,' Erlendur said. 'From way back. Involving youngsters. Possibly two of them. There was a breakthrough yesterday after decades of impasse. Admittedly, it's based on very slight evidence but I felt I should at least talk to you. For the sake of my conscience.'

'In other words, you want to shift the guilt on to me,' Thorbergur said.

'I couldn't think of anyone else. I don't know any better man for the job.'

'You know I've quit, like I just told you. The only thing I investigate now is engines.'

'I understand perfectly,' Erlendur said. 'I would have quit myself if I was trained for anything else.'

'What was the breakthrough?' Thorbergur asked.

'In the case?'

'Yes.'

'We've always treated it as two unrelated missing-person cases but there's a possibility that they were together when they disappeared: a boy in his last year of sixth-form college and a girl, slightly older, who was studying biology at the university. There's really nothing to link them but we haven't had any luck finding them separately either. The case had gone completely cold until recently and had been that way for decades. Then yesterday I learnt that the girl, whose name was Gudrún or Dúna, might have been seen at Thingvellir on her way to Lake Sandkluftavatn. I checked the dates this morning. Of course they don't tally. The girl might have been spotted at Thingvellir in late autumn. She was probably alone that time. The young couple didn't vanish until several months later. The boy's disappearance was reported at the end of February 1976. The report about the girl's disappearance reached us in the middle of March that year. Since then nothing has been heard of either of them, which is unusual in itself; that two incidents occurring a short time apart should leave absolutely no trace. Generally there's a trail somewhere. But there was none to be found in either of these cases.'

'It's unusual for kids in their twenties to get together with teenagers,' Thorbergur commented. 'Especially when the girl's older.'

Erlendur nodded. He could tell that the diver was becoming interested in spite of himself.

'Exactly,' he said. 'There was nothing to link them.'

They were sitting in Thorbergur's office at the garage. Three other employees were hard at work repairing cars and occasionally darted glances into the office. It was little more than a glass cage and was easily visible from the workshop floor. The phone rang at regular intervals, interrupting their conversation, but Erlendur didn't let this put him off his stride.

'I checked the weather that day too,' he said. 'It was unusually cold. Most lakes would have iced over.'

'I can tell that you've already formed a theory.'

'I have, but it's incredibly tenuous.'

'Is no one allowed to know about this?'

'There's no point complicating matters,' Erlendur said. 'If you find something, give me a call. If not, the case is as dead as ever.'

'I've never actually dived in Sandkluftavatn,' Thorbergur said. 'It's too shallow in summer and doesn't get much deeper, except in the spring thaw. There are other lakes out there. Litla-Brunnavatn, Reydarvatn, Uxavatn.'

'Sure.'

'What were their names? The couple?'

'Davíd and Gudrún. Or Dúna.'

Thorbergur looked out at the workshop floor. A new customer had arrived and was looking in their direction. He was a regular and Thorbergur nodded to him.

'Would you be prepared to do this for me?' Erlendur asked, standing up. 'I'm rather up against it, timewise. There's an old man lying at death's door who's been waiting for an answer ever since his boy disappeared. It would be good to be able to bring him news of his son before he goes. I know the chances are pretty slim but it's the only thing I've got to go on and I want to give it a stab.'

Thorbergur stared at him.

'Hang on – are you expecting me to drop everything and go this minute?'

'Well, maybe not before lunch.'

'Today?'

'I . . . just whenever you can. Do you think you could do this for me?'

'Do I have any choice?'

'Thank you,' Erlendur said. 'Call me.'

Erlendur had some difficulty locating the holiday cottage and drove past the turning twice before finally catching sight of the sign, which had almost been obscured by low-growing scrub: 'Sólvangur'. He took the turning, drove down to the lake and parked by the cottage.

This time he knew what he was looking for. He was alone and had told nobody what he was doing. He wouldn't do so until the case was solved, if it ever was. It was still too vague; he still lacked evidence; he himself was still unsure whether he was doing the right thing.

He had talked to the police pathologist who'd performed the post-mortem on María and had asked if she had taken any sleeping pills shortly before the time of her death. The pathologist said he had found a small amount of a sleeping drug but nowhere near enough to explain her death. Erlendur asked if it was possible to calculate how long before her death María had taken the drug but the answer he received was inconclusive. Possibly the same day.

'Do you think a crime's been committed?' the pathologist asked.

'Not really,' Erlendur said.

'Not really?'

'Did you find any burn marks on her chest?' Erlendur asked tentatively.

The pathologist had the post-mortem report open in front of him. They were sitting in his office. He looked up from the document.

'Burn marks?'

'Or bruises of any kind,' Erlendur added hurriedly.

'What are you looking for?'

'I hardly know.'

'You'd have been informed if we'd found burn marks,' the pathologist said dismissively.

Erlendur did not have the keys to the holiday cottage but that didn't matter; his interest was in the veranda, more specifically in the hot tub and its distance from the water's edge. The lake was covered by a thin film of ice and the waves clinked against the frosted rocks of the shore. A short distance away a small sandbank extended into the water, intersected by a rivulet that was now frozen. Erlendur took out a sample jar that Valgerdur had lent him and filled it with water from the lake. He paced out the distance from the lakeside to the veranda, five paces, then from the end of the veranda to the hot tub; six paces. The tub had a cover made of aluminium and plexiglas, which was locked with a small, simple padlock. He fetched a tyre iron from the Ford and bashed the padlock until it opened, then lifted the lid, which turned out to be extraordinarily heavy. It was held open by a hook fixed to the wall of the house. Erlendur didn't know much about hot tubs; he had never sat inside one, nor did he feel the slightest urge to do so. He assumed the tub would not have been used since María killed herself.

Before leaving town he had gone to a builders' supplier and spoken to an employee who presented himself as something of an expert. Erlendur's interest was directed at the waste pipe and the technology used to fill hot tubs. Empty and fill, he said. The employee was keen initially, but when he realised that Erlendur was not intending to buy he quickly abandoned his sales patter and became more bearable. He showed Erlendur a model with computer-controlled draining and filling, assuring him that it was very popular these days. Erlendur hemmed and hawed.

'Is it the best system?' he asked.

The employee frowned.

'Lots of people just prefer to control it manually,' he said. 'They want to be able to turn on the taps themselves and then turn them off when the tub's full. Like filling a bath. You control the heat with regular hot and cold taps.'

'And if it's not manual?'

'Then there's zero-crossing technology.'

'Zero-crossing technology?'

Erlendur looked the employee up and down. He was barely out of adolescence, with a fine down on his chin.

'Yes, an electronic remote-control system, usually located in the toilet. You press a button and the tub begins to fill with hot water at the required temperature. Then you press another button and it empties.'

'Are the inlet and outlet separate?'

'No, it's the same pipe. The water is sucked out through a filter in the bottom, and when you want to fill it the water flows up the same way.'

'Hardly the same water, surely?'

'No, of course not. Fresh water is piped up through the filter but some people see this as a bit of a fault in the system. I wouldn't buy one like that.'

'Why not? What's the problem?'

'The pipe is supposed to be self-cleaning but sometimes small particles of grit get left behind from the last time it was emptied. You know, something that's been lying in the pipe. That's why people prefer to do it manually. Though it may be nonsense, of course. Some people swear by this system.'

After talking to the salesman, Erlendur had a short conversation with a forensic technician with the CID who had been in charge of the operation at the holiday cottage. He thought he remembered seeing a little control panel in the lavatory for filling and emptying the hot tub.

'So the tub is electronically controlled?' Erlendur asked.

'From what I could tell,' the forensic technician answered. 'But I'd probably have to take another look.'

'What's the advantage of an electronically controlled system?'

'Well, it employs zero-crossing technology,' the technician explained and was a little startled when Erlendur hung up on him with a heavy sigh.

Erlendur stared into the tub for a long time, then peered round in search of the taps but couldn't spot any. The sales employee had told him that they might be anywhere near the tub but were usually located under the veranda. Erlendur couldn't find any trapdoor in the veranda that could conceal the taps, so he assumed that the technician had been right about its being electronically controlled. Clambering down into the tub, he bent over the filter in the bottom and managed to prise it loose. Dusk was falling but he had a torch and shone it down the drain. A little water had frozen in the waste pipe. Erlendur took out another sample jar, snapped off a piece of ice from inside the pipe, and placed it in the jar.

He closed the tub again with the heavy plexiglas cover and replaced the broken padlock.

After that he walked round the cottage until he encountered a shed behind it which he assumed was the boathouse. Pressing his face against a small window he made out a boat inside. He wondered if it was the same boat that Magnús and Leonóra had been in on that fateful day long ago. There were low piles of logs stacked against the shed.

The boathouse was locked with a small padlock that Erlendur smashed with the same ease as he had the other. He shone his torch inside. The boat was old and crumbling as if it had not been used for a long time. There were work tables on either side of it and shelves against the far wall, reaching from floor to ceiling. On one of them, down by the floor, he noticed an old Husqvarna outboard motor.

Erlendur carefully shone his torch beam over the shelves and floor. The boathouse contained various objects that one would expect to find at a holiday cottage: gardening tools such as a wheelbarrow and spades, a gas container and barbecue, cans of paint and wood varnish, and a collection of other tools. Erlendur didn't know exactly what he was looking for and had been standing in the shed for nearly quarter of an hour, lighting up every nook and cranny, before it dawned on him.

It was neatly stowed. Not as if anyone had been trying to hide the machine, quite the reverse, but neither was it in any way obvious. It was part of the furnishings, part of the mess, yet it drew his attention once he realised what he was looking for. He flashed his torch over it: a square box like a large, thick briefcase. Despite its unobtrusiveness, the machine awakened in Erlendur a strange old sense of dread, dating back to the time when he had almost frozen to death on the moors out east.

Leonóra had always said that the accident was their secret and that no one must ever know what had really happened. Otherwise they might be forcibly separated. It would be best if they didn't talk about the terrible event. Accidents happened which were nobody's fault and this was one of them. Nothing could be changed now, nothing would be achieved by explaining exactly what had happened on board the boat. María listened to her mother, placing all her trust in her. It was not until much later that the long-term consequences of the lie began to emerge. María's life could never be the same, however much her mother wanted it to be. It could never be made whole again.

As time passed, María recovered from the hallucinations and depression that had afflicted her after her father's death and even her anxiety diminished, but the guilt was always there inside her and hardly a day passed for the rest of her life when she did not think of the incident on Lake Thingvallavatn. It could happen at any time of the day or night. She had learnt to smother these thoughts at their birth but they were unrelenting and the pain of not being allowed to tell anyone what had happened, not being allowed to lighten her burden by talking about the incident was so unbearable that she sometimes thought of taking her own life, of putting an end to her suffering and anguish. Nothing was worse than the oppressive silence that clamoured for her attention every day, sometimes many times a day.

She had never been allowed to mourn her father in the normal way, never been allowed to say goodbye to him, never had the opportunity of missing him. That was the most painful aspect of all, because she had always been deeply attached to him and he had always been good to his little girl. Nor did she indulge in any memories of him from before the incident. She wouldn't allow herself that luxury.

'Forgive me,' Leonóra whispered.

María was sitting by her mother's bedside as usual. They both knew there was not much time left.

'For what?' she asked.

'It . . . was wrong. All of it, from the beginning. I . . . Forgive me . . .'

'It's all right,' María said.

'No . . . It's not all right. I thought . . . I was thinking of you. I did it for you. You . . . you must understand that. I didn't want anything . . . anything to happen to you.'

'I know,' María said.

'But . . . I . . . I shouldn't have kept quiet about the accident.'

'You wanted the best for me,' María said.

'Yes . . . but it was selfish of me, too . . .'

'No,' María said.

'Can you forgive me?'

'Don't worry about this now.'

'Can you?'

María was silent.

'Are you going to tell people what happened once I'm dead?'

María didn't answer.

263

'Tell . . . people,' Leonóra groaned. 'Please . . . for your own sake
. . . Tell people . . . Tell them the whole thing.'

31

Erlendur spent the next two days gathering further information about what he suspected might have happened at the cottage the evening María was found dead. He was not yet ready to present his hypothesis and wondered if it would be better to interview Baldvin and Karólína separately or together. He hadn't discussed his investigation with anyone else. Sigurdur Óli and Elínborg were aware that he was extremely busy, though they didn't have a clue with what, and even Valgerdur had heard from him less often than usual. The case occupied all his thoughts. He was also waiting for a phone call from Lake Sandkluftavatn that still hadn't come.

Over the past few days the desire that sometimes seized him to go east to the derelict farm and on to the moors had been growing in him.

He was sitting at home over a bowl of porridge and pickled liver sausage when he heard a knock at the door. He went out and opened the door to Valgerdur who kissed him on the cheek and slipped inside past him. She took off her coat, laid it on a chair and sat down in the kitchen.

'I don't hear from you any more,' she said, helping herself to a bowl of porridge. Erlendur cut her a slice of liver sausage. It wasn't nearly sour enough for his taste, although he had insisted that it should be taken straight from the pickling vat while he waited at the meat counter in the shop. The teenage boy who served him obeyed with a look of disdain, and obviously took no pleasure in plunging his hand into the sour whey. On the same shopping trip Erlendur had also bought some sour-lamb rolls, fatty breast meat on the bone and a portion of sheep's head in jelly that he kept in a tub of pickling whey out on his balcony.

'I've been busy at work,' Erlendur said.

'What are you up to?' Valgerdur asked.

'The same case.'

'Ghosts and apparitions?'

'Yes, something like that. Would you like some coffee?'

Valgerdur nodded and Erlendur got to his feet to turn on the machine. She remarked that he looked tired and asked if he had any leave saved up. He said that he had plenty of holiday owed to him but so far hadn't found any use for it.

'How did the meeting go the other day? The meeting with Halldóra?'

'Not too well,' Erlendur said. 'I don't know if it was a good idea to see her. There are so many things we'll never see eye to eye on.'

'Like what?' Valgerdur asked warily.

'Oh, I don't know. Lots of things.'

'Nothing you want to talk about?'

'I don't think there's any point. She feels I wasn't honest with her.'

'And weren't you?'

Erlendur grimaced. Valgerdur turned to face him as he stood by the coffee-maker.

'That probably depends on how you look at it,' he said.

'Oh?'

Erlendur heaved a sigh.

'She went into the relationship wholeheartedly. I didn't. That's the great betrayal. The fact that I didn't enter wholeheartedly into the relationship.'

'I don't think I want to hear about that, Erlendur,' Valgerdur said. 'It's nothing to do with me. It was a long time ago and has nothing to do with us. With *our* relationship.'

'Yes, I know. But . . . perhaps I understand her better now. She's been brooding over it ever since, for all these years. I think that's where her anger stems from.'

'From unrequited love?'

'What she says is true. Halldóra was honest in what she did. I wasn't.'

Erlendur poured two cups of coffee and sat down at the kitchen table.

' "The greatest pain is to love, but love in vain," ' Valgerdur quoted.

Erlendur raised his eyes to her.

'Yes, I suppose that's true,' he said, then changed the subject. 'I'm investigating another relationship and I don't really know what to do about it. Something that happened years ago. A woman called Sólveig started having an affair with her best friend's husband. The relationship ended in disaster.'

'Dare I ask what happened?'

'I don't know if we'll ever uncover the full story,' Erlendur said.

'I'm sorry – of course you can't discuss it with every Tom, Dick and Harry.'

'No, it's all right. The man died; drowned in Lake Thingvallavatn. The question is how far his wife was implicated in his death. And to what extent their little daughter blamed herself.'

267

'Oh?'

'It might have been a great deal,' Erlendur continued. 'The little girl got mixed up in her parents' quarrel.'

'Do you have to do anything about it?' Valgerdur asked.

'I don't think it'll achieve anything.'

Erlendur fell silent.

'What about all your leave, don't you want to do something with that?' Valgerdur asked.

'I should try and use it.'

'What have you got in mind?'

'I could try to lose myself for a few days.'

'Lose yourself?' Valgerdur asked. 'I was thinking maybe the Canary Islands or something like that.'

'Mm, I've no experience of that sort of thing.'

'What? You mean you've never left Iceland? Never been abroad?'

'No.'

'Don't you want to go?'

'Not particularly.'

'The Eiffel Tower, Big Ben, the Empire State Building, the Vatican, the pyramids . . . ?'

'I've sometimes felt a curiosity to see the cathedral in Cologne.'

'Why don't you go, then?'

'My interest doesn't amount to any more than that.'

'What do you mean when you talk about losing yourself?'

'I want to go out east,' Erlendur said. 'Vanish for a few days. It's something I do from time to time. Mount Hardskafi . . .'

'Yes?'

'That's my Eiffel Tower.'

*

Karólína did not seem surprised to see Erlendur on her doorstep in Kópavogur again and she invited him in straight away. He had been keeping her under casual observation for several days and had established that she lived a fairly monotonous existence, going to work at nine and coming home around six, stopping off on the way at the local corner shop to buy her supper. Her evenings were spent at home, watching television or reading. One evening a woman friend came round. Karólína drew the curtains. Erlendur sat tight in his car and saw the woman leave shortly before midnight. She walked down the road in her long red coat and disappeared round the corner.

'Still snooping for information about Baldvin's wife?' Karólína asked bluntly as she showed Erlendur into the sitting room. The question was posed without any apparent interest in an answer. Karólína seemed determined to behave as if she wasn't unnerved by receiving two visits in short succession from the police. Erlendur couldn't tell if she was acting.

'Have you and Baldvin been talking?' he asked.

'Of course. We find it funny. Are you seriously trying to suggest that we did something to María?'

Again the question was posed as if the answer hardly mattered, as if Erlendur's believing such a thing was too bizarre to be taken seriously.

'Would it be absurd to think that?'

'Ludicrous,' Karólína confirmed.

'There's money at stake,' Erlendur pointed out, his eyes wandering around the sitting room.

'Are you seriously investigating this as a murder?'

'Have you ever wondered about life after death?' Erlendur asked, taking a seat.

'No – why?'

'María did,' he said. 'Almost all the time. You could say she didn't think about anything else in the weeks before she died. She tried to find answers by going to mediums. Does that sound familiar at all?'

'I know what a medium is,' Karólína said.

'We know about one she visited. His name's Andersen. He gave her a recording to take home with her. We know about another medium she went to see, too; a woman I haven't been able to trace yet. She's called – or calls herself – Magdalena. Ring any bells?'

'No.'

'I'd quite like to meet her,' Erlendur said.

'I've never been to a medium in my life,' Karólína said.

Erlendur gave her a long look, wondering if he should disclose what he thought had happened instead of continuing to pussyfoot around the subject. He had a theory but couldn't prove it. He had gone back and forth over the possibilities without reaching any conclusion. He knew it was time to take action, set the case in motion, but had been dithering because he had so little to go on, not much more than suspicions, based on frail foundations that would inevitably be easy to deny. There was a possibility that he might be able to dig up some evidence, given time, but he was fed up with the whole case and wanted to finish it so that he could turn to other things.

'Have you ever played a medium?' he asked.

'You mean on stage? No, I haven't,' Karólína replied.

'And you say that you don't know a medium who goes by the name of Magdalena?'

'No.'

'The same name as the character you played on stage?'

'No, I don't know any Magdalena.'

'I had my people check up on it,' Erlendur said. 'There is no medium with that name in the whole Reykjavík area.'

'Why don't you just say what you're going to say?'

Erlendur smiled.

'Maybe I should.'

'Please do.'

'I'll tell you what I think happened,' Erlendur said. 'I think you and Baldvin pushed María into suicide.'

'Oh?'

'She was in a terrible state after her mother died. María had watched Leonóra fighting the cancer for two years, watched her endure dreadful pain and suffering before the end. She started imagining all sorts of things and began looking for signs that her mother had intended to give her as proof that she was safe or that there was some kind of life after this one that might even be better than this vale of tears. It didn't take much to push María over the edge. She was absolutely terrified of the dark – in fact, she was a bundle of nerves after her mother died, desperate for reassurance that Leonóra was feeling better in some better world. She might have been an academic but this was not a question of rationalism, rather it was one of deeply rooted faith and hope and love. She started imagining all kinds of things. Leonóra appeared to her at their house in Grafarvogur. María turned to psychics. I expect you had some part in that? In tipping her over the edge?'

'What do you mean? Have you any proof?'

'None,' Erlendur said. 'You both planned it well.'

'Why on earth should we have done something like that?'

'There's a lot of money at stake. Baldvin is seriously in debt and is hardly the type to pay it off, despite the fact that as a doctor he's on a decent salary. You two get rid of María and live in the lap of luxury for the rest of your lives. I know of murders that have been committed for much lower sums.'

'You're calling it murder?'

'I don't know what else to call it. When one thinks about it. Are you Magdalena?'

Karólína gave Erlendur a long look, her expression very sober.

'I think you should go now,' she said finally.

'Did you tell María something that might have triggered the events that ended in her suicide?'

'I have nothing more to say.'

'Did you play some part in María's death?'

Karólína was on her feet. She walked into the hall and opened the front door.

'Get out,' she said.

Erlendur had also risen to his feet and followed her out.

'Would you admit that you played even the tiniest role in what happened to María?' he asked.

'No,' Karólína said. 'She was unhappy. She committed suicide. Will you please leave now?'

'Has Baldvin ever told you about an experiment that he performed when he was a medical student at university? He was involved in causing a young man to die and then bringing him back to life. Did you know about that?'

'What are you talking about?'

'I think it was the tipping point,' Erlendur said.

'What?'

'Ask Baldvin. Ask him if he knows a man called Tryggvi. If he has any contact with him today. You ask him that.'

'Will you get out now?' Karólína said.

Erlendur stood in the doorway, refusing to give up. Karólína was crimson in the face.

'I think I know what happened at the holiday cottage,' he said. 'And it's not a pretty story.'

'I don't know what you're talking about.'

Karólína pushed him out of the door but Erlendur still refused to give up.

'Tell Baldvin I know about the defibrillator,' he said as the door slammed shut.

32

Erlendur sat waiting in the dark, in a state of uncertainty.

He had woken late that morning. Eva Lind had dropped by on the previous evening and they had talked about Valgerdur. He knew that Eva wasn't very keen on her and that if she saw Valgerdur's car parked in front of his block she would sometimes wait for Erlendur's girlfriend to leave before knocking on his door.

'Why can't you just be nice to her?' Erlendur asked his daughter. 'She's forever taking your side when we talk about you. You could be good friends if you'd only let yourself get to know her.'

'I'm not interested,' Eva Lind said. 'I'm not interested in the women in your life.'

'Women? There are no women. There's Valgerdur and that's it. There never have been any women.'

'Relax,' Eva Lind said. 'Got any coffee?'

'What do you want?'

'Oh, you know, I was just bored.'

Erlendur sat down in his chair. Eva Lind was lying on the sofa opposite him.

'Are you planning to sleep here?' Erlendur asked, looking at the clock. It was well past midnight.

'I dunno,' Eva Lind said. 'Would you mind reading me the chapter about your brother again?'

Erlendur looked at his daughter for a long time before getting up and going over to the bookcase. He took out the book containing the account and, taking his seat again, began to read about the incident and his father's ineffectiveness and how he himself was described as gloomy and withdrawn and how he had searched for his brother's remains. He glanced over at his daughter when he had finished reading. He thought she had fallen asleep. Putting down the book on a small table beside the sofa, he sat with his hands in his lap, thinking how angry his mother had been with the man who wrote the account. A long time passed, until Eva Lind eventually sighed.

'You've been trying to keep him alive ever since,' she said.

'I don't know if . . .'

'Isn't it time to let him die?'

Eva Lind opened her eyes and, turning her head, fixed her father with her stare.

'Isn't it time you let him die?' she asked again.

Erlendur still did not answer.

'Why are you interfering in this?' he asked at last.

'Because you're unhappy, probably even unhappier than me sometimes,' Eva Lind answered.

'I don't know if it's anything to do with you,' Erlendur said. 'It's my business. I do what I have to.'

'Then go out east or wherever it is you were born. Go out there and do what you have to do. Get rid of him and free yourself. You owe it to yourself after all these years. And him too. Let him die. You owe it to yourself and to him. You have to free yourself from him. You have to free yourself from this ghost.'

'Why are you interfering in this?' he repeated.

'Says you who can never leave anyone alone.'

They were both silent for a while until Eva Lind asked if she could sleep on the sofa since she couldn't be bothered to go home.

'Be my guest,' Erlendur said. 'Sleep here.'

He stood up to get ready for bed.

'If I ever needed to, I did it ages ago,' Eva Lind said, turning her face into the corner of the sofa.

'Needed to what?'

'Forgive you,' she said.

Erlendur was startled out of his reverie by the sound of a car stopping in the drive. A door opened and he heard footsteps on the gravel outside, coming in the direction of the boat shed. Daylight shone in through two little windows, one on each side, illuminating the dust motes in the air. Outside he could see the sunlight gleaming on Lake Thingvallavatn, which was as smooth as a mirror in the still autumn weather. The door opened and Baldvin stepped inside, closing it behind him. There was a slight pause before the light came on overhead. Baldvin didn't notice him at first and Erlendur saw him search for something, then bend down and straighten up again with the defibrillator in his arms.

'I thought maybe you weren't coming,' Erlendur said, rising from the corner where he had been sitting, and stepping into the light.

Baldvin started, almost dropping the machine.

'Christ, you startled me,' he gasped, before regaining his composure and trying to put on a show of anger and outrage. 'What . . .? What's this supposed to mean? What are you doing here?'

'Isn't it rather a question of what *you*'re doing here?' Erlendur asked levelly.

'I . . . This is my holiday home . . . What do you mean, what am I doing here? It's none of your business. Won't you . . . Why are you following me?'

'I'd begun to think that you weren't coming,' Erlendur said. 'But you couldn't stand it any longer and were going to dispose of the defibrillator in a safe place. Your conscience was starting to plague you. Perhaps you're no longer as confident of getting away with it as you were.'

'I haven't a clue what you're talking about. Why won't you leave me alone?'

'It's because of María; she's haunting me like an old ghost story. There are a number of things concerning her I want to talk to you about, various questions that I know she herself would have wanted to ask you.'

'What bullshit is this? Did you break the lock on the door?'

'I did that the other day,' Erlendur admitted, 'when I was trying to fill in the gaps.'

'What rubbish is this?' Baldvin asked again.

'I was hoping you'd tell me.'

'I'm here to tidy up the boathouse,' Baldvin said.

'Yes, of course. And there's another thing. Why were you using water from the lake in your hot tub?'

'What?'

'I took a sample from your hot tub, from the waste pipe. The water supply to the cottage and hot tub comes from the wells up the hill. It's heated by electricity inside the cottage and then pumped into the system. So why should there be fine silt from Lake Thingvallavatn in the waste pipe of your hot tub?'

'I don't know what you're talking about,' Baldvin said. 'We

sometimes . . . we used to take a dip in the lake in summer and get in the hot tub afterwards.'

'Yes, but I'm talking about a much larger volume of water. I think the tub was filled with lake water,' Erlendur said.

Still holding the defibrillator, Baldvin backed out of the boathouse, obviously with the intention of putting the machine in the back of his car. Erlendur followed him and removed the machine from his grasp. Baldvin did not put up any resistance.

'I spoke to a doctor,' Erlendur said. 'I asked him how someone would go about causing heart failure without anyone noticing. He said you'd need determination and a large amount of cold water. You're a doctor. Do you agree?'

Baldvin stood by the boot of his car without answering.

'Wasn't that the method you used on Tryggvi in the old days?' Erlendur said. 'You couldn't use any drugs on María. Couldn't risk any trace being found, could you? In case they did a post-mortem. The only thing you could use was a tiny dose of sleeping pills to dull the cold.'

Baldvin slammed the boot of the car.

'I don't know what you're talking about,' he repeated furiously. 'And I don't think you do either. María hanged herself. She didn't sleep in the hot tub if that's what you're imagining. You should be ashamed of yourself!'

'I know she hanged herself,' Erlendur said. 'I want to know exactly why. And just how you and Karólína persuaded her into it.'

Baldvin seemed to be ready to drive away rather than have to listen to Erlendur any longer. Going round to the driver's door, he opened it and was about to get into the car when he paused and turned to face Erlendur.

'I'm tired of this,' he said roughly, slamming the door. 'Tired of this bloody persecution. What do you want?'

He walked towards Erlendur.

'It was Tryggvi who gave you the idea, wasn't it?' Erlendur said calmly. 'What I want to know is how you two persuaded María to enter into it.'

Livid with rage, Baldvin glared at Erlendur who stared back.

' "You two"?' Baldvin said. 'What do you mean, "you two"?'

'You and Karólína.'

'Are you out of your mind?'

'Why should you suddenly be concerned about the defibrillator now?' Erlendur asked. 'It's been sitting here untouched ever since María died. Why is it so important to spirit it away now?'

Baldvin did not answer.

'Is it because I mentioned it to Karólína? Did you get scared? Did it occur to you that you'd better dispose of it?'

Baldvin continued to stare at him without saying a word.

'Why don't we go and sit down in the cottage for a moment?' Erlendur suggested. 'Before I call for back-up.'

'What proof do you have?' Baldvin asked.

'All I have is a nasty suspicion. I would really like to have it confirmed.'

'And what then?'

'What then? I don't know. Do you?'

Baldvin was silent.

'I don't know if it's possible to prosecute people for assisting suicide or deliberately pushing someone into taking their own life,' Erlendur said. 'Which is what you and Karólína did. Systematically and without hesitation. The money probably came into it. It's a lot of cash and you're in dire straits financially. And then there's Karólína, of course. You'd get everything you wanted if only María would hurry up and die.'

'What kind of talk is that?'

'It's a hard world.'

'You can't prove anything,' Baldvin said. 'It's rubbish!'

'Tell me what happened. When did it start?'

Baldvin still vacillated.

'Actually, I think I know more or less what happened,' Erlendur said. 'If it wasn't the way I think, then we can discuss that. But you'll have to talk to me. I'm afraid there's no alternative.'

Baldvin stood silent and unmoving.

'When did it start?' Erlendur repeated, taking out his mobile phone. 'Either tell me now or else this place will be crawling with police officers before you know it.'

'María said she wanted to cross over,' Baldvin said in a low voice.

'Cross over?'

'After Leonóra died,' Baldvin explained. 'María wanted to cross over the great divide to where she thought she could reach her mother. She asked me to help her. That was all.'

'The great divide?'

'Do I have to spell it out?'

'And what?'

'Come inside,' Baldvin said. 'I'll tell you about María if you'll leave us in peace afterwards.'

'Were you at the cottage when she died?'

'Relax,' Baldvin said. 'I'll tell you how it was. It's time you heard. I'm not going to try to deny any responsibility. We weren't honest with her but I didn't kill her. I could never have done that. Never. You have to believe that.'

33

They entered the cottage and sat down in the kitchen. It was cold inside. Baldvin didn't bother to turn up the radiators; he wasn't intending to spin this out. He began to tell his story, methodically, point by point, in a clear voice, describing how he met María at university, their cohabitation with Leonóra in Grafarvogur and the last two years of María's life following the death of her mother. Erlendur thought the story sounded a little rehearsed at times but in other respects Baldvin's account seemed both plausible and consistent.

Baldvin's affair with Karólína had been going on for several years. They had briefly gone out together when they'd been at drama school but their relationship had come to nothing. Baldvin married María, Karólína lived either with boyfriends or alone. Her longest relationship lasted four years. Then she and Baldvin met again and revived their old association that María had never known about. They met in secret, not regularly but never less than once a month. Neither wanted to take the affair any further until, shortly before Leonóra was diagnosed with cancer, Karólína began to say that maybe Baldvin should leave María so that they could live together. He wasn't averse to the idea. Living with his mother-in-law had put a strain on his marriage. Increasingly he had started to point out to María that he had not married her mother and nor did he wish to.

When Leonóra fell ill, it was as if the ground had been snatched from under María's feet. It transformed her life just as much as it did Leonóra's. She would not leave the patient's side. Baldvin moved into the spare room while María slept beside her dying mother. She gave up work completely, cut off almost all contact with friends and became isolated in the home. Then one day a building contractor got in touch with them. He had discovered that Leonóra and María were the joint owners of a small plot of land in Kópavogur and wanted to buy it from them. The area was up and coming and the price of land there had rocketed. While they had known of the existence of this property, it had never crossed their minds that it would bring them any wealth and they had almost forgotten about it by the time the constructor made them the offer. The amount he wanted to pay for it was astronomical. Baldvin had never seen such figures in writing before. María did not turn a hair. She had hardly ever taken any interest in mundane matters and now all she cared about was her mother. She let Baldvin see to the sale. He contacted a lawyer who helped them agree on a price and payment schedule, stamp documents and register the sale. All of a sudden they were rich beyond Baldvin's wildest dreams.

María became increasingly isolated as her mother's health deteriorated, and during Leonóra's final days she did not leave her room. Leonóra wanted to die at home. Her doctor paid regular visits to check on her morphine supply but no one else was allowed in to see her. Baldvin was sitting alone in the kitchen when Leonóra departed from this life. He heard María's wail of grief from the bedroom and knew that it was all over.

María was incapable of social contact for weeks afterwards.

She told Baldvin what had passed between them just before her mother died. They had agreed that Leonóra would give her a sign if what they called the afterlife existed.

'So she told you about Proust?' Erlendur interrupted.

Baldvin took a deep breath.

'She was in a very agitated state, on sedatives and anti-depressants, so she forgot about it immediately afterwards,' he said. 'I'm not proud of all the things I did – some of them were downright sordid, I know that, but what's done can't be undone.'

'It started with Proust, did it?'

'*In Search of Lost Time*,' Baldvin confirmed. 'Fitting title. It was always as if they were harking back to a lost time. I never understood it.'

'What did you do?'

'I took the first volume off the bookshelf one night last summer and left it on the floor.'

'So you and Karólína had started laying traps for her?'

'Yes,' Baldvin said quietly. 'It had started by then.'

He had not pulled the curtains and the cottage was cold and dark inside. Erlendur glanced into the living room where María's life had ended.

'Was it Karólína's idea?' he asked.

'She began to wonder about the possibilities this might open up. She wanted to go much further than I did. I felt . . . I was prepared to help María if she wanted to explore these issues: the afterlife, life after death, to find out if there was anything on the other side. She had talked about it often enough, to me and, of course, most of all to Leonóra. She took great solace in the thought of an afterlife. She took solace in the idea that our existence here on Earth was not the end of everything. She preferred the idea that it was the beginning of something. She read books. Spent hours on the Internet. Researched the whole subject very thoroughly.'

'So you didn't want to go all the way, then?'

'No, definitely not. And I didn't.'

'But you both exploited María's vulnerability?'

'It was a dirty trick, I know,' Baldvin said. 'I felt bad about it the whole time.'

'But not bad enough to stop?'

'I don't know what I was thinking of. Karólína was on my back. She made all sorts of threats. Finally I agreed to try it. I was curious, too. What if María regained consciousness with memories of visions from the other side? What if all this talk of an afterlife was true?'

'And what if you didn't resuscitate her?' Erlendur said. 'Wasn't that the main issue for you? The money?'

'That too,' Baldvin admitted. 'It's a strange feeling, having someone's life in your hands. You'd know that if you were a doctor. It's a strangely powerful feeling.'

One night Baldvin tiptoed into the living room, went to the bookcase, located *Swann's Way* by Proust and placed it carefully on the floor. María was sleeping in their bed. He had given her a slightly larger dose of sleeping pills than normal. He also gave her other drugs that she knew nothing about, psychedelic drugs with disorientating properties. María trusted him to administer the drugs. He was her husband. And moreover a doctor.

He got back into bed with her. Karólína had suggested that she should play the role of the medium in their conspiracy. Baldvin was to encourage María to talk to a medium called Magdalena whom he had purportedly heard someone recommend. They knew María would make no enquiries. She was in no state to be suspicious of anything. She had blind faith in Baldvin.

She was almost too easy a prey.

Baldvin slept badly that night and, waking up before María in the morning, got out of bed and watched her sleep. She hadn't slept so peacefully for weeks. He knew she would suffer a shock when she woke up and went into the living room. She had long given up sitting staring at the bookshelves, but he noticed that her gaze strayed to them many times a day. She had been waiting for a sign from Leonóra and now she would receive it. She would be too overwrought to suspect Baldvin. He doubted whether she even remembered telling him about the book. Now she would receive her confirmation.

He woke María gently before going into the kitchen. He heard her get up. It was a Saturday. Before long María appeared at the kitchen door.

'Come here,' she said. 'Look what I've found!'

'What?' Baldvin asked.

'She's done it!' María whispered. 'The sign. Mum was going to choose that book. It's lying on the floor. The book's lying on the floor! She . . . she's making contact.'

'María . . .'

'No, really.'

'María . . . you shouldn't . . .'

'What?'

'Did you find the book on the floor?'

'Yes.'

'Well, of course, that's . . .'

'Look where it had opened,' María said, leading him over to the book which was lying open on the floor.

She read the words of the verse aloud. He knew that it was by pure chance that the book had opened at that point when he put it on the floor.

'The woods are black now,
yet still the sky is blue . . .'

'Don't you think it's fitting?' María said. 'The woods are black now, yet still the sky is blue . . . That's the message.'

'María . . .'

'She sent me a message just as she said she would. She sent the message.'

'Of course it's . . . It's unbelievable. It's what you had discussed and—'

'Exactly like she said. It's exactly what she said she'd do.'

Tears welled up in María's eyes. Baldvin put his arms round her and led her to a chair. She was in a highly emotional state, wavering between sadness and joy, and in the following days she experienced more peace than she had for a long time; the sense of reconciliation that she had so long desired.

A week or so later Baldvin asked out of the blue:

'Might it make sense to talk to a medium?'

Not long afterwards Karólína received María at the flat of a friend who was away in the Canary Islands. María had no idea that Baldvin and Karólína had studied drama together, let alone that they had been romantically involved. She and Karólína had never met before. María knew little about Baldvin's friends from his years as a drama student.

Karólína had lit the incense, put on some soothing music and wrapped an old shawl around her shoulders. She was relishing the make-believe, had enjoyed making herself up with eyeshadow, pencilling on thick eyebrows, sharpening the lines of her face, adding a slash of scarlet lipstick. She had rehearsed on Baldvin who gave her various items of information that might come in useful during the demonstration of her psychic powers. Various facts from María's childhood, some from her life with Baldvin, her close bond with her mother, Marcel Proust.

'I sense you're not happy,' Karólína said once they were seated and her show of clairvoyance could begin. 'You've . . . you've suffered, you've lost a great deal.'

'My mother died recently,' María said. 'We were very close.'

'And you miss her.'

'Unbearably.'

Karólína had prepared herself with professional thoroughness by going to a medium for the first time in her life. She didn't take much notice of what the medium said but attended carefully to his use of language, how he moved his hands, head and eyes, his breathing. She wondered if she should pretend to fall into a trance in María's presence or emulate the medium she had visited and simply sit and sense things and ask questions. She had never met Leonóra but had been given a good description of her. Baldvin lent her a photograph that she studied in detail.

Karólína decided to give the trance a miss when it came to the point.

'I sense a strong presence,' she began.

As María and Baldvin lay in bed together that night, she reported to him in detail what had happened at the seance. Baldvin lay without speaking for a long time after María had finished her story.

'Have I ever told you about a guy I knew when I was studying medicine? His name was Tryggvi?' he asked, turning to look at María.

34

Baldvin avoided meeting Erlendur's eye as the detective sat opposite him at the kitchen table, listening to his story. He looked either past Erlendur into the living room or down at the table or up at Erlendur's shoulder, but never met his eye. His own eyes looked shifty and ashamed.

'And in the end she pleaded with you to help her cross over,' Erlendur said, the disgust plain in his voice.

'She . . . she took the bait immediately,' Baldvin said, lowering his gaze to the table top.

'And so you were able to dispose of her without anyone realising.'

'That was the idea, I admit it, but I couldn't go through with it. When it came down to it, I didn't have it in me.'

'Didn't have it in you!' Erlendur burst out.

'It's true – I couldn't take the final step.'

'What happened?'

'I . . .'

'What did you do?'

'She wanted to proceed cautiously. She was afraid of dying.'

'Aren't we all?' Erlendur said.

They lay in bed until the early hours, discussing the possibility of stopping María's heart for long enough to enable her to pass into the next world but not long enough to risk her suffering any harm. Baldvin told her about the experiment that he and his friends in medicine had performed on Tryggvi and how he had died but they had succeeded in bringing him back to life. He hadn't felt anything, had no memories of his death, had seen no light or human figures. Baldvin said he knew how to manufacture a near-death experience without taking too great a risk. Of course, it wasn't completely without danger, María should realise that, but she was physically fit and really had nothing to fear.

'How will you bring me back to life?' she asked.

'Well, there are drugs,' Baldvin said, 'and then there's the usual emergency first aid of heart compressions and artificial respiration. Or we could use electric shocks. A defibrillator. I'd have to get hold of one. If we do this we'll have to be very careful that no one finds out. It's not exactly legal. I could be struck off.'

'Would we do it here?'

'Actually, I was thinking of the holiday cottage,' Baldvin said. 'But it's only a fantasy, anyway. It's not as if we're really going to do it.'

María was silent. He listened to her breathing. They were lying in the dark, talking in whispers.

'I'd like to try it,' María said.

'No,' Baldvin replied. 'It's too dangerous.'

'But you were just saying it was no big deal.'

'Yes – but it's one thing to talk about it, another to do it, actually put it into practice.'

He tried not to sound too off-putting.

'I want to do it,' María said in a more determined voice. 'Why at the cottage?'

'No, María, stop thinking about it. I . . . it would be going too far. I don't trust myself to do it.'

'Naturally,' María said. 'There's a danger that I might really die and leave you in the lurch.'

'There's a real danger,' Baldvin said. 'There's no need to take a risk of that kind.'

'Would you do it for me anyway?'

'I . . . I don't know, I . . . we shouldn't be talking about this.'

'I want to do it. I want you to do this for me. I know you can do it. I trust you, Baldvin. There's no one I trust more than you. Will you do it for me? Please?'

'María . . .'

'We can do it. It'll be all right. I trust you, Baldvin. Let's do it.'

'But what if something goes wrong?'

'I'm prepared to take that risk.'

Four weeks later María and Baldwin drove up to the holiday cottage at Lake Thingvallavatn. Baldvin wanted to be certain that they wouldn't be disturbed and it had occurred to him that the hot tub on the sun deck would come in useful. They would need a large amount of cold water if they were to use that method of lowering María's body temperature until her heart stopped. Baldvin mentioned other methods but regarded this as the best and least risky. He said that volunteer searchers and mountain-rescue teams were trained to resuscitate people under similar circumstances. They sometimes came across people lying in snow or water and needed to act quickly if it was not already too late; they needed to raise the body temperature with warm blankets, and if the person's heart had stopped they needed to get it going again by any means possible.

Husband and wife began by filling the hot tub with cold water and pieces of ice fetched in buckets from the lake. It didn't take long because it was only a few yards to the water's edge. The weather was cold and Baldvin told María that she should wear as little as possible outside so as to accustom herself to the cold before immersing herself in the tub. Finally he bashed ice off the rocks on the shore and filled the tub with it. By now María had taken two mild sleeping tablets that he said would help to dull the cold.

María recited a psalm and a short prayer before lowering herself slowly into the tub. The cold was like knives driving into her but she put a good face on it. She entered the water slowly, first up to the knees, then the thighs, hips and stomach. Then she sat down and the water reached above her breasts, shoulders and neck until only her head remained above it.

'Are you okay?' Baldvin asked.

'It's . . . so . . . cold,' María gasped.

She couldn't control her shivering. Baldvin said it would stop after a while when her body had given up fighting the cold. It wouldn't be long before she lost consciousness. She would begin to feel drowsy and she shouldn't resist it.

'Normally, the rule is that you're supposed to fight off drowsiness,' Baldvin said, smiling. 'But not in this case. You *want* to fall asleep. Just let it happen.'

María tried to smile. Before long her shivering ceased. Her body was completely blue with cold.

'I must . . . know . . . Baldvin.'

'I know.'

'I . . . trust . . . trust you,' she said.

Baldvin held a stethoscope to her heart. Its beating had slowed rapidly. María closed her eyes.

Baldvin listened to her heartbeat growing feebler and feebler. Finally it stopped. Her heart had stopped beating.

Baldvin looked at his watch. Seconds passed. They had discussed waiting one to one and a half minutes. Baldvin reckoned that was safe. He held María's head out of the water. The seconds ticked away. Half a minute. Forty-five seconds. Every second felt like an eternity. The second hand hardly seemed to move. Baldvin became uneasy. A minute. One minute, fifteen seconds.

He reached under María's arms and with one good heave hauled her out of the tub. He wrapped a woollen blanket round her body, carried her into the cottage and laid her down on the floor by the largest radiator. She showed no sign of life. He began to administer mouth-to-mouth respiration and then to massage her heart. He knew he didn't have much time. Perhaps he'd left her in the water too long. He blew air into her lungs, listened for a heartbeat, massaged her heart again.

He laid his ear against her chest.

Faintly, her heart began to beat. He massaged her body with the wool blanket and moved her closer to the radiator.

Her heart began to beat more rapidly. She drew a breath. He had managed to resuscitate her. Her skin was no longer bluish-white. It had regained a slight flush.

Baldvin heaved a sigh of relief and sat down on the floor, watching María for a long time. She looked as if she were sleeping peacefully.

She opened her eyes and stared up at the ceiling, a little bewildered. Then, turning her head towards him, she gazed at him for a long time. He smiled. María began to shiver violently.

'Is . . . it over?' she asked.

'Yes.'

'I . . . I . . . saw her,' she said. 'I saw her . . . coming towards me . . .'

'María . . .'

'You shouldn't have woken me.'

'It was more than two minutes before you came back to life.'

'She was . . . so beautiful,' María said. 'So . . . beautiful. I . . . wanted to hold . . . to hold her. You shouldn't have . . . woken me. You shouldn't . . . have . . . done it.'

'I had to.'

'You . . . shouldn't . . . have . . . woken me.'

Baldvin looked gravely at Erlendur. The doctor was on his feet, standing by the radiator where he claimed that María had lain when she had come back to life after dying in the hot tub.

'I couldn't let her die,' he said. 'It would have been easy. I wouldn't have needed to revive her. I could have laid her in the bedroom and she'd have been found there the following day. No one would have noticed anything. An ordinary heart attack. But I couldn't do it.'

'Oh, aren't you noble?' Erlendur sneered.

'She was sure that there was something there on the other side,' Baldvin said. 'She claimed she'd seen Leonóra. She was very weak at first after she woke up so I put her to bed. She fell asleep and slept for two hours while I emptied the tub, cleaned it out and tidied up.'

'So she wanted to go back for good this time?'

'It was her choice,' Baldvin said.

'Then what? What happened after she woke up?'

'We talked. She had a clear memory of what had happened when she'd crossed over, as she called it. Most of it was like what people describe: a long tunnel, light, friends and relatives waiting. She felt she had found peace at last.'

'Tryggvi said he'd seen nothing. Just blackness.'

'I expect you need to be receptive to it. I don't know,' Baldvin said. 'That was María's experience. She was in a very good state of mind when I left to go back to town.'

'You came in separate cars?'

'María was going to stay here a bit longer to recover. I spent the night here with her, then went back to town at lunchtime the following day. She called me in the evening, as you know. By then she had recovered completely and seemed very cheerful on the phone. She was intending to be home before midnight. That was the last I heard from her. You couldn't tell she was planning something stupid. It didn't occur to me that she would take her own life. Didn't even cross my mind.'

'Do you think your little experiment was the trigger?'

'I don't know. In the period immediately after Leonóra died I had the feeling that María might do something like that.'

'Don't you feel the slightest responsibility for what happened?'

'Of course . . . of course I do. I feel responsible but I didn't kill her. I could never have done that. I'm a doctor. I don't kill people.'

'There are no witnesses to what occurred when you and María were here?'

'No – we were alone.'

'You'll be struck off.'

'Yes, probably.'

'But that'll hardly bother you now that you've inherited María's money?'

'Think what you like of me. I don't care.'

295

'And Karólína?'

'What of her?'

'Did you tell her that you'd changed your mind?'

'No, I hadn't talked to her . . . I hadn't spoken to her yet when I was told that María was dead.'

Erlendur's mobile phone started ringing. He retrieved it from his coat pocket.

'Hello, it's Thorbergur,' a voice said at the other end.

'Who?'

'Thorbergur, the diver. I've made a few trips to the lakes east of Reykjavík. I'm there now.'

'Oh, yes, Thorbergur – I'm sorry, I was being dim. Is there any news?'

'I think I've found something that will interest you. I've ordered a small crane and notified the police, of course. But I daren't do anything more without you here.'

'What have you found?'

'A car. An Austin Mini. In the middle of the lake. I didn't find anything in Sandkluftavatn, so I thought I'd check out the lakes round about. Was it freezing when they went missing?'

'Yes, it's not unlikely.'

'She must have driven out on the lake. I'll show you when you get here. I'm up at Lake Uxavatn.'

'Was there anyone in the car?'

'There are two bodies. A man and woman from what I can tell. Unrecognisable, of course, but it looks like they're your people.'

Thorbergur was silent for a moment.

'It looks like they're your people, Erlendur,' he repeated.

35

On his way to Lake Uxavatn Erlendur called the nursing home where the old man was lying at death's door. They wouldn't put him through. Apparently the old man was unlikely to survive the night and it was only a matter of time. Instead, Erlendur was connected to the doctor on duty who said that the patient might only have a couple of hours – or possibly even only a matter of minutes – left to live. It was impossible to say exactly how long but his time was running out swiftly.

Darkness was falling when Erlendur drove the Ford across the plain of Hofmannaflöt, past Mount Meyjarsaeti, along the shore of Lake Sandkluftavatn and then took a left turn in the direction of the Lundarreykjadalur valley. He saw a small crane taking up position at the northern end of Uxavatn. Thorbergur's jeep was parked not far off. Erlendur parked his car on the road and walked over to the diver who was putting on his oxygen tanks. He was preparing to dive with the hook from the crane.

'I was lucky,' Thorbergur said after they had exchanged greetings. 'I actually bumped into the car with my foot.'

'You think it's them?'

'It's the same car, at any rate. And there are two of them inside. I tried to shine a light on them. It's not a pretty sight, as you can imagine.'

'No, of course. Thank you for doing this for me.'

Thorbergur took a large hook from the crane driver and waded out with it until the water was waist deep, then submerged himself.

Erlendur and the crane driver stood on the shore, waiting for Thorbergur to resurface. The crane driver was a tall, thin man who knew only that there was a car in the lake, a car which probably contained two corpses. He tried to extract more information from Erlendur who was non-committal.

'It's an old case,' he said. 'A tragic old case that we'd long forgotten about, as it happens.'

Then he stood in silence, staring out over the lake, waiting for Thorbergur to re-emerge.

There had been little in the way of goodbyes when he'd left Baldvin. Erlendur had wanted to tell him how disgusted he was by what Baldvin and Karólína had done to María but he supposed there was little point. People who were capable of such an act would not be bothered by admonitions. They were not motivated by conscience or morals. Baldvin didn't ask what would happen now concerning the investigation and Erlendur himself was in two minds. He didn't know what to believe. Baldvin could deny the whole thing in court. He hadn't told anyone except Erlendur what had really happened and Erlendur would have difficulty proving any of it. Baldvin would very probably be struck off if he admitted to having stopped María's heart and resuscitated her again but that wouldn't matter to him in the circumstances. It was impossible to say whether he would receive any punishment. The burden of proof lay with the prosecution and Erlendur's investigation had not really produced any solid evidence. If Baldvin chose to change his statement when threatened with legal proceedings, he could simply deny having encouraged María's death wish and having temporarily stopped her heart, let alone having murdered her. Erlendur had certain clues about the sequence of staged events that had tipped María towards suicide but the evidence was extremely tenuous. It was not possible to prosecute people for playing tricks, no matter how immoral those tricks might have been.

He saw Thorbergur's head emerge from the water. The crane driver climbed into his vehicle. Thorbergur gave him a sign to start winding in the cable. Two police cars appeared on the road, driving fast, lights flashing. The winch on the crane started up. A thick steel cable moved slowly, inch by inch, under the winch that was winding it up.

Thorbergur climbed out on shore and took off his diving apparatus. He walked over to the Ford where Erlendur was standing with the passenger door open, listening to the evening news.

'Well, you must be pleased,' Thorbergur said.

'I'm not sure,' Erlendur replied.

'Are you going to tell the families yourself?'

'It may be too late in one case,' Erlendur said. 'The boy's mother died some time ago and his father is on his deathbed. They say he could go any minute.'

'You'll have to hurry, then,' Thorbergur said.

'Is it yellow?' Erlendur asked.

'The car? Yes, it's yellow.'

The crane roared. The two police cars drew up; four officers got out and walked towards them.

'Are you chucking that out?' Thorbergur asked.

He gestured at the defibrillator that Erlendur had put in the passenger seat of the Ford, the one from María and Baldvin's boathouse. He had shoved it in the car after his conversation with Baldvin.

'No,' Erlendur said. 'It's connected to another case.'

'Always plenty to do,' Thorbergur said.

'Yes. Unfortunately.'

'It's a long time since I've seen a piece of junk like that. Does anyone have any use for broken defibrillators?'

'Yes,' Erlendur said, absent-mindedly.

The steel cable made the water ripple and before long the car appeared.

'Hang on – what do you mean, broken?' Erlendur asked, giving Thorbergur a puzzled look.

'What?'

'You said the machine was broken.'

'Can't you tell?'

'No, I don't have a clue about these things.'

'It's completely useless. Look, this plug is kaput. And the wire here, the connection to the electrode is broken. No one can use this.'

'But . . .'

'What?'

'Are you sure?'

'I was in the fire brigade for years. This is just a piece of scrap.'

'He said that he . . .'

Erlendur stared at Thorbergur.

'It's broken?' he groaned.

The winch on the crane screeched as the Austin Mini reared slowly out of the water and crawled up the shore. The crane driver stopped the winch. The police officers drew nearer. Water, sand and mud poured from outside and inside the car until it was drained. Erlendur saw the shapes of two human bodies in the front seats. The car was covered in slime and pond weed but the yellow paint was still visible here and there on the sides. The glass in the windows was intact but the boot had opened.

Erlendur tried to open the passenger door but it was stuck fast. He went round to the driver's side and saw that it was open a crack and there was a dent in it. Peering inside, he made out two skeletons. Gudrún, or Dúna, was sitting at the steering wheel. He could tell by her hair. He assumed that it was Davíd sitting beside her.

'Why is the door dented?' he asked Thorbergur.

'Do you know what state the car was in?'

'Not necessarily good.'

'They wouldn't have had much time,' Thorbergur said. 'She must have tried to open the door on her side but could only do so to a very limited extent. There was a rock lying against the car on that side. The passenger doesn't seem to have been able to open the door on his side. Perhaps it was broken. The handles for winding down the windows probably didn't work either, or they would have tried to wind them down. It's the first resort in circumstances like these. The car was probably a bit of a wreck.'

'So they were trapped inside?'

'Yes.'

'While their lives ebbed away.'

'Hopefully the struggle wouldn't have lasted long.'

'How did they get so far out in the lake?' he asked, gazing over Uxavatn.

'The only obvious explanation is that it was covered with ice,' Thorbergur said. 'That she drove out on the ice. Maybe in a moment of madness. She must have thought that she knew what she was doing. Then the ice cracked. The water was cold. And it's deep enough.'

'And so they disappeared,' Erlendur said.

'There isn't much traffic here by the lake at this time of year nowadays, let alone thirty years ago,' Thorbergur said. 'There were no witnesses. A hole in the ice like that would soon close up again without anyone noticing that it had ever been there. Although the road must have been passable, since they managed to drive all the way out here.'

'What's that?' Erlendur asked, pointing to a lump between the seats.

'Is it all right to look at it?' Thorbergur asked. 'Don't forensics need to examine it?'

Erlendur wasn't listening. He reached over the driver's seat and grabbed the object that had caught his attention. He prised it carefully out of the car but it still fell apart. Holding the two pieces, he showed them to Thorbergur.

'What have you got there?' the diver asked.

'I think it's . . . I think it's a book,' Erlendur said, inspecting the two halves.

'A book?'

'Yes. Probably about the lakes in this area. The boy must have bought it for her.'

Erlendur placed the book in Thorbergur's hands.

'I must go to his father before it's too late,' he said, checking his watch. 'I believe we've found them; I don't think there's any doubt. He must hear what happened. His son was in love, that's all. He never meant to leave them with all that uncertainty. It was an accident.'

Erlendur walked quickly towards the Ford. He was in a hurry because before he went to the nursing home he had another call to make, in search of the truth.

She was a small child, sitting alone on the shore of the lake, listening to the whispering from the water. She was a young woman, gazing out at the lake, and saw its beauty and the light emanating from it. She was an old woman, kneeling beside the child, and she was a small child again, listening to the whispering and hearing the forgiveness in the words, and the whispering carried from the water and the whispering said: My child.

It took her a long time to regain consciousness; she was so infinitely tired and lethargic that she could hardly open her eyes.

'Bald . . . vin,' she sighed. 'It was an accident. What happened when Daddy died . . . it was an accident.'

She couldn't see Baldvin but sensed his presence.

She was no longer cold and it was as if a heavy burden had been lifted from her. She knew what she had to do. She would tell. Everything. Everything that had happened at the lake. She would tell anyone who would listen what had happened.

She was about to call Baldvin when she discovered that she couldn't breathe any more. Something was tightening on her throat.

She opened her eyes and looked for Baldvin but couldn't see him.

She clutched weakly at her throat.
'This isn't right,' she whispered.
'This isn't right . . .'

36

Erlendur drove down the cul-de-sac to Baldvin's house in Grafarvogur. He parked by the drive to the garage and stepped out. He was in a hurry. He wasn't sure if he was doing the right thing; he would have preferred to have gone straight to the old man but on the other hand he was tormented by questions about the defibrillator that Baldvin alone could answer.

He pressed the doorbell and waited. As he rang the bell again, he noticed Karólína's car parked in the road a little way from the house. When he had rung a third time he heard a sound from inside before the door opened and Baldvin appeared.

'You again?' he said.

'Can I come in?' Erlendur asked.

'Haven't we been over this?' Baldvin asked.

'Is Karólína with you?' Erlendur said.

Baldvin's gaze travelled past him to her car. He nodded and let Erlendur in. Closing the door behind him, he invited Erlendur into the sitting room. Karólína emerged from the bedroom, tidying her hair.

'We saw no point in hiding any longer,' Baldvin said. 'I've told you what happened. Karólína's going to move in with me next week.'

'You needn't tell him anything,' Karólína said. 'It's none of his business.'

'Quite right,' Erlendur said, smiling. He was in a hurry to get to the hospital but made an effort to appear relaxed. 'But one would have thought you'd have wanted to be careful,' he said, 'not attract too much attention.'

'We have nothing to hide,' Karólína said.

'Are you sure?' Erlendur asked.

'What do you mean?' Baldvin asked. 'I've told you the whole thing. I left María alive at the holiday cottage.'

'I know what you told me.'

'What are you doing here, then?'

'You lied about the whole thing,' Erlendur said, 'and I wondered if I could persuade you both to tell me the truth this time. It would make a refreshing change.'

'I didn't lie about anything,' Baldvin said.

'Why do you think he's lying?' Karólína asked. 'That *we*'re lying?'

'Because you're both liars,' Erlendur said. 'You lied to María. You plotted behind her back. Put on a whole play for her. Even though Baldvin claims he backed down at the last minute, it's still a crime. You've both lied to me from the beginning.'

'That's bullshit,' Baldvin said.

'How do you intend to prove it?' Karólína asked.

Erlendur smiled thinly and looked at his watch.

'I can't,' he said.

'Then what do you want?'

'I want to hear the truth,' Erlendur said.

'I've told you the truth,' Baldvin said. 'I'm not proud of what I did but I didn't murder María. I didn't do it. She committed suicide after I left for town.'

Erlendur stared at Baldvin for a long time without saying a word. Baldvin's gaze flickered over to Karólína.

'I think you did it,' Erlendur said. 'You did more than just push her towards suicide. You killed her. You put the noose round her neck. You hanged her from the beam.'

Karólína had sat down on the sofa. Baldvin was standing in the kitchen doorway.

'Why are you saying this?' he asked.

'You two spun a web of lies for María and you're still lying. I don't believe a word you say.'

'That's your problem,' Karólína retorted.

'Yes, it's my problem,' Erlendur agreed.

'You don't know . . .'

'How do you sleep at night?'

Baldvin didn't answer.

'What do you dream about, Baldvin?'

'Leave him alone,' Karólína said. 'He hasn't done anything.'

'He told me you pushed him into it,' Erlendur said, his eyes fixed on Karólína. 'That it was your fault. I got the impression he was shifting all the blame on to you.'

'He's lying,' Baldvin said.

'He said you were the moving force behind this.'

'Don't listen to him,' Baldvin interjected.

'Calm down,' Karólína said, her gaze on Baldvin, 'I know what he's trying to do.'

'Was Baldvin the prime mover, then?' Erlendur asked.

'You won't succeed,' Karólína said. 'Baldvin can say what he likes.'

'Yes, of course,' Erlendur said. 'I don't know whether to take any notice of anything he says. About himself. About you. About María.'

'What you believe is your problem,' Karólína said.

'You're actors,' Erlendur said. 'Both of you. You acted your roles for María. You wrote a scenario. You chose the setting. You chose the backdrop. She never suspected anything. Unless she found out about the defibrillator.'

'The defibrillator?' Karólína said.

'Of course it was only there to flesh out the background,' Erlendur said. 'It was a – what do you call it? – a prop. It was never intended to work. It was never intended as a safety precaution. The machine was never intended to save María's life. It was only a prop on the set you designed for an audience of one – for María.'

Karólína and Baldvin's stares locked for an instant. Then Baldvin lowered his gaze to the floor.

'The machine is broken,' Erlendur told Karólína. 'That's why he had to retrieve it from the cottage. He used it to fool María. It was supposed to show that he was in earnest, that he would do everything in his power to ensure her safety.'

'What do you think you know?' Baldvin demanded.

'I'm *sure* I know: you murdered her. You needed money that she alone had access to, unless she died before you. You were having an affair with Karólína and didn't want María to know; you couldn't divorce her because of the money. But you wanted Karólína. And I imagine living with María must have been wearing in the long run. Her mother was always there and even after Leonóra was gone it was as if she was still present in the house. María thought of nothing else. I expect you'd lost interest in her long before and that she was just in the way. In your way, in the way of both of you.'

'Can you prove this bullshit?' Karólína asked.

'Were you here the evening we came to inform Baldvin of María's death?'

Karólína hesitated a moment, then nodded.

'I thought I saw a movement at the sitting-room window as I was driving away from the house.'

'You should never have come here,' Baldvin said, rounding on Karólína.

'What happened at the cottage?' Erlendur asked.

'What I told you,' Baldvin said. 'Nothing else.'

'And the defibrillator?'

'I wanted to reassure her.'

'I expect most of what you told me about causing her death is correct. And I expect she allowed you to kill her voluntarily. But she wanted to live, too. I assume that everything you told me about what happened after she passed out in the tub is a lie.'

Baldvin didn't answer.

'Something went wrong and you felt you had to stage a suicide,' Erlendur said. 'It would have been tidier if she had died as you wanted and as you had arranged so neatly; if she had died in the hot tub. But she didn't, did she?'

Baldvin continued to stare at him in silence.

'Something went wrong,' Erlendur continued. 'She regained consciousness. You had probably taken her out of the tub and were ready to lay her in bed. You had induced cardiac arrest. No one would have noticed anything. A post-mortem would have shown a heart attack from natural causes. You're a doctor. You knew this. You'd got away with it. María had taken the bait. All you needed to do was betray her. Betray her trust. Break trust with an innocent who had long been teetering on the edge of despair. Not particularly noble – but then, you're not much of a hero, are you?'

Karólína lowered her eyes to the floor.

'Maybe you'd put her in bed,' Erlendur said. 'You were going to check her pulse one last time before hotfooting it back to town. You'd rung home and Karólína had taken your call. You wanted it to look as if María had called. You checked on her one last time and to your horror she was still alive. She wasn't dead. Her heartbeat was weak but it was there. She had started breathing. There was a danger that she would wake up.'

Karólína listened to Erlendur in silence. She avoided looking at him.

'Perhaps she did wake up. Perhaps she opened her eyes as you described and had crossed over into another world. Perhaps she did see something, but it's more likely that she saw nothing. Perhaps she did tell you something about her experience but she didn't have much time. And, anyway, she was exhausted.'

Baldvin didn't answer.

'Perhaps she realised what you were doing. She would probably have been too weak to fight. We saw no sign of a struggle. We know María suffocated when the noose tightened round her neck.'

Karólína stood up and went over to Baldvin.

'Gradually her life ebbed away and María died.'

Karólína put her arms round Baldvin and stared at Erlendur.

'Wasn't it something like that?' Erlendur asked. 'Wasn't that how María died in the end?'

'It's what she herself wanted,' Baldvin said.

'Some of it, maybe. Not all.'

'She begged me to do it.'

'And you did her a favour.'

Baldvin stared expressionlessly at Erlendur.

'I think you should get out,' he said.

'Did she tell you something?' Erlendur asked. 'About Leonóra?'

Baldvin shook his head.

'About her father?' Erlendur asked. 'She must have said something about her father.'

'You should go,' Baldvin said. 'You're deluded. I should sue you for harassment.'

'Didn't she say anything about her father?' Erlendur asked again.

Baldvin didn't answer.

Erlendur stared at them for a long time before making his way to the hall.

'What now?' Karólína asked. 'What are you going to do about this?'

Erlendur opened the front door, then turned back.

'It looks as if you've done it,' he said.

'Done what?'

'What you meant to do,' Erlendur said. 'You deserve each other.'

'Aren't you going to take any action?' Karólína asked.

'There's not much I can do,' Erlendur said, making to close the door behind him. 'I'll report the case to my superiors but—'

'Wait,' Baldvin said.

Erlendur turned back again.

'She did mention her father,' Baldvin said.

'I thought so,' Erlendur said. 'That she would probably have done so at the very end.'

Baldvin nodded.

'I thought she wanted to make contact with her mother,' he said.

'But that was wrong, wasn't it?' Erlendur said.

'Yes,' Baldvin said.

'She was longing to meet her father, wasn't she?' Erlendur said.

'I didn't quite understand what she said. She wanted him to forgive her. What was he supposed to forgive?'

'You never will understand.'

'What?'

Baldvin stared at Erlendur.

'Was it . . . was it . . . María? She was with them in the boat when Magnús died. Did she blame herself for what happened to him?'

Erlendur shook his head.

'You couldn't have found a more helpless victim,' he said and closed the door behind him.

Erlendur rushed into the nursing home and up to the old man's ward. He was not in his room and Erlendur was informed that he had been moved to another. Erlendur hurried there and was shown in to see the old man who was lying under a thick duvet, invisible except for his head and his gaunt face and the bony hands lying on the cover.

'He died a short time ago,' the nurse who accompanied Erlendur said. 'It was a peaceful death. He was never any trouble.'

Erlendur sat down by the bed and took the old man's hand in his.

'Davíd was in love,' he said quietly. 'He . . .'

Erlendur brushed a hand over the old man's forehead. He pictured Gudrún and Davíd as it finally became apparent that they would not be able to escape from the car and they held hands, resigned to their fate, as their life ebbed away and their hearts stopped beating in the cold water.

'I wish I could have come a bit sooner,' he said.

The nurse crept out of the room, leaving them alone.

'He'd met a girl,' Erlendur said after a long silence. 'He didn't die alone. It was an accident. He didn't commit suicide. He wasn't depressed or unhappy when he died. He was happy. He was in love with a girl he had met and they were fooling around – they were in high spirits; you'd have understood. They died together. He was with his girl and he was probably going to tell you about her when he got home, that she was at the university and was great fun and absolutely obsessed with lakes. That she was his girl. His girl, for ever.'

37

Erlendur stood by the derelict farm that had once been his home, looking up at Mount Hardskafi. It was difficult to see the mountain because of the icy fog that was sinking ever lower over the fjord. He was well equipped, in his old walking boots, thick waterproof trousers and a warm down jacket. After gazing at the mountain for a long time in solemn silence, he set off on foot, with a walking stick in his hand and a small pack on his back. He made quick progress, enfolded in the hush of nature now fallen into its winter sleep. Before long he had disappeared into the cold fog.